MW00532042

Flora Qian

Proverse Hong Kong

2023

Supported by

Hong Kong Arts Development Council fully supports freedom of artistic expression. The views and opinions expressed in this project do not represent the stand of the Council.

SOUTH OF THE YANGTZE starts with the protagonist, Qian Yinan, taking the high-speed train through the landscape of Jiangnan ("South of the Yangtze River") with her American husband. Now in her mid-thirties, Yinan recalls her first trip along the same route in the late 1980s, as well as her Shanghai childhood with her "historical counter-revolutionary" grandfather, semi-literate grandmother, philosophy professor father and former "red guard" mother. Later in school, while receiving a nationalist education and witnessing the booming market economy, she becomes close to Jie, a classmate who aspires to join the Communist Party. And a few months before the new millennium, Yinan finds herself trapped in a secret love affair with her Mandarin-speaking high school teacher, who was once an activist during the political turmoil of 1989.

In the midst of these formative relationships, Yinan contemplates the impact of the nation's ideology, tradition and even its written language, and pushes the boundaries of thinking which are restrained by these tools. Later, she decides to write and read in English as much as possible, and eventually leaves her home town. But what is the price to pay when she adopts a new language and a new way of thinking? After the SARS epidemic in 2003, would her reunion with a psychologically troubled Chinese American friend bring Yinan real hope for love, understanding and peace? While this thoughtful novel is a meditation on both physical migration and migration between languages, it also provides a moving portrait of China's only child generation.

FLORA QIAN was born and raised in Shanghai. She left home in her early twenties and has spent most of her time since then in Hong Kong. She has also lived in Washington D.C. and Singapore. Her short fiction has appeared in the *Asia Literary Review*, *Eastlit* and a few anthologies. A graduate of Fudan University in Shanghai, she has an MFA in Creative Writing from the University of Maryland and an MA in Translation from The Chinese University of Hong Kong. *South of the Yangtze* is her first novel.

SOUTH
OF THE YANGTZE

Flora Qian

Proverse Prize 2022

Proverse Hong Kong

South of the Yangtze
By Flora Qian
First published in paperback in Hong Kong
by Proverse Hong Kong,
under sole and exclusive right and licence,
21 November 2023
ISBN 13: 978-988-8833-44-3
Alternate Edition: ISBN-13: 978-988-8833-45-0
Copyright © Flora Qian 2023.

Distribution (Hong Kong and worldwide)
The Chinese University of Hong Kong Press,
The Chinese University of Hong Kong,
Shatin, New Territories, Hong Kong SAR.
E: cup@cuhk.edu.hk; W: https://www.cup.cuhk.edu.hk
Proverse page: https://cup.cuhk.edu.hk/Proversehk
Distribution (United Kingdom): Stephen Inman, Worcester, UK.

Enquiries to Proverse Hong Kong
P.O. Box 259, Tung Chung Post Office,
Lantau, NT, Hong Kong SAR, China.
E: info@proversepublishing.com.
W: https://www.proversepublishing.com

The right of Flora Qian to be identified as the author of this work
has been asserted by her in accordance with
the Copyright, Designs and Patents Act 1988.
Cover image, "Gathering at the Orchid Pavilion",
hand-scroll by Qian Gu, Wang Guxiang, datable to 1560.
(Metropolitan Museum of Art, CC0, via Wikimedia Commons.)
Cover design by Artist Hong Kong.

British Library Cataloguing in Publication Data
A catalogue record for the first paperback edition
is available from the British Library

Prior Publication Acknowledgements

An earlier version of Chapters 10 to 13 was first published as a short story under the title, 'Early June' in *Asia Literary Review*, No. 32, Winter 2016, pp. 55-69.

Author's Acknowledgements

I wish to thank the editors at Proverse Hong Kong, and especially co-founder Dr. Gillian Bickley, for your insight, encouragement, and dedication towards South of the Yangtze. Thank you to the judges at the Proverse Prize, who picked the novel as a 2022 winner. I'm also grateful for the generous support from the Hong Kong Arts Development Council.

Many thanks to my parents and to my in-laws, Carol and Herb, for your faith in my first novel. Geoff, thank you for reading some of the earliest drafts and for your wisdom and help throughout the years. Emily, I was fortunate to be in your workshop and have your kind feedback when the tiniest saplings of my novel appeared. My gratitude also goes to my friends including Dami, Prasenjit, Diana and Crystal, for being my readers who inspired and encouraged me.

And thank you, Scott, for taking the trip with me to my ancestral village in Jiangnan five years ago before I sat down to write the first full draft of the novel. What a journey it has been since then. Thank you for being here with me.

Author's Note

The chapter titles of *South of the Yangtze* contain both Chinese characters and *pinyin*, as well as their English translation.

Chinese characters are an essential part of the story, as the protagonist considers the history, custom and form of these characters. She separates some Chinese characters into semantic components, referred to as "radicals", in order to analyze and reflect on the shared imagination of Chinese speakers.

Pinyin − the Romanized phonic system − is also included in the chapter titles to help readers pronounce these Chinese characters. In general, after the first appearance of special terms in Chinese characters, their subsequent appearances are in *pinyin*.

In *South of the Yangtze*, quotation marks are used around Chinese characters with the exception of radicals that are not stand-alone characters in order to distinguish between the two, similar to distinguishing words from letters.

For Scott

South of the Yangtze

Table of Contents

SOUTH OF THE YANGTZE

South of the Yangtze

1
South of the Yangtze
江南 (*Jiangnan*)

It was the second year of our marriage. My husband and I were taking a high-speed train southward from Shanghai to Zhuji, my late paternal grandparents' hometown. The distance was roughly 240 kilometers, a short ride of less than two hours. Through our windows, we watched as the city landscape quickly receded, and gave way to low-rise farmhouses, rice paddies and distant hills.

I was traveling through the landscape of Jiangnan, once again.

The last and only previous time, had been in the early-1990s, when I was seven years old. The trains were slow then, crowded and rudimentary, and painted in a uniform shade of deep green. The journey had taken nearly half a day. My parents and I got the "hard seats" and we shared a small tray table in the middle of the two facing rows with a stranger. It was considered a good arrangement at the time as many passengers, who took as long a journey as us, got the "standing" tickets. The corridor was filled with people sitting on their bags and suitcases. When we left to use the bathroom, we found our seats temporarily taken by those who were in desperate need of a rest.

But I was excited about my first trip outside Shanghai as a child. I watched people smoke as they hung their heads out of the windows. Our tray neighbour had brought a large pack of peanuts to crack on, covering the floor with shells. Many kids took off their shoes and laid their feet on the opposite seats, between two other strangers. The smell in the car was a mix of sweat and the delicious cooked food people had packed to save money. I had heard from my parents that during the long-haul train rides in those days, people made friends. Some youngsters found their partner, such as the well-known 1980s' poet Gu Cheng, who later murdered his wife whom he had met on a train ride and committed suicide afterwards.

I still remember a whole pomegranate, which my parents gave me to entertain myself during the journey. I savored every red seed, one by one, so that it would last until the end of the trip. However, when the slow train stopped at a small city called Jiaxing, my father treated us to *zhongzhi*, pork dumplings wrapped in reed leaves sold by venders on the railway station platform. The smell of meat must have made our peanut-eating neighbour feel jealous. A few stops later, in Hangzhou, she bought a packet of sweet-looking lotus powder, which turned into a fragrant jelly after she poured hot water over it, and she ate it in front of us in triumph. In my childhood memories, the local specialty food was always the highlight of a journey.

It made me hungry just thinking about them. Today, alongside the silver bullet trains, there was no sight of the vendors. From station to station, the platforms looked modern, with identical designs. A family with two children sitting across from us on the train were playing games on their digital devices. Here we were after decades of economic reform and industrialization. I wondered if I could explain in English to my American husband the cultural treasures, as my father used to do when the train stopped at each small town in Jiangnan: silk, porcelain, tea, wine, literature, calligraphy... It was the beginning of my fascination with a classical culture that had captured the imagination of Chinese literati for generations.

My name, 憶南 (Yinan), was an homage to the twenty-seven-syllable poetic form "憶江南" (*Yi Jiangnan*), meaning "Remembering Jiangnan," or "Remembering the

South." The Tang Dynasty official and poet Bai Juyi, who had been governor of both Hangzhou and Suzhou, was a master of this form and one of my father's favourite poets. Though Bai was originally from the central plain and eventually retired there, he spent his late years composing nostalgic songs about the south. My father, who chose my name, shared Bai's nostalgia even though he had never lived outside the geographical Jiangnan at the time when I was born – to me, his loss of anchor was a cultural one.

***

Just a day ago, before our trip to my grandparents' hometown, I took my husband to Duolun Road in Shanghai where I grew up. The street had become a site of historical tourism since the beginning of the new millennium, pedestrian only and dotted with museums and cafés. Once called Darroch Road during the International Settlement days in the 1920s and 30s, its name changed in the early 40s when it became part of the Japanese quarter. Duolun Road had been a bustling neighborhood of political leaders and left-wing writers before and during the Second World War.

The five hundred meter long street my husband was seeing now kept the façade of its golden times. Like many of the "revival" cultural scenes in Shanghai, it was trendy and it was escapism, rather than education. As a former resident who had a private history with it, however, I remembered the years when it was reduced and forgotten in the public eye. I remembered the wet market my family used to pass by every day on our way home in the 1980s, and the sound of vendors' peddling and housewives' bargaining. I remembered that at a young age, I didn't cringe at the sight of a chicken being slaughtered, and rather welcomed the close proximity of ice cream carts and spring onion pancake stands in the market.

The kindergarten my grandfather had walked me to every day was only a few minutes away from the house we used to live in. The *longtang* was still there, so was the original stone arch surmounted at its entrance. But I didn't see any sign of a still-operating kindergarten. Our house was long gone. A small new shop was selling "retro ice cream brick" wrapped in wax paper, a summer favourite of mine as a child for its rich flavour. I had liked it more at the time, knowing that ice cream and ice cubes were only available in the summer months – I was drawn to every local seasonal ritual.

My grandfather used to tell me the Wu and Yue Kingdom stories of Jiangnan, even though I couldn't understand them properly at that age. But early memories always left imprints. I had heard these stories far more often than his own life story. As a result, I didn't know that before I was born, he had spent twelve years in a labour camp as a "historical counter-revolutionary." No one in my family talked about it then, not until much later, when I no longer lived in Shanghai. My husband didn't have a chance to meet my grandparents.

I am in my mid-thirties. My childhood already feels far distant in time, so unindustrialized in its pace, and so small in the geographical radius it covered. My husband went to New Zealand with his parents when he was eighteen-months old, his first trip abroad. I had my first travel document at the age of twenty, to go to Hong Kong. The 1980s in America were the Ronald Reagan years, followed by triumphant milestones in the Cold War. The last year of the same colorful decade ended abysmally in China, silencing the most daring and searching voices after the reign of the current Communist régime began.

My childhood in the 1980s was far from affluent, yet not without freedom and happiness. And only looking back, I could see how the short-lived, spirited time after the end of the Cultural Revolution had made my parents optimistic – I was, however, too young to remember many details. What I recalled vividly were the drastic economic shifts in the 1990s and how it had impacted our daily life in both good and bad ways. And the coming of a new millennium separated my life into two halves, one lived in the Chinese language and less documented, and the other lived in the English language, uprooted and much more visibly metamorphic.

Riding the train to Jiangnan again, decades later, made me realize, all of a sudden, that it was the first half that I wished to tell my husband about most urgently, yet somehow it was largely left out in our conversations: those days lived in the *longtang*, school years and the first favourite books that I curled up to sleep with, the time when I felt that I had to lose my native words so that I could speak my true mind, and the unbearable loneliness that came with early love and friendships. I wanted to tell him about Jie and Simon, too, even though they had not come to my mind for a long time. The love I have for today nonetheless contains the love I had for the past.

*****

My husband was leafing through a "Fun with Chinese" language book we had bought a few days ago in Shanghai. We both liked it for the cartoonized explanation of the original logographic script of the Chinese characters and their evolution. The Mandarin tones, however, were less fun for him.

"*Jiang-nan*," he read from the two characters I showed him from the book. He said it half joking and half frustrated, and his pronunciation was a little off as usual.

"First tone for '江' (*jiang*) and second tone for '南' (*nan*). Even tone and then rising. Imagine a robot speaking for the first tone, and a question for the second. The two characters mean 'river' and 'south.'"

"*Jiangggg-nannnn?*" he tried again, this time making dramatic head movements to make me laugh.

And our journey was just beginning.

2
The Lane and its People
弄堂 (longtang)

As I was growing up, I pronounced "弄堂" in the Shanghainese way, *"lhongdhang"*. This is a little different from the Mandarin pronunciation, *"longtang"*. In fact the term had originated in Shanghai. Entering a straight alley, one can see these lane houses on both sides, a blend in style of Western terrace houses and Jiangnan architecture, mostly built from the mid-19th century to the 1930s, when people started to move to the still young city from their neighbouring Yangtze River Delta farming towns.

By the time I was a child, many of these *longtang* houses had already passed their glory and been divided up. The house we lived in had once belonged to a concubine of the Chief Police Officer in Hongkou District during the Nationalist régime. It had three stories with one toilet and one south-facing balcony. The police officer and his concubine had both been executed when the Communists took over in 1949 and the house was appropriated by the government. In the 1980s, the five of us – my grandparents, my parents and I crammed into the third floor. The balcony was set up as an outdoor kitchen and shower area. On the first and second floor, there still lived the concubine's son and his family, now as renters. My youngest uncle, unmarried at the time, occupied the small storage room next to the communal toilet in between the second and third floors.

We didn't enjoy much privacy with these living conditions. The shower area on the balcony was only separated by a wooden screen. And since the screen was not very tall and our house was not too far away from the neighbouring houses, we often took quick showers sitting on a plastic stool, and poured water onto ourselves with a basin. Luckily, there was a drain on the balcony so water did not flood the kitchen. On winter days, we used a wet towel to wipe our bodies carefully instead. Both my parents and grandparents had a colorful spittoon with a big double-happiness character on it, which we used as bed pans on chilly winter nights so that we wouldn't have to venture down to the toilet through the dark, squeaky stairs and wake up my uncle. As a result, our rooms often didn't smell very nice in the mornings.

I had always known that my father was the favourite first-born son of the family. It could be seen from the way my grandmother treated us. When in rare cases she cooked a whole chicken, my father always got the drumsticks – "dark meat is more active, therefore more delicious," we believed. Sometimes, my grandmother would serve me a wing because she said that I was also a Qian, although a girl, but never my mother. My grandmother herself, often claimed that she particularly liked the fatty tail end of a chicken and the chicken feet, and I believed this for many years in my childhood.

My mother, then a young wife, often had conflicts with my father and grandparents. One day, she complained that my grandparents were selfish for suggesting that the two families eat separately. "But I have a full-time job," she said to my father, "so when I start cooking after work, it will be late. While you can still join your parents for dinner, it will be mainly me and our daughter to suffer." My father was quite shocked when he learned of the suggestion and finally talked my grandparents out of it. Another day, my mother told me in good humour that my grandmother had seen the large pile of dirty clothes that she didn't have time to attend to until the coming weekend – we had to hand-wash our clothes at the time – and my grandmother had picked out only my father's clothes to wash and hang dry while leaving the rest alone. "Can you believe it," my mother sighed, "quite funny, in fact, isn't it!"

My father had bad, decayed teeth filled with cavities, which had started in his youth. And it became a pain to tackle this later in his life. At first, I thought it was just due to the lack of public health care in the old times. Only in the 1980s had schools started to have cavity screening for students. My mother, on the other hand, as a health professional, had always taken good care of her teeth despite limited resources in her younger years. Later I learned that my father's teeth were really a product of his family's favoritism. When my father was born in the old family house in Zhuji, Zhejiang Province, in 1944, his restaurant-owning and country gentleman grandfather had celebrated his birth with firecrackers and a feast that went on for days. Every country neighbour who came to their house could enjoy a meal. As a child, my father would receive a candy from his mother every night before sleep, behind my grandfather's back, and put it on his tongue to melt as he lay in bed. This had lasted until his teenage years in Shanghai where the family had moved in 1946. In contrast, one year after my father was born, my grandmother gave birth to a baby girl. My great-grandfather was rushing up the stairs to my grandmother's room, when he heard the midwife announcing that it was a girl. My great-grandfather then stopped and turned around without seeing the baby at all.

I heard from my mother that an aunt of mine died when she was a toddler. She was playing with some fish that somebody had caught and put in a small basin. All of a sudden, one fish jumped high over her hand. She was startled and scared to death. I wasn't convinced when I heard the story in my twenties. "How could that happen?" But my father didn't have any memory of the incident, or much recollection at all of his little sister. So that was the only version of the story we knew. With my grandparents both passed away, the life of my aunt would remain a family mystery.

***

I wondered what our downstairs neighbours thought about us. I thought they were a strange family. The parents who lived on the second floor would often fight or curse each other. My father once intervened when the husband had pinned down his wife on the bed, and was choking her with both hands around her neck. My father thought that he had saved the wife's life, but she was nevertheless still not friendly towards my family. On the first floor lived the wife's younger brother, who had stayed single into his late thirties or early forties, during a time when people generally got married earlier. He was a gentle and decent-looking man. I didn't understand at the time that men from certain families had much less promising prospects to find a wife.

The second-floor daughter, Weiwei, was my own age. I didn't really like her. She had crooked teeth, and an unhappy, mouse-like face. Like her mother, her voice was always high-pitched as if being too defensive. But we spent a lot of time together, as there were not many other children I knew. And because we were both lonely only children of the 1980s, we liked plants and animals very much.

Weiwei used to have a pet pigeon when we were around five years old. At first, I noticed that she had a bird cage hanging on the bamboo drying racks outside the second floor window. The pigeon was an ordinary colour, dark silver and white. At the time, I didn't know any neighbours who had more colorful, exotic singing birds, so I found the coo coos of the pigeon interesting enough. Unlike the skinny, wild ones we often saw on the streets, Weiwei's pigeon had grown very big from the millet bowl she had been feeding on. Her feathers looked smooth and young. Weiwei was very diligent in taking care of her pet and refilling the bowl. In the early morning, she would mimic the coo coo sound when opening the bird cage, as if telling her friend to go out and get some exercise for the day. Once she told me with pride that they didn't really need that bird cage now as the pigeon would always circle back before the evenings to rest outside their window. Weiwei's mouse-like face seemed to light up a little and get less wrinkled when I saw her playing with the pigeon.

I think it happened a couple months after Weiwei and the pigeon became inseparable. My mother had somehow already guessed the fate of the little creature, because one day when I talked to her about Weiwei's obsession, she went on to educate us about the nutritious value of pigeon eggs. "It is comparable to ginseng," she said. "When I was a child, our Cantonese next-door neighbours in the *shikumen* always used to give us a few. Good for women's skin, too." I wasn't sure why Weiwei had never picked up on any warning signs over the months. But she came back from kindergarten one winter afternoon and wailed loudly into the evening. The second-floor wife had decided that it was the day to enjoy their pet on the dinner table.

"Well, well," my mother commented as both Weiwei's cry and the meat smell travelled up to our floor, "they surely waited until the Winter Solstice, so the bird was fed well."

The three months of Shanghai winter were both humid and cold. The temperature often dropped below zero Celsius. We didn't have any heating systems inside the rooms, like those in the provinces north of the Yangtze River. And the provinces further south had pleasant, milder winters. On our third floor, wind often blew in from the open balcony. I was always bundled up in layers at home. Perhaps because our clothes were not made of good quality fabric, or because I didn't like to wear mittens, I got purple chilblains on my fingers each year. My mother then made me soak my hands in hot pepper water, and applied medicine to them. When the chilblains were healing, my skin got very itchy. I always dreaded winter.

That year, I noticed that Weiwei, who used to laugh at my chunky, purple fingers, also got chilblains on her ears. I felt bad for her. She had now joined her family's noisy quarrels and would stand next to an open window looking down at the street. I wondered if she was observing wild pigeons on chilly days.

When spring came in the next year, my mother bought us a pair of chicks from the wet market for one *yuan*. What lovely yellow things they were! A chick's fluffy body could fit into the palm of one hand; and I could feel their warm beating hearts when I held them. One *yuan* was a big sum of money when my parents' monthly salary was only 70-80 *yuan* combined. So we put them carefully in a wooden basin, laid some dry grass underneath, and covered them up in the evenings with a big mesh food cover. As the days grew warmer and my chilblains healed, I enjoyed sitting on the balcony with the chicks, peeling green edamame dutifully while waiting for my mother to return from work.

My father didn't really enjoy having animal companions. He was often at home on the days when he didn't teach at the university, using our room as a study. My grandmother was good at tiptoeing around when she was busy with household chores. I, however, was a trouble-maker. Once, I was trying to show him a giant green caterpillar that I had caught on the balcony and carried it to our room. The little thing unfortunately escaped from my hands onto my father's desk and, trying to catch it, I knocked down a porcelain tea mug that he had been using for over ten years. After that, I was scolded and was not allowed to take my animals beyond the balcony.

When I invited Weiwei upstairs to play with the chicks, I must have shared the recent mug incident with her. Weiwei suggested that we build them a stone home outside in the *longtang*. In those days, the *longtang* was where we played hide and seek in the bushes, played jump rope and featherball with other neighbours' children, and dared each other to taste the supposedly poisonous oleander leaves. On stifling summer evenings, it was also where the community gathered in their lounge wear and bamboo deck chairs to get away from the hot rooms. So I considered the *longtang* as an extension of home and didn't think it was such a bad idea. While I had my mother's promise that the chicks Huanghuang ("yellow") and Cuicui ("emerald") wouldn't end up in dinner bowls, there seemed no harm in being more cautious based on Weiwei's experience, and my father and grandparents' complaints of chicken poop often seen on the balcony. As six-year-olds, we had learned not to take adults' words at face value.

One evening, before my mother came home, I found a big cardboard box that used to carry fruit, and layered some small pinewood branches and grass on the bottom. Weiwei helped me transfer Huanghuang and Cuicui into the box. We also threw in some millet and bun crumbs, together with a bowl of fresh water. The chicks made a few squeaks as if happy in their new environment. We then carried them out to their new "home" in a corner of the *longtang*, where we had already marked a square behind the bushes with bricks. None of my family members seemed to notice what we were up to.

The next day, when Weiwei accompanied me to feed Huanghuang and Cuicui in their new home for the first time, we were shocked to find that they had gone missing! The cardboard box and the half-full water bowl were still there. Yet a few bricks seemed to have been pushed down. We searched the entire lane and couldn't see even a shadow of the chicks. Later on, after hearing my story, my mother sighed for my poor judgement. "An alley cat might have got them. What were you guys thinking, to smuggle them out like that! Isn't our home good enough for you? Being little, you already have an arm that stretches out towards others instead of your own family!"

The arm comment was a harsh one, coming from Chinese parents. Both frustrated and humiliated, I thought that Weiwei was the cause of my distrust of my mother, whom I had considered more of a predator than alley cats! Not wanting to end up in tears like Weiwei when she had lost her pigeon, I was extremely mean to her that day, calling her the stupid, jealous daughter of trashy parents and granddaughter of a convict's concubine. Weiwei's face turned red from anger and fought back immediately.

"You think you are so much better? The whole house was always ours, and should still be. Your family are here only because you are pitied! And my mom told me that your grandfather was a labour farm convict himself!"

"Liar! My grandfather was a doctor before he retired. Unlike your convict family, he has saved lives!"

"Only saved lives for the enemies, I'm sure."

The dichotomy of family versus others, and friends versus enemies had been passed down to us from an older generation very easily, and was very hard to shake off or sometimes even notice later in life.

I cursed Weiwei for making things up, pulled her braids, got kicked by her in return, and stopped speaking to her for days. I blamed it all on her to my mother and perhaps she believed me. "No ivory comes out of a dog's mouth," my grandmother frowned when she heard what the neighbouring girl had said, with a phrase often used in our daily relations with other people. I didn't realize then how similar our two families' fates in fact were, bringing us together under the same roof, and how foolish it was to attack each other.

Weiwei was the first one in my childhood who brought up questions about a history not really distant, yet a history that everyone seemed so eager to push further out of sight, or to accept and bury, and to carry on without looking back.

And most of my generation, a generation of only children, grew up without speaking about, or sharing history. We didn't feel safe enough to do so with someone outside our families. I only understand years later, following the trajectory of my peers, that loneliness was what we had most in common.

South of the Yangtze

3

Five Black Categories
黑五類 (*hei wu lei*)

My grandfather was once labelled a "historical counter-revolutionary." And therefore my father belonged to one of the "黑五類" (*hei wu lei*, "Five Black Categories"), a title he had inherited rather than earned, and which included landlords, rich peasants, counter-revolutionaries, bad elements and rightists. The character for "black," "黑," has evolved from its original logographic script, which resembles a face bearing ink tattoos, as ordered by a court to show that a person is a criminal.

My grandfather's life, however, wasn't coloured or tattooed in the beginning. He was the middle son of a landowner in Zhuji, Zhejiang Province. My great-grandfather had 33 *mu* of farmland, approximately 5.4 acres, and a restaurant in a commercial street in Zhuji where he had hired a few *changgong*, long-term workers with food and accommodation provided. Referred to as a "country gentleman" in the old days, my great-grandfather wasn't rich, but had a comfortable life with some influence. When his daughter-in-law, my grandmother, married my grandfather from her poorer village seven miles away in the same county, all her friends had remarked that "she must have done enough good deeds in the past few incarnations to have this luck." Who would expect then that during the Land Reform in the 1950s, my great-grandfather would be killed and have all his properties taken by the government?

Among the three sons, my grandfather was the only one who went to a university in Shanghai. During the Sino-

Japanese War in the late 1930s and early 1940s, he had worked in an Army Hospital behind the frontline, and was a young Lieutenant Colonel in the Nationalist régime. In the old photographs we had kept of my grandfather, he was always dressed in a suit and tie, the fashion style he had picked up in the Westernized city, and groomed himself with shiny hair gel. We didn't have any photos of him after the time when the Communist régime came to power in 1949, however, until his old age. And in those recent photos, there was no trace of his former dapper self. He had become a very different person.

My grandmother used to claim that it was out of the "love for our country" that my grandfather had turned down the Taipei-bound plane tickets for the entire family and a management position in the Health Department in Taiwan in 1949. She said that my grandfather had determined to retire from clinical work during the Civil War but would continue to contribute to public health care – he discovered that plague had killed more than firearms in war times. And after 1949, he was hired as an ophthalmologist with a 200 *yuan* monthly salary in Shanghai. The government had changed, but he didn't seem to be concerned at first.

The three-year "Campaign to Suppress Counter-revolutionaries" soon started in 1950, together with a sweeping Land Reform in the country. My grandfather's history of working under the Nationalist régime was revealed. Later, before he was sent to labour camp in Anhui Province, all his bank savings were frozen. My grandmother was left alone with four children and only twelve *yuan* a month to live on. The few gold bars that he had saved up were kept in the home of his younger brother, who used to have the "good background" of a factory worker. However, at the beginning of the Cultural Revolution in 1966, even his younger brother's home was raided because the Red Guards found out that he was the descendent of a landlord, one who had already been punished with execution during the Land Reform. My grandfather received news of his father's public trial and death months after the tragedy, while in the labour camp.

My father, as a *hei wu lei*, was denied a higher education at the age of eighteen, even though he had high marks in the university entrance examination and passed the admission criteria. He spent the next fourteen years working in a chemical factory. Only in 1979, when he was in his mid-thirties, was he able to skip undergraduate studies and go straight to graduate school at Nanjing University, the same one he had applied to as a teenager.

By the time I was born, my parents' life had finally settled into a quiet rhythm, even in our compromised living condition. My father had secured an assistant professorship at one of the most well-regarded universities in Shanghai. Although an intellectual didn't earn more than a factory worker in the beginning of my father's career, he was content. And my mother was working as a pharmacist and studying for a university degree at the same time throughout the 1980s, as her school years were largely interrupted by the Cultural Revolution.

***

Financially, we had only begun to make ends meet when we lived on Duolun Road. Once an earthquake came in the middle of the night, and I realized how few possessions we had. At first, we felt our beds and the house shake, and soon heard neighbours shouting from the *longtang*: "Earthquake, earthquake!" Suddenly, all the lights in the neighborhood were turned on. We put jackets over our pajamas and quickly gathered the family. Everybody seemed to head to the open space on Duolun Road. It took my parents only a moment to decide that there was nothing of material value worth burdening themselves with. The single exception was a flashlight.

Our neighbours were mostly in the same situation, sleepy-eyed and empty-handed. Weiwei and her family came out before us, not carrying anything either. Only one older neighbour had his small television in his arms. We all had a black and white television at home. But the news didn't usually cover these events. Adults still had memories of the devastating earthquake in Tangshan that had killed over 200,000 people, a decade earlier, the year Mao died, and I heard some people talk about hanging a pot lid from their ceiling for years as an earthquake predictor, which made them act faster tonight. My mother had volunteered to walk to her hospital thirty minutes' away to make a long-distance phone call to a friend who worked at the Beijing weather bureau. Thanks to her, we later confirmed that it had been only a magnitude 5 earthquake, and there was no need to go into an "air-raid shelter" nearby.

"Well, if we had to go hide," my mother said to my father later as we went back to our room, struggling to sleep again, "there were quite a few air-raid shelters within walking distance. We left elementary school in the fifth grade to build them, after all!"

"Why did you have to build air-raid shelters?" I asked.

"Because the 'American Imperialists and Russian Revisionists' were going to bomb us at any moment in the 60s. So every family had a brick quota…we had to use a mold to build bricks and find raw materials for them. My classmates and I even dug up some graves for coffin wood. As we opened up a coffin, we saw a dead body in a shroud floating in the water. I had already given up; but some brave boys used a stick to poke the body…"

I was quite terrified by the picture I imagined in my mind. Didn't my father teach me that we should always respect our ancestors? It sounded that at the time my mother was not only disrespectful, but almost a gangster. No wonder she was never afraid of the dark and ghost stories like I was. My father only shook his head in disapproval. My mother kept murmuring about fighting for leaflets and taking the trains to other cities to exchange revolutionary ideas, until we eventually fell asleep again.

It was only a couple of days later when we heard the rumor that even though the buildings in Shanghai were mostly intact during the earthquake, people were quite panicked because of their lack of information. Over 90 people were injured from jumping off their buildings and 3 people had died that evening. These numbers, of course, never made it into the official papers.

***

Even as a young child, I had a rudimentary sense of equality, which is achieved in our society not really by the fairness of the game rules, but by the absence of class security. An earthquake just might come at any time. Or a family would fall from grace very quickly. I didn't have proper words for it then. Adults in my family didn't discuss their own history freely. They would rather channel their emotions and find solace in other people's stories.

My grandparents enjoyed watching Yue Opera on their black-and-white television. My semi-literate grandmother didn't care for Peking Opera where "you can see 'red face' and 'white face' from the beginning," she claimed. Besides, the singing in the Yue Opera was very similar to the dialect they had spoken in Zhuji. So before I learned to read the subtitles, I could rely on my grandparents to interpret the singing.

The story we had watched the most was "The Legend of Xi Shi," one of the oldest tales of Jiangnan. In fact, it was a story more about two warring states than about a beautiful woman. In the Spring and Autumn period (770 - 476 B.C.), there were two states, Wu and Yue, in the Yangtze River Delta area. Both had a temperate climate, green mountains and wet farmlands good for tea and rice paddies. The two states were old enemies, and each of them had won in turn. In 496 B.C., the Yue army killed the old Wu emperor in a battle; and two years later, the young son of Wu got his revenge and captured the Yue emperor as a slave. All the smart councilors of Wu had advised their emperor to execute his enemy. But the Wu emperor was too arrogant and he fell into the trap of the Yue emperor's schemes.

First, the Yue emperor laid his head low as a slave, and even once volunteered to taste the Wu emperor's stool to diagnose diseases. So after a few years, he was seen as inconsequential and released back to his home country like a tiger going back to the woods. Once he was back in his old capital, he paid his tribute of grain seeds in full. But he had the seeds cooked in advance so that the Wu farmers who planted these seeds later would suffer from a famine. Then, he sent the young Wu emperor the most alluring woman in Yue, Xi Shi, so that his enemy would happily ignore state affairs. And lastly, to remind himself of the humiliation he had previously endured, for a period of twenty years, he kept his slave habit of sleeping on uncomfortable brushwood every night and additionally tasted every day the bitterness from an animal gall bladder that he had hung from his study ceiling. As the Yue army grew strong again, in 473 B.C., they took Wu's capital and trapped the Wu emperor on a mountain. The Wu emperor pleaded for surrender, but was denied as the Yue emperor knew all too well about keeping his enemy alive. Eventually, Yue took all of Wu's territory after the Wu emperor committed suicide.

"What becomes of Xi Shi, then?" I asked.

"Well, from the opera, we know that she eloped with Fan Li, who had been the Yue emperor's top councilor and the man who discovered Xi Shi when she was a washerwoman by the river…" my grandmother said.

My grandfather interrupted her. "Fan Li was a smart man," said. "He knew that the Yue emperor would only value people in miserable times. 'When the birds are all gone, the good bow will be hidden; and when the rabbits have all been killed, the hunting dog will be cooked.'"

"They lived happily together in the Five Lakes after the fall of Wu," said my grandmother.

My father, also quite familiar with the story, put down his books and walked into my grandparents' room. "There was another version," he said, "that Xi Shi had returned to Yue with the Wu emperor's posthumous child. The Yue emperor treated her badly, as did her old lover Fan Li. And the Yue people gossiped behind her back. So Xi Shi was disappointed with her homeland and jumped off a cliff."

"That doesn't sound like a happy ending," I said.

"In reality, it is often the case, and different from either the stories told by the winning party's historians or the stories people would rather believe," my father said. And my grandmother gave him a look.

"Always a woman," my grandfather said, "a woman who brings down a nation...Da Ji ruined Shang, Bao Si ruined Zhou, Empress Yang almost ended the Tang Dynasty, and Mao's wife..."

I thought that if my mother were here, she wouldn't like such a comment. And then my grandmother said, "No matter what you men say, I still believe that she and Fan Li went to the Five Lakes, living like celestial beings."

My grandmother was still a romantic after all these years. But if not so, how would she have survived for more than a decade while her husband was in the labour camp without communication, or the madness of the 1960s when they had my grandfather's "self-criticism" glued on both the house entrance and their third-floor front door? She did many odd jobs to support the family, including working in a spun silk factory and coloring black-and-white photos in a photo studio. When the Cultural Revolution started, the "bourgeois" photo studio was shut down and all the employees made Mao Zedong badges instead. Before my grandmother retired in the late 1970s, she worked as a cashier at a public bathhouse, where her husband and sons often went for free showers.

When I was a child, I was confused about my father and grandfather's tone when referring to women, as if I myself also carried some destructive force that could bring down a civilization. When I asked about Xi Shi's fate at the end of the story, it seemed to lead to a familiar conclusion, despite the various endings. In many of our cultural narratives we are encouraged, instead of facing history head on, to understand it in terms of scapegoats. The one who started the violence wished to burden their victim with criticism, as well as repentance. And narratives were passed down through the vehicle of our language – *hong yan huo shui*, "beautiful women are the roots of bad karma" – a phrase I had learned very early on.

In our day-to-day life, on the other hand, I noticed how reliant my father and grandfather were on their wives and mothers. For example, my father never learned to cook ("Confucius said that 'a gentleman should stay away from the kitchen'"), but he was never shy in letting my mother know that her cooking would never live up to the standard of my grandmother's.

4
Allowing Temperament
任性 (*renxing*)

At seven years old, I had a chance to visit Zhuji, the old capital of Yue and my grandparents' hometown. Even though my memories of the trip mostly consisted of the local specialty food from station to station, my parents said that, during the train ride, they pointed to the fields of crops outside the windows and quizzed me. They teased me for being born to be *wu gu bu fen* (not knowing what the five major grains were), despite having a healthy appetite. They said that I belonged to a new breed of city-bred only children born after the 1980s, a generation that seemed to be spared the acute sufferings which had defined China's contemporary history in the past century.

My father had two siblings who were "Sent-down Youths" in the 1960s, among the 16 million educated city youngsters rusticated to the country. My uncle and aunt had considered themselves fortunate to go to Zhuji at the time. Granted, there were those happy-go-lucky youngsters who didn't go beyond the outlying islands of Shanghai such as Chongming and Hengsha. But think about the ones who went all the way to the northern-most Heilongjiang Province where there were only sweet potatoes to eat! On the train, my father had told me that the quota to stay in a "rice eating province" was very tight at the time for Shanghainese; and my grandparents were comforted by the idea that at least their children went back to where their roots were.

Both my uncle and aunt married a local in Zhuji and had a child. After they got married, they waived their right to return to Shanghai. Perhaps they were not strong-willed enough to wait a decade in their best years for a change of the political wind. Perhaps as children belonging to the "Five Black Categories", they were hoping to improve their lives by marrying a good "Poor and Lower-middle Class Peasant." Or they simply fell in love while looking for solace, as people did in the harsh and lonely working environment. When my parents narrated marriage stories of their generation, circumstances often weighed as much as attraction, if not more.

During the late 1970s, when the "Sent-down Youths" were allowed to return to the cities, many families broke up. In one Xishuangbanna farm, located among the Dai ethnic minority villages in Yunnan Province, 3,000 couples filed for divorce within five days of the new policy. I didn't know where this province was until the early-1990s, when a popular television show told the story of five beautiful, mixed race teenage children coming to Shanghai to look for their birth fathers, all of whom had moved on and built new families. My parents and I would gather near our television at 8 o'clock sharp, so that we wouldn't miss even the opening theme song – *"The beautiful Xishuangbanna, cannot keep my baba..."* In the show, these five Yunnan children were eventually disappointed with Shanghai and went back to their mothers. I remembered that in those evenings, even the neighborhood streets would be very quiet, as everyone sat in front of the television and had their hearts tied to the fate of these characters.

It was the first time I became aware of the history of the Cultural Revolution and its aftermath, through fictional stories.

My aunt and uncle had remained in Zhejiang Province. Aunt Jingyun's son died from rabies at age five after being bitten by a wild dog. She didn't have another child afterwards. This meant Uncle Jingchuan's son, Xiaolong ("small dragon"), was the only third-generation son of the Qians. And because he had carried an atrial septal defect since childhood, he was spoiled rotten by his parents.

***

During our visit, we stayed at the riverside house Uncle Jingchuan had built just a year earlier. On the first floor, they had opened a grocery store that sold shampoo, water bottles, cigarettes and lighters, as well as packaged snacks. My uncle and his family were more weather-beaten than us. But after a week of swimming in the river in front of their house, I soon became as tanned as a country kid.

My cousin Small Dragon, 11 years old and chubby, had kept his wary distance from me at first. But as I turned darker by the day, he started to regard me as one of his peers, and let me follow him to dig up earthworms or catch green locusts. "However," he said, "now I'm too embarrassed to introduce you to my friends as 'my cousin from Shanghai,' because you don't look like a city girl anymore!"

Four years younger than him, I didn't care who I looked like at all. I felt free with all the open dirt roads, chickens roaming in the backyard, and pink lotus flowers occasionally spotted in the river. I had never swum in a pool before. So I had to learn swimming like the village kids, who were just thrown into the river by their parents, and left to flop about freely until they figured out a way to stay afloat. My father watched us from the bank, however, ready to jump in in case of emergency. The river was, after all, over two meters deep.

"Relax more," my father said as I clung on to the steps near the bank, "don't kick your legs too hard. The thing about swimming in the river is that the more you resist, the more the current works against you and exhausts your energy. You need to submit to it, feel the motion of the water and borrow its movement. Allow the water to work for you. Observe your cousin!"

Small Dragon had already gone further out with his friends to pick lotus seedpods and water chestnuts. They laughed as they kicked, and moved as swiftly as frogs. I was eager to be one of the frogs. It took me a few days to catch up with my primitive "dog crawling style," as my father called it. But I got much more comfortable with the river over time, and started joining the local boys and girls' later excursions such as diving for winkles.

"Very well done," my father praised me as we ate winkles cooked with soy sauce one evening. "Swimming is a good skill to have. Your mother never learned it, although we went to the beach on Putuo Island a few times…"

My parents had the habit of putting each other down in front of other relatives for modesty, which sometimes bothered me. But my mother wasn't really listening at the time. She told me later that over the course of dinner, she was simply amazed to see that Uncle Jingchuan's family had used their mouths to suck out the winkle meat and ate all of it, including the tail! When at home, we would use a toothpick to pull the meat out and would eat only the head. "Your poor uncle," she said, "look at how far down he has fallen. Who would think that he was a doctor's son? And your own father, with a mouthful of bad teeth!"

My mother was a little more relieved a few days later. When we went sightseeing to a Taoist temple on top of the Rock Bucket Mountain near my uncle's house, I drew a divination stick from a bamboo pot to tell my fortune, and found out that I had the top luck to become a doctor in the future. "Reincarnation of Hua Tuo, the most skillful physician in ancient times. Very nice," my mother said.

Uncle Jingchuan was even more pleased that Small Dragon would turn into a *guan*, referring to an imperial official in the past, and a government official now. He patted the back of my cousin and said, "Xiaolong, our family relies on you!" Back home, my uncle's wife bought some Shaoxing rice wine to commemorate the occasion. I didn't understand at the time what a big deal a *guan* was, that people had treated it as *guang zong yao zu*, bringing honor to our ancestors. It certainly seemed to have a better prospect than my grandfather's profession, a doctor, based on everyone's reaction. I didn't think too much of the predictions afterwards, one way or the other.

Small Dragon, however, became more and more ridiculous after our fortune-telling. At first, he had gone around announcing to his friends that since he was born to be an official, he would now be the leader of the group, and everyone should listen to him or he would beat them up. Since my cousin was a big boy and the eldest, nobody said anything. He then started to ask other kids to give him "tributes," in the form of fragrant erasers, cigarette cards and the glass marbles that we liked to collect in the 1980s and early-1990s. I got sick of him just taking the possessions of others, who had spent months of pocket money to accumulate these valuables. As a result, I was less enthusiastic about hanging out with the group, and volunteered to my uncle that I could help look after the grocery store when he and his wife needed to run a quick errand.

Noticing that I no longer trailed behind him, Small Dragon stayed with me one day in the store while our parents went to visit my aunt Jingyun. He didn't seem pleased with me that afternoon and bossed me around to fetch things from storage for him from time to time. It was a rainy day. And there were hardly any customers. I started reading a picture book about a legendary monk with supernatural powers and a magical fan. "Hey, show me your city girl tits," Small Dragon said out of boredom, "take off your top and let me take a look."

"No!" I wasn't happy with the way he was telling me what to do, and felt annoyed with being distracted from the picture book.

"Well, Xiaoting always takes her clothes off for me when her parents are not around. She has very fair skin." Xiaoting was the prettiest girl among my cousin's friends, always wearing two "sheep horn" braids. And she was of similar age to him. I found it hard to imagine the shy and pretty Xiaoting doing such a thing.

I decided that I was just going to regard his words as noise.

"Forget about it then! I bet you have nothing yet, like an airplane field. You are so boring."

A few minutes later, Small Dragon came up with another idea.

"I want to try something now. You better sit where you are behind the counter and don't move." And before I could understand what he was getting at, he leapt over and bit my lips with his teeth. "Ah, how disgusting kissing is! Now I need to rinse my mouth." As he announced his disgust, he put his head under the sink for a long time as if making a point to me, drank some water and spat it out.

I felt that his teeth might have broken my skin, and felt humiliated, so I started crying. And when my parents came back, I was still in tears. "What happened?" My mother asked. Small Dragon had already sneaked out before the adults were home, and went out to seek his tyrant fun with others.

Too embarrassed to recount what had happened, I said that Small Dragon had kicked my face with his shoes.

My mother was angry, and complained to my father, loud enough for my uncle and his wife to hear: "You see, these lawless 'little emperors' really need to be disciplined these days! Even worse than those in the city!"

"My sister-in-law, you don't know, boys are like that," my uncle was smiling, trying to bribe me with a candy from the shelf. "I'd say, only with a lawless personality can he become a *guan* one day!"

Later that night, I asked my parents when we were returning home.

"Yinan, we are guests here," said my father. "And we don't see your uncle and aunt very often. You shouldn't be

too '任性' (*renxing*), having that princess attitude."
Growing up, my father's worst accusation for me was always "任性," meaning "allowing temperament," or "following your own temperament." The character "性" is made up of the "heart" radical 忄 and "生" – the original logographic script of "生" resembles a growing plant. "Allowing temperament," however, was a derogatory adjective in Chinese.

"I am not *renxing*!" I said.

"Don't talk back to your parents!" he said. "You should learn from your cousin – he's older than you and hasn't minded showing you around all this time."

"Well, he stinks."

I didn't describe the incident to my parents in the end, sensing the failure in my own personality, and was disappointed that no criticism was laid upon Small Dragon from my father. In hindsight, I wondered if this memory had become the meaning of *renxing* for me, so that when, years later, Mr. Yang used the same words about me, it evoked similar confusion, anger and shame.

How many years would go by before I allowed myself to follow my own temperament again without self-indictment! I simply didn't remember this conversation until much later.

"Okay, okay," seeing that both my father and I were stubborn, my mother jumped back in then. "We only have a few more days – your father has the summer holiday; but I need to go back to work. After taking you to see Aunt Jingyun, we will head home. Stop arguing with your father now. You already look like a wild girl in the country."

5
Foreign Air
洋氣 (*yangqi*)

After my mother came back from Zhuji, she wore the pearl necklace Aunt Jingyun had given her to go to work every day. Pearls were rarely seen on Shanghai streets in my childhood. My mother still remembered reading about President Liu Shaoqi's wife being publicly denounced during the Cultural Revolution, wearing a string of ping pong balls on her neck to mock her "capitalist style." My mother grew up never owning any jewelry, nor wanting any when she was younger. However this time, after the Zhuji trip, she got many compliments for her pearls in her hospital.

"Are they real?" One of her colleagues had asked.

"Of course they are." My mother said, "my in-laws' hometown is famous for freshwater pearls. My sister-in-law and her husband have turned their fish ponds into a pearl cultivation farm now. Mostly exporting to foreigners!"

Her colleagues gathered their heads around her neck and studied closely. "They do look real," another pharmacist said, "the fake ones would be more perfectly shaped. But these are not so round if you look carefully."

"Yueling looks very '洋氣' (*yangqi*) with the necklace," they decided. "洋氣" was a popular Shanghainese phrase in the 1980s and 90s, meaning putting on a "foreign air." "洋," meaning both "ocean" and "foreign", is made up of the "water" radical 氵 and "羊" (sheep). Women of my mother's age were usually very pleased to receive this compliment.

My hand-me-down clothes in my childhood were mostly from stores that sold "export rejects." Aunts and older cousins on my mother's side liked to shop for these trendier items rather than local brands. It also seemed that the local brands and traditional industries were not doing well in those days, since everybody was making things for export. The "export rejects" clothes were usually cheaper, more colorful, and baggier, perhaps partly because of the fashion style at the time and partly because they were not designed to fit Chinese bodies. Growing up, my clothes were always a size too big.

One of my mother's sisters had moved to New Mexico in the early-1990s and would sometimes mail us her daughter's old clothes. I didn't really mind wearing second-hand clothes as a child, and felt rather excited to see novelty items. But once my mother went too far and bought me a second-hand suede jacket and my father a cashmere sweater from Huating Road, a popular clothes market at the time in the French Concession for new and old "foreign designs." My father was not impressed.

"I'm not wearing some foreign man's unwanted garbage." He said.

"You are strange. Look at this, a hundred percent cashmere and almost new!"

"Anyway, I don't want it. Can't believe you paid for this," my father said.

"But cashmere…"

"Not half as comfortable as my silk floss wadded jacket. From Zhuji."

My grandparents also came over to inspect the clothes. My grandmother turned the sweater inside out and sniffed the armpits. "Well, I've heard that they all have the 'foxy smell,' isn't it? And who knows if they have AIDS or not."

"They don't have AIDS," said my mother. I could see that she wasn't really sure, though, and didn't know how to talk back. AIDS was a strange concept to us back then, sometimes branded in the news as a capitalist vice. When it came to foreign influence, like many people in China at the time, neither the supporters nor belittlers in my family seemed to understand much about it.

"Call me superstitious," said my grandfather, "but I don't think it brings any good luck to wear a dead man's clothes. You also have a job, Yueling. There is no need to skimp on your husband and daughter's clothes."

My mother must have thought this funny coming from my grandfather, who used to tailor his three-piece suits in the most fashionable Western style when he was a young man. She often said that my grandfather had now turned into a stingy person, and "would break a coin into two to use if he could," given that his small retirement salary came from Anhui Province instead of Shanghai.

"At least I'm not breaking the rough toilet paper into half pieces each time to conserve it," she murmured only to me later, knowing that I was her ally against the household toilet paper policy. "I actually earn more than your father, but they acted as if I'm only your father's helper! Well, luckily you won't be that picky."

I had no choice but to put on that suede jacket with odd shoulders that winter.

However, one type of "foreign air" that my mother didn't approve of was Kentucky Fried Chicken (KFC). She said that Coke tasted like cough medicine, and the fried chicken only smelt good and was nothing compared to traditional Shanghainese steamed chicken or delicate drunken chicken cooked in wine. KFC had opened its first outlet in Shanghai in 1989; and a chicken and salad set used to cost one-tenth of most people's monthly salary. Even so, when the first restaurant opened in a historical building on The Bund, my youngest uncle Jingzhang put on a suit and tie and took his then fiancée there for a date. They had to stand in line for an hour to get in, and later brought back home paper placemats as souvenirs for their first "authentic American cuisine" experience. My uncle told me that there were even couples holding their wedding parties at KFC back then.

In the early-1990s, however, as people's salaries increased quickly, so did their understanding of the outside world after decades of lockdown. Even though a taste for novelty and imported brands stayed, within just a few years, KFC was no longer the only foreign chain in Shanghai. While many shared my mother's opinion about the "cough medicine," American fast food restaurants soon became an ordinary place mostly for young students to camp in with their friends and homework.

***

A year after we had visited Zhuji, when I was eight years old, my father was finally allotted an apartment near his university. It was a moment my mother had been waiting for ever since she married into the Qian family. She urged my father to move out as soon as possible, even though our new apartment was bare without any interior decoration.

I still remember the moving day. Some of our *longtang* neighbours stood nearby to watch us, many in their usual white-turning-yellow vest undershirts or pajama sets. One or two women were puffing the quilts that had been laid outside under the sun. A few children were kicking a featherball back and forth in a circle. We said goodbye to Weiwei and her family. And it didn't come to my mind then that I would not see them again, because I didn't know that my grandparents would also move out a few months later. Four of my father's graduate students came to help. They had borrowed a couple of three-wheeled rickshaws to carry my parents' wedding furniture: a bed, a wardrobe, a chest of drawers, a nightstand, a desk, a bookshelf and some chairs. We didn't have a sofa. I was excited by the prospect of having my own bed soon.

There were no professional movers around then, so people usually sought help from their relatives or acquaintances. My father seemed to be popular among the students, as I saw them being very chatty with him. I felt curious about these university students, who were all thin and wore black framed specs. At least two of them didn't speak Shanghainese. "What do these Philosophy students do after graduation?" I asked my father. And he said that they could do anything they pleased because their major would help them become a more insightful person. It was probably at that time when I started to realize that my father didn't have the conventional utilitarian approach towards teaching unlike most adults I knew. Although on the other hand, his students were already helping my family in the most utilitarian way on our moving day. I didn't imagine then that more than ten years later, one of them would even hire me for my first job.

***

Our new neighborhood was in the urban-rural fringe. There was nothing around the residential complexes that the university had built for its professors and employees. Within five minutes' walking distance from us, there was still lots of wasteland. Over the years, we would see it slowly turning into construction sites. My parents said that the small green hill five or six blocks away from us used to be the Japanese army's execution site in the 1930s and 40s, and again an execution place during the Cultural Revolution in the 1960s for those found "guilty" after public trials. One day, when our bus passed by the hill on our way home, we saw some workers building a pavilion on the top. "The government must think that there are many bitter and furious ghosts wandering about on the hill. A pavilion will give them a place to rest," said my father. My mother told me to stay away from the hill altogether as she had heard that in recent years a few deserted babies had been found dead there, possibly due to the strict One-child Policy in the city.

A few weeks after we had moved in, one of my mother's colleagues came with her husband and helped us put up cupboards. We set up a round table in the kitchen and used that room for dinner as well. Chinese apartments built in the 1990s had big bedrooms and small living rooms – few were really entertaining much outside the family. So my parents took the only bedroom we had and I took the dark "living room" as my bedroom. Even during the day, I had to turn on a lamp to read or work on my homework; and my new room had no doors. I was nonetheless very happy with it.

My parents started to use liquefied gas instead of a coal stove. I often saw my father returning home with a new tin of gas on the back of his bicycle in the evenings, which he then had to carry up the stairs to the fourth floor. Our neighbours were doing the same. But we were only nodding acquaintances with them now. Having a private bathroom was a big improvement, even though my parents had moved in too quickly to pre-install a water heater or a shower head, or even a flushing toilet. So for the first few months before we found a contractor, we were still using the double-happiness spittoon, and pouring warm water from a big plastic wash basin for showers.

I was transferred to a new elementary school nearby after spending the first year in my old one. My mother had already bribed my class teacher with next year's wall calendar and a face cream sent from New Mexico. All parents seemed to give teachers gifts when I was a child, so that they felt their children would receive fair treatment in school. My transfer seemed to be quite smooth. And I found out that many classmates were transferred children of university professors as well.

It was in the new elementary school that I first learned to sing our national anthem. Teachers asked us to be loud, clear and high-spirited when we sang the song. The lyrics started with these lines:

Arise, ye who refuse to be slaves!
With our flesh and blood, let us build a new Great Wall!
As China faces its greatest peril,
From each one the urgent call to action comes forth.

Arise! Arise! Arise!...

The tune was very catchy and had the effect of waking us up before the first class. Our class teacher said that the song was composed during the Sino-Japanese War. And it was used as the theme song of a popular Communist film in the 1930s, "Children of Troubled Times." In my textbook, I saw the photographs of two young men. They were the lyric writer and the composer of the song. I was sad to learn that the composer Nie Er had drowned in Japan at the age of 23, while swimming with friends. Our class teacher played us a short documentary to learn about Nie Er's life. The class was intrigued by the short-lived but prolific composer, as well as by the new teaching format. At the end of the class, one student raised his hand and asked, "Are we watching another documentary about the lyric writer Tian Han tomorrow?"

When the teacher said that there were no more documentaries, my classmates were a little disappointed. Later, I went home and described the class to my parents.

"Well, Tian Han lived to old age," my father answered my question. "He died during the Cultural Revolution. Does it mention that in your textbook?"

As a child, I had rationalized the textbook's decision, thinking that perhaps writing a tune was harder than writing lyrics. And the photo of Tian Han in the textbook didn't look as handsome as Nie Er's. So I didn't discuss it further with my father. Years later, when I read about Tian Han's incarceration and unnatural death, his picture rose up in my mind again. I wondered what difference it would have made if we had been given the chance to see his documentary in primary school instead, and learn about what happened to him after he wrote our national anthem.

I didn't like the song's lyrics in primary school. The "flesh and blood" image was too much to imagine. And mention of the Great Wall reminded me of the sad story of

Lady Mengjiang, which I remembered from watching Yue Opera with my grandparents.

My grandparents had explained to me that Lady Mengjiang lived during the Qin Dynasty in 221-206 B.C., when all the small and prosperous kingdoms such as Wu and Yue during the Spring and Autumn and Warring States periods had been defeated by the militarily superior Qin from the northwest. After conquering all the central plain and east coast territories, the Qin emperor announced himself to be the First Emperor of the "land under heaven," and required people under his rule to use a unified written language and follow identical rules of conduct. During the years when the Qin was expanding and waging war with northern nomadic countries, the First Emperor called for millions of civilian labourers to build the Great Wall, including Mengjiang's husband, originally an east-coast Qi state citizen before the unification.

Mengjiang's husband left for service three days after their wedding, and never sent a message to his wife for months. As winter approached, Mengjiang worried about the harsh climate in the north and decided to take her husband some padded winter clothes herself. After a long journey, she finally reached the Great Wall, but was told that her husband had already died. Hearing the long-feared news, Mengjiang wept for her husband, whose life was wasted and his body nowhere to be found. Her sorrow and anguish eventually made 400 kilometers of the Great Wall collapse, revealing the white bones of all the labourers who had died for the Qin tyrant.

Every morning, I started a new school day singing our national anthem.

Arise, ye who refuse to be slaves!
With our flesh and blood, let us build a new Great Wall! ...

6
Ready Language
成語 (*chengyu*)

Ever since I entered primary school, I noticed that many of my classmates had started to wear glasses. I was lucky, my mother said, that I was born far-sighted as a child. When we lived on Duolun Road, my grandfather, the ophthalmologist, had always assured her that my eyesight would be "cured" when school began. And it turned out to be the case.

I started to bring home many assignments to work on under the yellow lamp in my room. Even though our new complex had a large garden and nice woods, I didn't have much time to play outside after school. When we heard in the news that there was a crazy woman who poured sulfuric acid on a young child's face because of her frustration with the child's married father, and later an exhibitionist who liked to ambush school children, not far from where we lived, my mother got a little nervous and sometimes even locked me in the apartment when neither of my parents were home. Many of my only-children peers had a similar arrangement with two busy working parents.

On weekends, I went to cram schools. These cram schools usually borrowed the classrooms of our district's elite middle schools, in order to inspire applicants. Once my mother even ran into a colleague there. They became good friends, sharing information about secret cram schools and city-wide competitions for primary school students. I went to quite a few competitions as a result of my mother's new friendship, including singing and dancing, acting, essay writing and calligraphy. Perhaps the friendship wasn't the healthiest of its kind, created on such a basis; but it was quite normal in my mother's eyes and standard in the world in which I was brought up.

But with all the assignments and extracurricular competitions put together, I dreaded nothing more than the mandatory "Weekly Diary." Instead of writing one piece a day as advised, I often waited until Sunday evenings to finish seven entries all at once. My class teacher required us to record only "meaningful incidents" or "good deeds" in the diary, and she would grade us with such parameters. I usually couldn't think of anything morally praise-worthy to say, and didn't want my week's memories to be directed and summarized in this way. As a result, my diaries were seldom selected to be read in front of the class.

Meanwhile, some of my classmates led eventful lives. They often described helping an elderly granny across the street and returning wallets they found on the sidewalk to police officers. One classmate helped his parents fight off two armed robbers in the evening when they broke into their apartment. Another had a brave face-to-face encounter with a thief, described as of the Uygur minority, and persuaded him to take up a better profession.

Thinking back, I remember that, in the early 1990s, primary schools launched a new wave of the "Learning from Young Soldier Lei Feng" campaign. Lei Feng had been a popular hero during the three-year famine of the 1960s. His motto then was that he wanted to become "a screw of the proletarian revolution that never rusts", and he often helped others in trouble "without any consideration of self." According to my parents, Lei Feng's image was revisited for a couple years after the end of the Cultural Revolution. And again, after 1989 a new generation of young students all over China — my entire generation — were required once more to learn from him, they said.

Lei Feng's parents were said to have been tortured to death by the Japanese and old-world landlords. As an orphan, he regarded the Communist Party as his family and Chairman Mao's words as his purpose in life. Lei Feng died in a car accident in 1962. He was twenty-two. Another more recent young hero we had learned from in primary school, was Lai Ning, a near-sighted fourteen-year-old, who died in 1988 when helping to put out a forest fire. Perhaps I felt somewhat more distant from these heroes than my classmates did because I was neither near-sighted like Lai Ning nor did I hold a grudge against old-world landlords like Lei Feng. However, if I had known then that my great-grandfather was a landlord, I probably would have felt a little ashamed.

I realized that many exemplary people in our textbooks had died young, similar to the national anthem composer Nie Er. One could almost say that dying young was one of the pre-requisites of being exemplary.

"Consideration of the self," however, was not a notion that I could learn to expel easily. During some nights in my primary school years, I couldn't sleep well and found myself experiencing terrible fear for the first time in my life – thinking how provisional my presence in the world was – and woke up with a chill. The moment I opened my eyes, my pupils couldn't focus on the wooden furniture in the room anymore. It seemed to have had receded beyond my reach, all distant and blurry. It often took a good ten or twenty minutes for my eyesight to return to normal, my cold sweat to evaporate, and that sinking, helpless feeling to go away. In the bi-annual eye exams at school, however, the results showed that my childhood far-sightedness had now been replaced by normal "perfect" eyesight. So what I had felt in the evenings could only come from the depth of my own consciousness. It was my own demon made from my "consideration of the self."

Over time, the thing I found most helpful for my eyesight was watching the clouds outside the window. From my desk at school, I often saw a light gathering of white clouds against the sky on fair days, floating and parting with the wind, always changing shape and taking new forms. Clouds seemed never to need a boundary of the "self." And it amazed me how serenely they embraced each other, obtaining and losing at the same time, and became a new cloud with each encounter. I could watch the clouds for a long time until I heard the piercing bell at the end of those classes.

***

Once I had a bad bout of flu and was at home for a week. The following Monday, I handed in my "Weekly Diary" with one piece entitled "Happy to Have a Small Illness," in which I described in a jolly tone not having to show up at my cram schools and receiving more attention and candy bars from my parents. This time, I was selected to read my diary in front of the whole class as a lazy student's bad example. I remember that many of my classmates laughed as I read, and my class teacher laughed too. I realized that, in fact, my model classmates had all sympathized with and indeed shared my lack of the "selfless spirit." It was just that, at a very young age, they had already learned not to put it down on paper.

I was indeed not a fast-learning child. I resisted picking up the buzz words, the ones often heard in the news, entertainment programmes or on the streets. And I couldn't explain then why I didn't want my thoughts to be so easily shaped by the custom of our language. When, in primary school, we first started learning "成語" (*chengyu*), the four-character idiomatic phrases, everybody was very excited. Most *chengyu* derived from classic literature, from folklore or from historical events. They contained many entertaining stories and myths; and I was intrigued by them. Soon, my classmates started using these phrases in their diaries – for example, describing new buildings erected in the neighborhood as like "bamboo shoots sprouting after the spring rain," and people who couldn't see the entire truth as "a blind man feeling the elephant." My class teacher praised them for adding colour and dimension to their writing. However, after I had heard "bamboo shoots sprouting after the spring rain" in my classmates' reading many times, and frequently in the evening news too, I couldn't help feeling that learning too many *chengyu* would make me an even lazier person.

One evening after dinner, my father was smoking cigarettes on the balcony as usual. He was a heavy smoker and could consume three packs a day. I would usually leave him alone at these times, as my mother did. But that evening I had just come up with a question about my recent preoccupations that I wanted to talk to him about.

On the balcony, I asked him if it was possible that one life has only twenty-four hours – every evening we fall dead, and we wake up in another life the next day – only our memories trick us into believing that these days are continuous.

"Well, many philosophers have expressed similar thoughts in the past," said my father. *But I thought of it myself!* I wanted to say. However, I didn't interrupt as he continued, "One could compare floating life to a dream: 'passing clouds and morning dew' might be apt to describe such feelings, don't you think?"

"But that's not what I mean," I said.

"What do you mean then?" He knotted his eyebrows.

Years after that conversation, I finally read that *fu yun zhao lu*, "Floating clouds, morning dew," was a beautiful phrase coming from a Tang Dynasty history book, commenting on the ephemeral nature of human life, and the speaker's wish to attach to himself every landscape in sight with a long rope and not let it go.

"I don't really know…" I said, "there are so many ready-made phrases out there for me to borrow, but they are usually not what I mean. I'm always debating what to say. But in class, many people's diaries have started to sound like the news now…"

I knew that my father also hated the news language in China, both in papers and on television. He had said before, that it had its own system and linguistic style of hypnotizing and telling people nothing within half an hour. And apart from its abstractness, the news language usually omitted the subject of sentences, which my father believed to work in favour of the political narratives of the ruling group.

He took me more seriously at last. "Granted, these words come to your mind, before you could even think. Most people prefer not to think, of course…that's the problem with learning language in general though," he said, "it limits the boundary of your thinking before you know it. And no matter what language you learn, over time it becomes the only tool you have. Your mother, for example, only speaks in her Mao-style language."

"Talking behind my back, huh?" My mother heard herself mentioned and walked to the balcony to drag me away from my father's cloud of cigarette smoke. "I no longer have any choice, marrying into a home of second-hand cigarette smoke. But spare our daughter!"

I realized that ever since I first attended school, I had turned a little more towards my father for advice, and often took his side in my parents' arguments. My mother wasn't happy about my team-switching and liked to remind me that my father had never changed any of my diapers or walked me to kindergarten even once. "But now he reaps what I have sowed and poisons your mind with his strange bourgeois theories," she said.

While I agreed that my mother liked to slip in phrases now and then from the "Little Red Book," I thought it would be fair to say that my father also quoted a lot from Confucius classics such as the *Analects*, *Great Learning*, *Doctrine of the Mean* and *Mencius*. Perhaps that was why I didn't fully understand what he said.

The phrase, "Floating clouds, morning dew" had given me a comforting ink painting to land my thoughts on at the time, rather than a mirror to reflect the true shape of my musings. I realized just how much comfort some *chengyu* could bring – they made everyone feel that they could speak with a predecessor in time and space, echoing the same words. Even my father yielded to loneliness very quickly. I wondered if I noticed these things because I was an only child, and therefore had already learned to have low expectations for company.

A few days later, however, my father brought home four volumes of "New Concept English," a set of self-learning English textbooks which had been popular among his colleagues ten years previously, together with eight cassettes. After our little discussion, he had decided that learning English was a good way to expand my "boundary of thinking."

In Shanghai in the early 1990s, basic English was not introduced to students until the third grade of primary school. And the school textbooks put most of the emphasis on learning English verbs and their tenses. My father, on the other hand, wanted me not only to learn earlier than my peers, but also with an adults' textbook put together by an Englishman, with no grammar explained.

For the next few years, I listened to these cassettes hundreds of times, until I could recite each one of the essays in the four volumes, written by authors including Bertrand Russell and George Orwell. It had turned out that the Chinese method of teaching English was still very much like teaching Tang Dynasty poetry – "after one memorizes three hundred Tang poems, one can surely sing even if he cannot compose." I often cried at our dinner table and felt bitter about the extra work I had to commit to after school, apart from my other weekend classes. I had no energy left at the time to really understand or enjoy what I had recited, but I didn't want to quit and upset my father, who had put a lot of effort into learning the essays himself and teaching me.

Little did I know then that a decade later, after the new millennium, I would cling to the language of Russell and Orwell like clinging to a lifebuoy. English would become the language I used to speak, to write, and to think, even though moments of frustration came as often as moments of inspiration. Sometimes I wondered if I woke up only to find myself in a new dream, like in the epiphany I had discussed with my father. Or had I allowed myself to be bound at the ankles simply by a different tool? And I thought back to that evening conversation on the balcony with my father and how we realized only much later that those quiet, ordinary days were the days when we made some of the biggest decisions of our lives.

7
"Dream of the Red Chamber"
「紅樓夢」 (*Hong Lou Meng*)

When I graduated from primary school, I was one of only two students who made it to the best middle school in Hongkou District, a "key school" in our parents' terms. There were only a handful of "key schools" in Shanghai. And getting into one was considered a big milestone for a young contestant.

My mother said that my cram schools had paid off, otherwise I wouldn't have earned a score only one point above the admission line. One of my classmates, Qiong, a studious girl from a single-parent family and often the one with best scores in my cohort during mock exams, didn't get in because she was not able to solve the last Math question on the paper. I remember that she cried so hard after learning the results. "One exam decides your whole life" was a popular saying among students of my time. Parents mentioned it often to warn us that there was nothing else more important than running the academic marathon until we landed in a good university. And therefore, we had little time to look around at our fellow contestants, while fixing our eyes ahead in the race.

I don't remember making any close friends throughout my primary school years. I suppose it was the case for many of us only children born under the same one-child state policy. Back then, we didn't think about the cruelty of such loneliness.

That last year of primary school, a few days before the summer vacation, I heard that Qiong had had an accident, falling from the third floor while she was helping her mother clean the windows. Fortunately, they said, she fell into the bushes and merely broke one arm. Our class teacher arranged for us to send her a greeting card signed by all her classmates. We also donated our pocket money. My parents discussed Qiong's accident for a few days, especially her family's financial status, and how she must feel that many doors had already been closed to her at that young age. Nevertheless, when the summer vacation started, we who were merely more fortunate seemed to quickly forget about her. My parents now had frequent phone calls with the parents of the boy in my primary school who had also won admission to the same middle school.

For me, I was allowed to enjoy a rare break that summer, free from studies and competitions. My parents took me to Nanjing, where my father had spent his university days. And we went to Putuo Island in the East China Sea, one of the four sacred Buddhist retreats in the country and my parents' favourite summer destination. We dipped in the ocean near the Thousand Step Beach and visited many Buddhist temples. One night, through the windows of our mountain lodge, I woke up to a clear sky with thousands of stars that I had never seen before in the city. For days, I wished that I didn't have to return to my windowless bedroom and the dim yellow lamp.

However, when we were back home later, I didn't really miss our travel time as much as I had expected. I realized that the biggest freedom I had that summer was reading what my mother called the "leisure books" from my father's bookshelf. And I finally discovered the secret of fluidity in life through imagination – how we were not confined in our small circles merely because of our habits or circumstances, but that imagination could bypass the custom of our present-day language and speak to the hidden content of our hearts.

***

Among my father's collection, I had a particular fondness for 「紅樓夢」 (*Hong Lou Meng*, "Dream of the Red Chamber") as the main character, Jia Baoyu (his name means "false precious jade"), also disliked studying the textbooks assigned for the examinations to enter for the Imperial Civil Service, and preferred to read "leisure books" with his beautiful and spirited cousin Lin Daiyu ("wood ink jade"). The lovers' high ideals and their way of life, however, was crushed by the fall of the eminent Jia family, and Jia Baoyu's later arranged marriage with another cousin Xue Baochai ("snow precious hairpin") who exhibited more traditional traits and tactful manners favoured by the matriarchs of the family.

In the book, the marriage between Xue and Jia was referred to by the author as "a good union of gold and jade", while the covenant between Lin and Jia was "a previous covenant of wood and stone." *Hong Lou Meng* was originally entitled 「石頭記」 (*Shi Tou Ji*, "Story of the Stone," when the manuscript was first circulated in hand-written copies during the 1760s in the Qing Dynasty.

When I was walking or taking a bus to school, my mind often wandered off to "The Red Chamber." Like those tales in the Yue Opera that I grew up with, this story felt both old and new. Yet unlike a Yue Opera tale, which was often a vivid sketch of events, I found *Hong Lou Meng* to contain real portraits of the two lovers' souls, a rarity in classical Chinese literature.

The book was not completed, however, for the author, Cao Xueqing, died after finishing two-thirds of his manuscript. And the last forty chapters, added by Gao E, resolved the story in a conventional way often adopted by the Ming and Qing Dynasty's magnum opus novels, having Jia Baoyu walking away in the snow with a Buddhist and a Taoist monk at his either side after bidding goodbye to his Confucius father. I found this ending of my favourite novel in the Chinese language too convenient, and often wondered, had Cao Xueqing lived, what different answer would he have given to me, a stranger to whom he spoke so poignantly through time and space.

And before I realized it myself, my family noticed a change in me when middle school started.

My grandparents commented that I talked less than before. And they said that I didn't volunteer to entertain them anymore, such as by reciting a Tang poem or singing a popular children's song at family gatherings. My eyebrows were said to be often knotted sitting at the dinner table. When my parents and I visited them on weekends, I didn't have the same appetite for my grandmother's cooking that I used to have.

At the time, my grandparents had already moved into a new apartment which my youngest uncle Jingzhang had bought in the Pudong suburbs. It was an hour and half bus ride away from us, on the other side of the Huangpu River. My uncle, who used to live with us in the store-room on Duolun Road before he got married, was now the owner of two apartments and the wealthiest of all my relatives.

Shanghai had opened its first Stock Exchange in 1990, the first in mainland China since the beginning of the Communist régime. It started with only two stocks, and gradually increased to eight. In 1992, the government issued warrants for new stocks to balance the limited supply and a drastically increasing demand. Uncle Jingzhang bought a hundred warrants for 3,000 *yuan* at the time, after borrowing all the IDs he could get and queuing up for days, hoping to make some quick money for his wedding. What he hadn't thought of was that with the stock market reform in the same year, a lot more new stocks were issued than people had expected, pushing up the value of these warrants to a hundred fold of their original price. Uncle Jingzhang, who always had the gift of a business mind, didn't let his blind luck go. He sold them slowly on the black market and made a fortune. By the time I entered middle school, he had already quit his accounting job to become a full-time investor in the stock and real estate markets.

My grandparents were surprised by Uncle Jingzhang, to whom they hadn't given much attention before. I could see that even my parents were confused with the new reforms that happened one after another. My father had worked in the same university for over a decade and had waited many years for his turn finally to be allotted a university apartment. And the size of our apartment had been decided based on my father's associate professorship title, his age and working years. The system had turned many colleagues into enemies, I had heard, while they were fighting for the quota. However, in the mid-1990s, the housing market became fully commoditized very quickly. And many early stock market winners, like my uncle, had purchased apartments with their hot money. During my parents' conversations, I learned that even some of my father's colleagues from the university were now tempted by the new environment and started to "leave their academic temple and plunge into the commercial sea."

I realized that at the time, I didn't understand what big decisions every adult had to make in the face of new political winds. My mother, who had always been proud of both her and my father's professions, grew a little uneasy in Uncle Jingzhang's presence. It didn't help that my grandparents now gave more attention to my infant cousin, Uncle Jingzhang's daughter, than to me. At the same time, I seemed to have entered a stage of troubled adolescence.

Now thinking back, apart from the books I had been reading, perhaps my reticence and non-engagement with my surroundings was due to these social changes as well. Uncle Jingzhang and his wife started to appear annoying in my eyes when they developed a habit of ordering more than we could eat and being condescending to waitresses at restaurants. I wasn't happy with my father, either, who, after several arguments with my mother, had finally yielded and purchased stocks. Furthermore, I had learned after a few days in middle school, that besides admitting students through the entrance exam, admission could also be bought with 40 thousand *yuan*. My parents were as surprised as I when they heard this, but I was the one who quickly lost the initial excitement of earning my place after all the hard work.

***

The world I grew up in no longer responded to the ideals of "The Red Chamber," where one found poetry in the seasons and youthful longings. But in some way, it resembled everything outside Jia Baoyu and Lin Daiyu's small and protected circle – and Cao Xueqing had painted an equally compelling picture of that in the book. People's behaviour hadn't really changed since Qing Dynasty. The rules of the power game were subject to revision constantly, so those who were fortunate to rise always stood on shaky ground. And their descendants, like Jia Baoyu and Lin Daiyu, would sooner or later become victims of another violent cycle. When a family fell from grace and was put to the test of survival, to what extent could they still maintain the nobility of the soul? Or was there the nobility of the soul to begin with, without any worldly conditions? I thought of these questions day and night.

My best friend in the middle school, Jie, later said that I got it all wrong, since I read too much classical literature, which was only composed and appreciated by a privileged class in history.

"The ones who had lost their fortune and title, like the author of 'The Red Chamber,'" she said, "did not have the full courage to face life directly. How often did he quote comforting words from the past to avoid looking at his own situation? I doubt that he could come up with a different ending other than a daydream."

She was the one with whom I had talked so much about the book at the time, and the only person who understood my adolescent obsessions.

But I remember disagreeing with her. "If we simply behave like everybody around us, for example, analyzing the stock market each day or repeating the coarse, empty words of the evening news with words that "fit" our situations, how could we even begin to imagine something beyond that?"

And Jie laughed. She said that I spoke like someone who didn't belong to our times, from the first day we met. She joked that she would always be worried for me, who wanted to be seen for the parts that were not normally obvious. Maybe she did for a long time. However, I remember worrying for her instead throughout our younger years, for Jie was someone who did not believe that one could be loved for who she was, but only what she did for another.

8
Of the World
世俗 (*shisu*)

How do I translate the term "世俗" (*shisu*)? "世" refers to "the world" and "俗" combines the "human" radical 亻 with "谷" ("valley"). *Shisu* is what is ordinarily practised, and the antonym of "文雅" (*wenya*, "genteel elegance").

For example, "No ivory comes out of a dog's mouth" is a *shisu* wisdom of my grandmother, while "Floating clouds, morning dew" is a *wenya* phrase quoted by my father.

When in middle school, Jie and I couldn't reach an agreement about how to interpret *shisu*, or form a judgement against it one way or the other. Therefore even today, I still hesitate to translate it as a derogatory opposite of elegance and refinement. I think "of the world" could be a more neutral way to put it.

***

My middle school's main building was in the French renaissance style architecture of the 19th century. During the International Settlement days, it used to be a boarding school that only admitted Caucasian or Eurasian boys. While much of Shanghai's historical architecture had been bombed in the Sino-Japanese War before the city surrendered, my school survived to serve as the British and American diaspora's concentration camp in the district. After the Civil War, the school had become mixed-gender and was selected as a "key school" under the Communist régime in the 1950s. From our classroom windows, we could see that half of the campus' brick walls were covered with green ivy. As the seasons changed every year, I noticed that this archaic ivy changed colours like any other flora.

We started wearing a blue sailor's uniform with white collar to school in the mid- to late-1990s. Although I didn't like the colour, I appreciated that the uniform made dressing easier every morning. At least, we were fortunate not to wear tracksuits like other schools in the district. A school badge, however, was now mandatory and so was a "young pioneer's" red scarf. I often put them on in a hurry before I entered the campus, as there would be "on duty" teachers and students at the gate to check on everybody's appearance. Sometimes, they would point out that my badge was lopsided on my jacket or scarf tied in a knot too loose. Like others who were found flawed in these details, I suffered punishment a couple of times. I had to stand at the gate alongside some teachers and take part in the duty of spotting other careless students. I did this very reluctantly.

On Monday mornings, the school assembly became longer than that of my primary school. We would often stand straight for two hours on the parade ground, while the headmaster, director of discipline, and student representatives took turns to give speeches, before we sang the national anthem in unison and saluted the flag. I don't know whether I had become less tolerant than previously, or whether I had low blood pressure entering adolescence, but I fainted a few times on such occasions and was taken to the clinic by my classmates. Jie was one of the classmates that accompanied me.

"No wonder they called you Lin Daiyu from 'Dream of the Red Chamber,' fainting like a willow tree," she said.

Jie was about my height and had a slightly tanned, round face. Her tied-up hair style was adapted from a television show about female volleyball players, making her look sportier even in our skirt uniform. She wasn't standing close to me that morning. But as our class president, Jie often took advantage of the situation and volunteered to bring the sick classmates to the clinic. As the nurse did a usual check-up on me, Jie went to the tuck shop and bought me a cup of warm hot chocolate.

"Ah, your class president is quite attentive!" The elderly nurse praised her and sent us to sit outside at the pantry.

I smiled and nodded at Jie. I felt a bit uneasy, and didn't know how to say thank you in those days. My parents had the same problem – they were much more used to snapping back when someone had been nasty to them.

"When did you read the book?" I asked Jie while sipping hot chocolate.

"I only watched the TV series," she said. "You couldn't really avoid it as they have shown 'The Red Chamber' during every summer vacation since I was a kid!"

"Well, it's either that or 'Journey to the West'."

"I like 'Journey to the West' better. But I'm not really a costume drama fan. Hong Kong series are more addictive, especially the industry ones. You could use some to toughen up."

I said that I would watch her shows if she would read "The Red Chamber" itself this year. And Jie agreed. She asked me about the poetry society I had started with some other girls, and I told her about the notebook that we circulated among ourselves to write classical Chinese poetry – it had so far only made one round. I didn't think Jie would be really interested in this, but she said, "Of course. I think your group has the prettiest girls in our class!"

***

I wasn't reflecting too much on our conversation that evening. A small pebble from the parade ground had cut into my knee when I fell. My mother discovered it in the evening and helped me treat the wound so that it wouldn't leave a scar. When I met Jie the next morning before class, she put a blue envelope containing a one-page letter on my desk, and didn't say a word. Perhaps her silence had added formality to the otherwise awkward gesture. After I read it during class break, I couldn't stop thinking about the content for an entire day.

It wasn't the most beautiful or eloquent letter. In fact, it was no more than an ordinary teenager's letter with descriptive feelings. But I couldn't forget about it for many years afterwards. This is what she had written.

"I was sitting near the bus window on my way home from school. Outside, the city lights blurred and connected together as usual. My mind, however, wanders afar...

"I suppose I have a 'sacred land' in my heart as well, like what you said yesterday, that I would want to cherish with all I have. You may not believe it, because I don't appear to be sentimental. Having divorced parents made me a little more premature than my peers, so I have probably buried the desire for anything that is out of reach. I have always known the right path for myself, and that I will have to go into the world for it.

"Yinan, our time at the clinic seemed to have left an imprint on me. I only wish to protect you, as if it was to protect my own 'sacred land.' P. S., I started the first chapter of 'The Red Chamber' last night – how nice it would be to have another person's lifetime of tears, only reserved for you. Although I would rather make her smile, and make her happy.

"I will bring you some Hong Kong drama VCDs tomorrow."

I noticed that Jie had used matching writing-paper and envelope, a fashionable set sold at stationary stores at the time. The pattern was simple wildflowers. In middle school, we always paid attention to these silly little details. Someone had told me before that if you want to send a love letter, you should glue the stamp in a 45-degree angle so that the receiver could guess. Of course, Jie's letter did not have a stamp on it. For myself, I only had a brief epistolary period with an unknown student that my primary school teacher had assigned as a "pen friend," and it didn't feel right to write to someone whom I had never met. The mentioning of her divorced parents had reminded me of my primary school classmate, Qiong, the one who had fallen from her building after the result of the exam. Jie's letter had evoked a strange feeling in me for the first time – that I could really get to know someone behind their exterior, and perhaps, to be known too.

The following morning, I left my reply letter on Jie's desk before she got in, covering it with a notebook. I didn't remember my own words as much as hers. But they were similar to these lines:

Jie,

I want to hear more of your experiences growing up. I have always liked the saying from the Qing Dynasty scholar Zhang Chao, 'As long as there is one confidant in the world, I hold no grudge against anything.' He went as far as to say that the confidant didn't need to be a person, but could be plum blossom and bamboo, lychee and tea, a white goose and a pipa. I still prefer the idea of enjoying all these with another person. What do you think?

I suppose I still haven't given up hope of finding such 'sacred land' within this world. Perhaps it is only something people of our age dream about? I don't know what will become of us in another twelve years – I'm not as sure as you are about what is the right path. But in any case, I won't forget about you...

P.S., here is the poetry society notebook, in case you want to write something in it. The theme for this round is 'spring rain.' It should be a wuyan – five characters for each verse.

***

Like Jie, I started building a collection of writing paper and envelopes. And we exchanged letters frequently for the first two years of my middle school. As we did in many early school relationships, we often talked in the future tense, showing each other that we were aware that an eventual parting was inevitable, that we had each other only for our school years, and even so, just for this romantic side of our lives. Jie had added to the sentiment by writing that she would reserve the right to marry me in my next life, when she became a boy. And we had made quite a deal on that, as if it was really up to us to map out our next life together. However, as the future tenses made our present school life more bearable, and even hopeful with the otherwise intolerable passing of time, talking about such prospects would still alter expectations. Neither of us was experienced enough to realize that at the time.

Jie continued to be the most reliable student in class, the one to whom our class teacher Mr. Zhu turned when discussing outings or arranging cleaning duties. I discovered that she also had a talent for writing poetry, pinning down raw, original ideas, instead of focusing much on rhyme, vocabulary or elaborate images like many other girls in our group. Was it just laziness, I used to wonder, or in fact a much deeper, more complicated contempt for our way of writing? I didn't know at first. Her approach somehow worked. And unlike most girls in the poetry society, Jie was also much better at playing volleyball and finishing the required sixty sit-ups within a minute in our P.E. classes.

I had wished that our next life would start earlier. And sometimes Jie had to defend herself to me that being nice and responsive to other classmates was her way of being "of the world," of being part of the community. "Not everyone can afford to pick and choose their favourite all the time," she said to me in a mocking tone. I only realized then that I had behaved as I had because I wanted to be Jie's only friend.

After school, we often walked to the bus terminal together through a small street lined with tall redwood trees. On the way, we discussed our teachers and talked about our day, as well as the upcoming big exam which would select students for the Advanced Science Class for our third year, one out of ten only from our cohort of four hundred students. In most cases, it equaled earning tickets to our high school without participating in the city-wide entrance exam again. In addition, we all knew that our school had assigned its best teachers for the Advanced Science Class, so that the students would soon be equipped to compete in the Math or Physics Olympiad on behalf of the school.

Most of our classmates didn't talk about their preparations, already an old habit by then as we were put under frequent, fierce competitions with each other ever since the beginning of our school years.

But Jie had already told me her worries about having too many administrative duties and not enough time to prepare for the exam.

"I hope we stay in the same class," she said. "My marks are not consistent lately, though. Too much to do organizing for the 'learning from farmers' trip."

"We can go over our notes together more." I said.

Wanting to stay in the same top students' bracket with Jie, I had worked harder in the second year, especially after we had added Physics and Chemistry, both giving me a greater challenge than Math.

"I would like that," Jie sighed, "your rankings have improved so much in the cohort. I don't know how you did it. Perhaps I need to think of a back-up plan."

"What's on your mind?"

And that was when Jie started to tell me her plan of participating more in the Communist Youth League activities, and joining the study group to apply for a probationary membership of the Party in four years. In our school, there was a very small quota for probationary members, only one or two each year. And Jie thought that would give her a leg up in our academic race in the future.

"But you don't believe in such a thing," I said. "You always said that your values were more like those in the Hong Kong drama, to become a capitalist entrepreneur rather than sell your skills to the imperial family. I can't bear to see you become so *shisu*."

Jie's face turned pale for a minute, because of my thoughtless bluntness. She started to talk more slowly than before, phrase by phrase, until her tone had evened. The whole time, Jie didn't turn to look at me.

"Well, I don't think *shisu* is such a derogatory term. It only sounds bad in the cloud of classical language you have woven yourself into. But people who have spoken that language met a bitter end, didn't they? Didn't Cao Xueqing's whole family eat only congee while he was trying to write 'The Red Chamber'? How could I do that to my mom? For one thing, we are still sharing a bathroom with our neighbours. You know that I'm not one of those who paid a 40 thousand *yuan* 'donation' to get into this school."

I was going to say "me neither," but then I remembered that because of my father's employment, I could earn ten extra points in my university entrance examination should I want to apply to his prestigious school. University was a long way ahead. Yet I couldn't deny that the policy had helped me be less concerned with which high school I would end up in. I had a security blanket that I had mostly taken for granted, even though it was only ten extra points. And Jie knew all of this.

"It's not about something I believe in or not. It's about doing the necessary, Yinan, and making longer-term plans."

She was one of the few people I knew in my teenage years who set difficult goals that could be achieved only in a few years rather than in a single year. I, on the other hand, had little imagination of the future at the time and would still write the dates on my homework as the previous year in February. So who was I to judge her decision, I thought.

"You know," I said, "my parents once told me that when they were young, not everyone would automatically qualify as a Youth League member at the age of fourteen. The quota was as small as the probationary Party membership quota in high school now. They remade the rules – but still a very old rule after all, loyalty over all other merits – and then set the bar high to make the prize appear more desirable. My father said that he had the best scores in class, and also did well in extracurricular activities, but still couldn't join the Youth League because of his "elements," his family background. My mother, on the other hand, had simply started a "Learning from Selected Works of Mao" study group with a friend and earned the right to become a member. So she did the same thing, you see, only she truly believed in it at the time."

"'Selected Works of Mao,' oh dear," said Jie, with the dismissive tone she usually used about the fashion trends of the previous generation, as if they were gold-rimmed glasses and bell bottoms. "It has never been a fair game, has it? But I still want to play it well, since it's the only game we have. Maybe I'll just sit in the back row and write a poem while pretending to take notes."

"Not bad," I said, trying to reciprocate her smile, even though her grinning face was still in profile. I wanted to make peace with her after she had said it was the only game. "Jia Baoyu could have learned from you when he had to suffer the four Confucian classics in his private school."

"He should have. I think if Cao Xueqing had brought his book to a conclusion, the characters who used to live in 'The Red Chamber' would eventually regret not staying strong for the family and protecting them."

At the time, I thought Jie was merely defending her own choices. Perhaps reading a great book in a certain, simpler way was how we could gain confidence in our own position. Later, I realized that she was also responding to my mention of my parents, and had already understood why I had spoken about them – understood more clearly than I did at the time – about their efforts and frustration in trying to stay afloat in the current for the sake of the family.

But could a person remain herself while her actions were constantly against her heart? I wondered. We didn't know the answer until we tried. It was not until years later that I would finally see how high a standard Jie had set for herself all along. She was in fact, always more of a believer than me, in a pure, autonomous mind separated from any "worldly," pragmatic actions.

I changed the topic as we kept walking towards our adjoining bus stops. I thought about these buses, which, for decades, were the only means of transportation between the commercial district of our school and our residential neighborhoods. The buses didn't run very frequently. And the distance was too great for riding a bicycle. As a result, the waiting lines at the bus terminal were always packed with people during rush hours. We often saw adults of our parents' generation push each other out of the way to get on the bus or to secure a seat. We heard quarrels almost every day between strangers on our overly crowded journeys.

Now, in the late 1990s, however, I noticed that some families had begun to own cars. My uncle Jingzhang was the first relative I knew to have purchased a Buick, at the time a brand that was everyone's envy. Additionally, in 1993, Shanghai had its first subway line running, and was planning to build more lines, soon reaching where we lived. At last people of my age would not need to fight for a bus seat in the future, I thought. We should consider ourselves a luckier generation at least. Even though I didn't wish to pursue the same political direction as Jie, I didn't feel my future was as doomed as my father had once felt. Nor did I believe, like many literary heroes in the classics, that a monastic life was the only path wandering off the main road.

As a young teenager who hadn't tasted real bitterness yet, I had even wished that Jie's bus would come first, so that I could wave her off with a little nostalgia, and see the red tail lights of the bus slowly disappearing into the early evening.

South of the Yangtze

9
Running Water Account
流水賬 (*liu shui zhang*)

I was in my final year of middle school when my grandmother started to lose her memory. My grandparents were living in Pudong at the time, across the river from the old city centre of Shanghai. Streets in Pudong were wider, and had less people on them. Only a decade earlier, Shanghainese had said that they would "have a bed in Puxi rather than own a house in Pudong." But nowadays, many people were moving there for bigger and more modern apartments.

However, Uncle Jingzhang's two-bedroom apartment didn't really suit my grandmother, who had spent all her life living with a big family and had been kept busy solving everybody's problems. Moving to Pudong must have felt like moving to another city for her, far away from the people who needed her to take care of them.

At first, she started repeating the sentences which she had said only a few minutes previously. For example, after hearing that my mother had a recent business trip to Singapore, she commented that "Singapore is very small, but very nice," and kept saying that during our later conversations. We were simply amused in the beginning. But it wasn't long before we realized that she could now take us for somebody else. And my grandfather was no exception. Often, she would call him Jingcheng, my father's name, and thought that he was only a young man. My grandfather said that she had travelled back to the twelve years when he was in the labour camp, and she was bringing up four children all by herself. Those were the memories which she had decided to stick with, he said. In the end, she didn't remember my grandfather at all.

"I didn't want to send him to the countryside," she pointed at my father. Later on, we realized that she was talking about my uncle Jingzhang, whom she had sent to Zhuji to live with a relative during the three-year Great Famine in the early 1960s, when she felt that she couldn't feed all her children. "Who would have known that it was even worse there than in the city? My aunt said that one day Jingzhang found a dry and chewed piece of sugarcane on the street and put it into his mouth. He was that hungry. And everybody laughed at him when he came back to the city, knowing no Shanghainese. He could only speak our countryside dialect...so dark and skinny too..."

Another time, she took me for my aunt Jingyun and gave me a bag of steamed buns she had made a few days earlier. My father told me later that when Aunt Jingyun was a child during the famine, she once got mugged on the street for eating a piece of flat bread in public. And Aunt Jingyun came back home crying for days. My father thought that my grandmother always regretted not being with her when that had happened.

To everybody's surprise, since the onset of my grandmother's dementia, my grandfather had mentioned more than once that he did not want to live with her. "I would rather live in a home now," he said, often in her presence. He also complained that my grandmother had lost her wallet several times after she went to the wet market, and forgot to buy the mandarins that he liked to eat, or peeled too many walnuts for him all at once.

"How could he behave like that," my mother said later to my father. "She did nothing in her life other than labour for the Qian family. Cooked every meal but was always the last to eat at the table. Do you know how many women divorced Rightists or Counter-revolutionaries at the time? And now she is too much trouble for him!"

My father would not respond to that but smoked more cigarettes for the day, so that he could be left alone on the balcony. My father was the one who often praised my grandmother for being an example of the older generation women that we didn't see in China anymore. She had even let my grandfather change her written character name from Qin ("seven-stringed zither") to Qing ("cloudless day") to suit his own aesthetics. But what kind of person was the one who got the most praise? The one who waived her rights the most, I thought. I felt disappointed with my grandfather, whom I used to spend so much time with as a child. And we talked about the possibilities of moving my grandmother to stay with us when my father would be allotted a bigger apartment next year.

My father had been made full professor recently. And we were looking forward to moving again, this time to a more mature and quiet neighborhood near the university. As I helped pack and declutter things before the move, I discovered my mother's candy wrapper collection – a tin of shiny, aluminum foil, all ironed flat and stacked neatly on one another.

"I almost forgot about them!" she said, running her fingers through the pile one by one with a smile, as the wrappers made faint rustling sounds. It seemed to me, though, that she remembered clearly the stories of how she had collected each particular one.

"It was the time when rice and oil were rationed, so we could have a few candies only during the Lunar New Year. Of course, if we were lucky and my parents happened to have important guests at home, they would sometimes serve them candies, too. My sisters and I would quietly wait for them to leave, like vultures waiting for a dying animal, so that we could at least pick up the wrapping paper, if not the leftover candies themselves. And then I soaked the paper in water, and stuck them on the windows overnight to flatten. The next day, I would put them inside my textbooks and bring them to school. Oh, what a competition at the time among me and my friends, to see who had the most, or the rarest ones that were part of a limited series!"

"My mother used to collect stamps," said my father. "Although during the house raid in the Cultural Revolution, I still remember, when she threw all of her collection into a nearby river before other people could find them, including the most precious Li Shizhen ones. You know, portraits of the Ming Dynasty herbalist. Hundreds of white stamps floating in the water…it was a sight quite hard for me to forget…"

"Well, she has started over later." My mother said. "That's why I asked my sister to mail me some from the U.S., for many years. Those aren't worth much like her old ones, although equally pretty to look at."

"I wonder where they are now," said my father, mostly talking to himself. I was not sure whether he was referring to the old stamps, or the replacements, the new foreign ones.

In the end, my mother didn't keep her candy wrappers when we moved. I wondered whether it was because of my grandmother's dementia, making her realize that she didn't want to attach too much meaning to mementos, while forgetting about people. Or whether she simply wanted to put an end to generations of Chinese women who were collectors of these seemingly insignificant items, of which only they knew the value; girls with no candies collecting candy wrappers and women who would never compose a letter collecting stamps. My mother had started writing diaries around the same time, mostly bare bones or "流水帐" (liu shui zhang), a "running water account" as we called them: about places she went to, friends and family she met, and bigger events such as our family trips, moving to a new apartment, me entering the Advanced Science Class or my father's promotion. In this way, her stories would not only live in her own memories or in a rusted tin.

My mother was the first in our family to have set her stories free.

**

I spent the first year of my Advanced Science Class studying on the old campus, still as a middle school student, and the rest in high school. During the first year, there was much construction noise around us. Because of the school's prime location in a commercial district, the management board had decided to make a bold financial move – "breaking the campus walls and opening shops" – by allowing a few restaurants and a Taiwanese-owned shopping mall to be its tenants. In return, the school made a profit so that our classrooms soon had televisions, and the new campus of our high school included a heated indoor swimming pool, a concert hall and dormitories for boarding students.

It was soon part of our everyday life to study with faint pop songs from the shopping mall in the background. In fact, I found it quite charming over time, especially the theme songs of popular television dramas. My favourite one was "Love in the Snow," a song from "Fox Volant of the Snow Mountain," adapted from a Hong Kong writer's *wuxia* novel: *"Long journey with falling snow, singing those songs, leaving the stars behind...and remembering our parting time, tear marks from unawakened dreams, only love in the snow..."* I found that the Chinese diaspora who lived in subtropical or tropical locales often liked to imagine their martial heroes' stories set in snow country. Otherwise, what do they do with all the wintery vocabulary in our language, in poetry, and in history books? During those long school days, with pop songs distracting me from difficult science classes, I often thought about such displacement, as if already practicing my own homesickness.

I realized that my family had not been adventurous people for generations, at least for a thousand years. My father said that the Qian clan in Jiangnan, south of the Yangtze River including Zhejiang Province, Shanghai, and parts of Jiangsu and Fujian Province, started to flourish when a former Tang Dynasty warlord, Qian Liu, had formed his own kingdom in the area in year 907. It was a time in Chinese history referred to as "Five Dynasties and Ten Kingdoms," when the northern part of China had five states succeeding one another within seventy years, and the southern part below the Yangtze River was divided into ten smaller countries. Since Qian Liu's kingdom had inherited both the ancient Wu and Yue territories from the first millennium B.C., he named it Wuyue, and honoured the area's tradition of agriculture and learning. The related dialects spoken in Wuyue had later shared an abbreviated umbrella name, the Wu dialect. In addition, Qian Liu was a patron of Buddhism in his late years as were all his successors. They had adorned the kingdom with temples, grottoes and pagodas, and encouraged cultural exchange and trade with friendly neighbouring countries across the ocean in modern-day Japan and Korea.

The Wuyue kingdom was prosperous and influential, but its sovereignty didn't last long. In 978, the fifth and last emperor Qian Chu had rendered his land to the strong Song régime to protect the region from war. And soon, Tang was succeeded by Song as another powerful dynasty. The last emperor of Wuyue had enjoyed aristocracy in the new régime, until ten years later on his 60th birthday, he was gifted a bottle of wine from the Song court and died of stomach pain the same evening.

However, the seventy-year reign had already given the Qian clan a chance to spread over the region and have a lasting influence. The founding emperor Qian Liu himself was said to have had more than a hundred children. My father kept a blue, thread-bound book researched by a Zhuji clan member who detailed the migration route of our ancestors' branch – that of the 8th generation descendants of Qian Liu who had moved to the county of Zhuji during the Song Dynasty and the 25th generation who had settled in my grandfather's village since the Ming Dynasty. Both my grandfather and father had taken the blue book quite seriously, and didn't appreciate my occasional joke that there could be a possibility that our ancestors were mere subjects or slaves of the Qians and later adopted the family name – they insisted that there was no such tradition throughout our civilization, and I didn't intend to argue with that. Nonetheless, for all I knew, over the past thousand years, our family line had remained in the former Wuyue territory.

Was this the reason my grandfather had decided against accepting a position in Taiwan in 1949? For certain last names, it was more difficult to leave. I started to wonder after learning more about Wuyue from my parents towards the end of my middle school. The old world seemed to carry memories of a faint ancestral prestige, and some pride in being the forefathers and long-term residents of Jiangnan's distinct, rich culture – my father said that the main river in Zhejiang Province, over which our slow train had quietly passed through in my childhood, still bears the name Qian River, or Qiantang River, honoring Qian Liu's contributions in constructing sea walls (*tang*) at the mouth of the river and enlarging city perimeters. Perhaps in my grandfather's imagination, the new world was only in the south of all directions, without a farming calendar or distinct seasons. But was Jiangnan still the Qian homeland? After all, the thirteen prefectures of Wuyue had long ago become part of the conquering dynasty, or more recently, after my great-grandfather was shot dead in the Land Reform of the 1950s as a landowner of a mere 33 *mu*? The little things that were still left after a thousand years, I thought, were finally wiped out in the recent generations. Perhaps it was only such circumstances that would force one to reconsider what all the glory of civilization really meant, and only such circumstances could force the lethargic Qian genes to become more adventurous.

As a teenager, there were so many ways to feel lonely. The one that I had spent the most time to put a name to throughout the years, was a feeling of already being part of a diaspora in my own country.

10
Mandarin
普通話 (*putonghua*)

I started to have Mandarin-speaking teachers in high school. Before that, my teachers had taught mostly in Shanghainese. After all, Shanghainese, one of the most widely spoken subgroups of the Wu dialect in Jiangnan, was my mother tongue.

"普通話" (*putonghua*, "Mandarin"), the Beijing dialect-based standard which had been the lingua franca only since the beginning of the 20th century, on the other hand, started to seep more into our daily life and earned its literal meaning, the "common speech." In the late 1990s, it seemed that Shanghai had loosened its grip to allow more university-degreed immigrants to move into the city. The new teachers we had were mostly younger, some only in their twenties and thirties, and struggled to fit in at first.

For example, the English teacher Mr. Chen was often talked about by students for having a strange accent and wearing clothes too casual for class. Once while Mr. Chen was sitting in front of him, listening to a group presentation, a mischievous boy made a cut in his hoodie, to show his opinion about the way he dressed. And nobody tried to stop him. Another time, our Advanced Science Class played a trick on a young Chemistry teacher Ms. Yan on April Fools' Day by switching classrooms with the adjoining class. And she didn't find out until twenty minutes later. Unfortunately, in that incident, the other teacher who had gone to the "wrong" classroom, Mr. Liu, hit his front teeth on the door when he was leaving in a hurry and cracked a tooth. Both classes were punished by the director of discipline afterwards. And we had to clean the campus for several weeks.

Like many fifteen- or sixteen-year olds, we had our ways of being cruel and a simple lack of empathy for anyone who was unfamiliar in appearance. It didn't help that, at the time, we couldn't fully understand our discontent at having to switch into a different vernacular language in class, a cultural majority suddenly subjected to a cultural minority. But instead of seeing the bigger picture of the aggressive state policy, helpless young people often channel their protests towards individuals. It was an environment to encourage a hidden, defensive feeling of false superiority over teachers who had never heard of April Fools' Day or appreciated popular desserts from the colonial era of Shanghai, such as an éclair.

Besides, the Advanced Science Class had already gathered the most high-achieving people in my cohort. We had a more intensive study schedule. And many of us had pursued science only because of the common belief that "there was a larger quota for science majors than for arts majors in universities." Therefore we were merely enduring it as a means to an end.

Sometimes I wondered whether it was the same in the case of our Physics teacher, Mr. Yang, also, when he chose his path of studies.

Mr. Yang was one of the newer, Mandarin-speaking teachers who was assigned to teach first-year high-schoolers. He was from Beijing and in his mid-thirties. My classmates were a little nicer to him because he was from the capital, had taught at a university, and was quite tall and fit. Some of us, however, including Jie, thought that he would be better off teaching a different subject.

Once I was called into the office by our class teacher Mrs. Xue, to talk about an article I had submitted to our school journal. I had questioned the need for having a camera at the back of each classroom to monitor our everyday lives – a new initiative for my high school to spend its "breaking the campus walls" profits. In the Advanced Science Class, some boys had tried to throw a dirty cloth on it to protest, or perhaps they were just letting off extra steam as usual. Nonetheless, I had described the protest in my article and had quoted from *1984*, one of the books on my father's bookshelf that he had saved from a library clearance in his university.

"I think it is mainly for educational purposes," said Mrs. Xue. "I hope you can help inform other classmates not to think in a wrong way." She didn't explain what purposes, though, and didn't give me an opportunity to ask.

"I understand the emotions. But as someone who has walked the younger paths before, I just want to let you know that at a certain age, many of these emotions are likely to be fights against your own men of straw. Ask yourself, is it really worth the energy? I'm a little worried that reading 'leisure books' will eat up your time for the more important tasks. And I just checked your fall semester's final scores with Mr. Yang. It seems that you and two others were barely above the passing mark this time."

She turned to Mr. Yang sitting at the neighbouring desk, and he nodded. I felt a little uneasy to be lectured in front of him.

"If they would like, I wouldn't mind tutoring them during the break," said Mr. Yang, in his Beijing-accented Mandarin, the "perfect" *putonghua*.

"Are you sure, teacher Yang?" Mrs. Xue pushed up the bridge of her glasses. She stuck to her Shanghainese. I could see that, for a moment, this made Mr. Yang uneasy as well.

"Not a problem," he said.

"That's very kind of you in that case." Mrs. Xue turned back to me, not giving the new teacher another glance. Her eyebrows were still raised, deepening the lines on her forehead. "Teacher Yang will set up appointments with you all then. I know there is a lot on your plate right now. But you will realize many years later how critical high school is for your future – try not to waste any more time. As for the article, since it was already published by our student editors, I guess there's nothing more we can do about it."

Of course, I thought I should agree with everything Mrs. Xue had said. She seemed to have genuine worries for us. Yet, I must have walked with a hunched back and low spirit coming out of the teachers' office, because Mr. Yang who walked behind me on his way to class, told me in a low voice to "cheer up."

"Big Brother is watching, you know." He smiled as I turned my head back in surprise.

Later on, I told Jie about the episode and she wasn't too impressed with Mr. Yang's knowledge of banned literature.

"I think it's weird that he made up a poem about energy and resistance in class the other day. That is just too much, especially for a science teacher," she said. And feeling embarrassed, I quickly dropped the topic.

After we both entered the Advanced Science Class, Jie and I didn't have as much time to hang out as we used to. She was often attending probationary Party member applicants' meetings and outings in her spare time. During the previous summer vacation, they had gone to the Red Army base in Jinggang Mountain and posed for a group picture with baggy military uniforms rented from the local tourist shop. I had swallowed my cynicism and comment when seeing that photo, knowing that she had valued the experience and maintained a good relationship with the leading teacher of their group, Mr. Lin. Mr. Lin was also our school's Party secretary, an older, stern Shanghainese teacher who had taught us Math before. I thought that he would surely frown on behaviour such as writing an impromptu poem on the class blackboard. I wondered though, how much Jie's contempt for Mr. Yang was because of the fact that he was an outsider.

***

That winter, in the beginning of 1999, my father had the opportunity to go to Germany as a visiting professor for a year. We were all excited for his first adventure living in another country since he had never even left Jiangnan before. My mother bought him an expensive long black trench coat so that he could put on a "foreign air" in the West – it met no resistance this time since we no longer bought second-hand "export rejects" like ten years ago – and a few silk scarves and tea as gifts for his future colleagues. My father left quickly after the Lunar New Year. And we started to communicate through long-distance calls once a week.

The university my father was visiting was in Konstanz, a city near the German-Swiss border. At first, over phone calls, he described the everyday "paradise-like" scenery of a beautiful lake and sunbathing youngsters in the spring. He sent photos of himself with red-beaked swans in the background, a bird we had often read about in European mythology and fairy tales, but had never seen in real life before. Later on, my mother and I laughed at all the Chinese professors' dull weekend activities, such as playing poker, and encouraged him to travel more. My father took our advice and visited a few neighbouring countries in Europe, including a nudist beach in the south of France, where according to him, he and his colleague "were the only two fully-dressed people walking around on the sand!"

His views on foreigners had changed as well, perhaps partly thanks to the shocking sight of Mediterranean nudity. During the first few months, he had complained about both German food and the fact that some of his female Chinese graduate students had ditched their boyfriends back home to go out with German-born Chinese or Caucasians. However, as time went by, my father grew to enjoy the local pork knuckle dish and even compared it to his favourite Shanghainese sweet and sour pork ribs. He seemed now to speak mostly positively of his students' German boyfriends who were good at being on time and occasionally hosted him for dinner. He soon extended these warm feelings to include the local community.

"Once I found myself without small change for the bus fare after I had boarded. It was not looking good, since the bus had already started moving. Then a stranger, about my age, walked up to me from his seat, spoke to me in English, and opened his wallet to help me out. It was surprising to realize how much I had not been used to small, kind gestures like this," said my father.

He added that he had purchased a German portable radio so that when he returned to Shanghai, he could use it to access the international news channels which Chinese-made radios couldn't.

"I finally watched the Beijing video of ten years ago, too," he told my mother one day. "You could see that the soldiers were of a similar age to the students. All were young kids who barely had hair on their faces."

"Who did you watch it with?" my mother asked, quickly. Whenever there was static or lag in the call, she was always worried that somebody could be listening.

"Well, just a couple of other visiting professors."

"Oh..." said my mother. "Speaking of them, if you are going to Switzerland with them next month, don't forget to check out watches and chocolates..." She mentioned that one of her colleagues had recently had a business trip there and gave everybody chocolates as souvenirs, and even the large quantity of army knives in her suitcases had passed border control.

Hearing my mother's enthusiastic enquiries about Swiss watches, I remembered a time when the "Shanghai" brand watch was a premium staple in China, and the only brand known to us. I felt a strange nostalgia for the 1980s, when everything was being picked up from the ruins and everyone was hopeful. But the decade ended and people started to shift their focus to things like Swiss watches. How my mother had responded to the mention of the video was just an epitome of the changing times.

"Alright, I will take a look. How are you getting on with your homework, Yinan?"

"Oh, the usual," I said.

"She got 82 in Math and 70 in Physics in the recent mock exam," my mother said.

"Seems like the tutoring has gone well, I guess," my father commented. At the beginning of the winter break, a couple of weeks before he left for Germany, my father had followed me on his bicycle to the meeting point with Mr. Yang, so that he could make sure that the new teacher who had offered free tutoring was decent. My father was a believer in judging people by their mannerisms – "a person can easily disguise their words, but not the way they walk," as he put it. This was a piece of wisdom which I thought came from the Cultural Revolution years when people with different thinking adopted the same vocabulary as others for self-protection. However, I had already told him that there were two other girls in the apartment, one of them the daughter of Mr. Yang's landlord. My father had concluded after his quiet observation from 50 meters away that even though Mr. Yang had a face too smooth for a man, he didn't look like a threatening person.

I was reluctant to discuss my tutoring in detail with my parents at the time, however. It was one of the few experiences I had that was entirely my own, a space I could finally put a door behind. In fact, I had already learned more about Mr. Yang than I had expected. For example, his studio apartment was quite humble – there was not much good furniture, but a big plastic box with a zip in the middle to serve as a wardrobe. When it was still winter, he had made a dumpling soup to keep us warm during the tutoring sessions. And once as we were eating dumplings together, we learned that Mr. Yang had been married ten years ago, to a senior Party official's daughter in Beijing, but the marriage lasted only one year. "She had kept a dozen lovers," Mr. Yang said. Therefore, when he allowed us to browse through his photo albums later on, I paid attention to the privileged-looking, smartly-dressed young adult women with him, posing in the Forbidden City, at Fayuan Temple, or rowing a boat on Kunming Lake. I couldn't tell which one could be the woman in question, and in the end didn't want to ask.

I only realized some time later that we were perhaps Mr. Yang's first friends in the city. At the time, I was simply mesmerized by the fact that a teacher would tell us so much about himself, even flattered. Mr. Yang had once shown me an essay he wrote. And from this, I learned that he had been orphaned in Henan Province during the Great Famine of the early 1960s. A couple of junior Party officials in Beijing had adopted him, and brought him up. He had always wondered about his birth parents, not knowing whether they were in fact dead or whether they had just left him behind in a local shelter. He would always have tender feelings towards them, he wrote. In those years, after all, there were worse stories in his part of Henan about parents who had to sell their children on the black market, or children being kidnapped and even cooked during the most desperate times.

In the essay, Mr. Yang used stronger, more emotional words than those I had been accustomed to. Some stories he mentioned were close to nightmarish. I wondered whether it was because of his age or his own particular use of the Mandarin language. He had painted his personal history with deep colours in contrast to my otherwise subdued aesthetics. I didn't know if he was exaggerating or whether I had the tendency of avoidance in my own personality. How much innocence should one trade for looking at life directly?

In 1999, I had not yet read anything about the Great Leap Forward, the national campaign to make steel out of pots and pans and killing sparrows, or the people's commune and how crops were taken away from farmers at the time. But I remembered what my parents had told me. My father had mentioned that even though things were bad in Shanghai and Zhuji, in poorer landlocked provinces such as Anhui, where my grandfather's re-education camp was, many more lives were lost. My grandfather was said to have had only skin on his bones during the famine and had been carried out by guards to be buried several times, until they realized that he still had breath left. His fellow prisoners had searched in the fields for anything they could find to eat, including mice, but some still died lying next to him in the evenings. After I read Mr. Yang's essay, my grandfather's dark and skinny face emerged in my mind, and become similar in appearance to that of Mr. Yang's birth parents. For days, I found myself immersed in that imagination, and wanted to see Mr. Yang as the orphaned boy he was when he was an adopted child in Beijing.

Mr. Yang had a large forehead. As a young boy, I thought, he would probably have been made fun of by his peers with the popular children's rhyme: "Big head, big head, of rain never afraid; others with umbrella, but I have my big head." And I had even allowed myself to imagine being the young boy's sole friend in the Beijing neighborhood where he grew up. Did he ever speak the Henan dialect, before adopting *putonghua*? Had his childhood accent caused him any trouble, or was it a memory too insignificant for him to remember? I imagined him confiding in me about these things. In the end, the scenes had become so vivid and nuanced that I almost thought it could be an anecdote Mr. Yang had shared with us. Naturally, I wondered why he had given me the essay to read.

***

Among his three students that winter, Mr. Yang had always said that Lily was the brightest and most sophisticated, and Xiaofen, the landlord's daughter was the dullest. They were both boarding students who had cars waiting outside our campus on Friday afternoons. Since high school, along with the discovery that boys my age had started to grow taller than me, I also noticed how much wealthier my classmates had become. In the students' journal where I had submitted the "1984" article, there were many interesting accounts of international travel to Venice or Sydney during summer vacations. Meanwhile, more classmates' parents were filing divorces. And a few boys began calling prostitutes with their parents' new cell phones. I had heard that those in my cohort with bad scores were talking about immigration to English-speaking countries as a new back-up plan. Even though my family's financial situation was hardly keeping up with that of my peers, I realized that we had at least moved to bigger and bigger apartments, and now enjoyed food, home appliances and vacations unthinkable only a decade previously. And unlike our parents, my peers born after 1980 wanted to be the first in Communist China to wipe away all traces of poverty from our lives, which of course included forgetting about what had caused such poverty.

I didn't know why Mr. Yang had left his university job in Beijing, and come to a city with a different culture to teach a bunch of newly-spoiled teenagers. The Wu-dialect-speaking Shanghainese had resisted cultural assimilation for decades, yet often, as seen in the people around me in a cowardly form. I doubted that Mr. Yang would feel much welcomed by everyday encounters such as those with Mrs. Xue.

But for someone with generations of her family tree rooted mostly in the Yangtze River Delta region, I was still envious of him. He had inherited a more ambiguous past, and was therefore freer to move, and freer to reinvent his life, at what seemed, at least to a teenager, a very settled age.

11
Year of the New Millennium
千禧年 (*qian xi nian*)

In May of that year, 1999, a few months before the new millennium, the bombing of China's embassy in Belgrade caught everyone's attention. May was often the best spring month in Shanghai, when the long-lasting humidity and drizzling rain had finally subsided and the oven-like summer air hadn't yet arrived. In school, my classmates talked all day about current events with extra excitement like singing birds.

As we watched on our classroom television in the mornings, the news was dominated by angry-sounding commentators. Words such as "a deliberate and barbaric attack" and "imperialist enemies" made recurring appearances. I was amused at first hearing such dated vocabulary from a generation back. However, the government seemed to mean business. The state channel reporters dismissed the U.S. President and his defense secretary's remarks that the NATO plane had "bombed the wrong target because of an outdated map" as a complete lie, because "our enemies were afraid of us helping Milosevic develop defenses against their missiles." In-depth interviews were given to the families who had lost their loved ones in the incident. We learned that two of the three reporters who had died in the bomb were young newly-weds – the wife was a pretty twenty-eight year old woman who had been a good daughter, student and employee. Her innocent smile in the black and white obituary photo lived in my mind for weeks.

The restless boys in my class now stopped hiding my pencil box or messing with the tea in my thermos. They declared war against KFC and McDonald's, which used to be their favourite after school hang-outs. Not only did they stop eating there, but one group of boys threw rocks at a nearby McDonald's and broke the restaurant's heavy glass entrance doors. At school, our only foreign teacher, Mr. Eriksson who taught music, had his bicycle tire punctured so that he would, "fall and hit his Clinton-like nose." I felt bad for him, because he had married a local wife and spoke a little Shanghainese. Besides, I simply felt distaste for those who rode on the current sentiment and targeted individuals. After I described the recent craze to my father, he told me that Mr. Eriksson's home country, Sweden, didn't even belong to the notoriously condemned NATO, and certainly was not the same as the U.S.

"Why do you think the government made such a big deal about the bombing of our embassy in Yugoslavia?" he said over the phone, "Not that this isn't newsworthy, but it seems that they put too much emphasis on it. It seems to me nothing more than playing a trick at a critical time to distract people's attention, as they often have."

I understood immediately what he had meant by "they." In my father's dictionary, "us" only included ordinary people like our family, and never grew to a behemoth including "all Chinese nationals" or large corporations, especially the government.

So when he mentioned that it was the tenth anniversary of the event in Beijing, I listened quietly with my mother. The former General Secretary's name, Zhao Ziyang, didn't ring a bell for me, nor did those of any of the former student leaders. I thought that perhaps I was too young to remember. Had my parents watched any news from Beijing through our old black and white television at that time? Based on my father's enthusiasm for the subject in recent months, it was more likely that they hadn't seen much.

"So they don't talk about the bombing at all over there? How strange – it is all we hear in the news lately," said my mother.

It must have been the first time in my life that I thought how naïve my mother still was for asking such a question, thinking that everyone in the world watches the same news. And with the heated, nation-wide discussions about the embassy-bombing incident, the spring of 1999 seemed to pass by very quickly. Pink peach-petals soon covered part of the school playground, and cicadas couldn't wait to perform their high-pitched chorus for the next season. I thought that I was already familiar with the script of time in my own city, moving from day to day without making too many decisions. It turned out that one could never be too used to such things. What happened on an early June day would change the rhythm of the rest of my high school life.

On that morning, Mr. Yang came to my Physics class as usual. But I noticed that he was wearing all white. A white shirt was common, but I thought it was unusual to wear white trousers too, even on a warm day. The only other occasion I had seen people in all white linen was at the funeral of one of my mother's colleagues. So who was Mr. Yang mourning? Even the most talkative boys seemed to sense the strange mood in the classroom and the atmosphere was subdued.

Ten minutes had passed when Mr. Yang stopped writing the Physics formulae on the blackboard. He turned around slowly and put the chalk down. His fingers gripped the edge of the lectern and he stared at his open textbook for a while. I thought that he was going to ask a question. Instead, Mr. Yang excused himself to the class and told us that he couldn't carry on today.

"It is not an ordinary day today for me," he said.

The classroom was quiet as we didn't know how to respond to such a situation. There were multiple times when teachers sent naughty students to stand at the back or outside the classroom as a punishment. Never had we seen a teacher who wanted to exile himself, especially for a personal reason.

Mr. Yang added that he couldn't teach today, because some people he knew had died ten years ago. I started to understand Jie's comment about him being sentimental and not trying to hide anything from us. Our other teachers had never voluntarily showed weakness in public. Jie never showed weakness in public.

After he walked out of the classroom, there was a minute of buzzing discussion, until Jie went ahead to fetch Mrs. Xue to manage the situation. We spent the rest of the class in self-study. Jie informed me that evening that Mr. Yang was told off by the headmaster for his irresponsibility in the classroom and had had his pay docked. In addition, he had received a serious warning from the school Party secretary, Mr. Lin. The official announcement was brought to the class later by Mrs. Xue, that Mr. Yang would take sick leave for a week.

We soon had a substitute teacher step in temporarily for a few sessions, a re-employed retired teacher with more experience. However, this time when I heard the Physics terminology in my familiar Shanghainese dialect, I found myself feeling disappointed.

How does it feel to have a memory about a certain time, or a certain historical event, so different from everyone else? I wondered about this in class while pretending to take notes. Truth be told, I thought, none of us shared the exact same memories about time and events. But many were willing to change their own memories to safely resemble a collective version, or to reiterate them with a convenient collective language. Over the years, where I grew up, I had seen very few people defend their memories in the form of white mourning clothes, or seek that kind of loneliness when they had other choices.

***

On the fourth day of Mr. Yang's absence, I went to his sixth-floor studio flat after school. On the way, I picked up a leafy plant from a flower shop. Neither of my tutoring classmates, Lily or Xiaofen, knew about this. And I didn't mention it to Jie, either. Mr. Yang seemed surprised when he opened the door, but he invited me in right away.

"I brought you a plant," I said. On the way, I had rehearsed a few lines of what to say for an unannounced visit, but nothing came to my mind when I realized that Mr. Yang wasn't going to question me. On the contrary, he seemed very quickly to take it for granted – a student visiting him on a balmy June day, a green plant in hand – there was nothing strange at all about this. I felt a little breathless since I had run up and down the six floors three times, before making up my mind to knock.

Mr. Yang was wearing clothes more casual than usual, an old, long-sleeved T-shirt and faded jeans. The flat was not as tidy as it had been when we came for tutoring. I thought perhaps that was why it felt like a different place altogether this time.

"Do you want some tea? I just made some," said Mr. Yang.

I followed him into the kitchen to get a fresh mug, and then to his desk where the pot of tea sat. After I leaned against the desk and had sipped some tea, my heart rate finally returned to normal. Mr. Yang sat down on the edge of his bed in the studio, facing me.

"So, how are you, Yinan? Tell me how you feel," he said.

I thought that I should be the one to ask him a question. Mr. Yang didn't really look sick, though.

"I wondered what happened at the time, in Beijing," I said. "Why did you leave?"

"Well, I shouldn't have cancelled class like that," Mr. Yang said. "You guys must be confused. Strange enough though, I thought that you might visit me for some reason."

How could that be possible? I thought. I didn't know that I would be visiting him until this morning, or not until the third time I had run up the stairs of the building. It was not like a chess game, where someone with more experience could predict an outcome several moves ahead of time. Or was I playing a game without the slightest awareness of doing so? I forgot that he had not yet answered my question.

"Yesterday was my birthday," he said. "Thirty-eight now. And you have brought life to my apartment. You are like a little sweetheart to me."

Before I tasted the meaning of his words, Mr. Yang came over and pulled me up by the hands. He took me into his arms and said something I didn't hear in a low voice. When I looked up to him, he lowered his head and started to kiss me. It was more salacious and possessive than I had imagined a kiss would be. My lips were pressed together. But Mr. Yang's tongue parted them and found his way in. His hands moved onto my buttocks at the same time and I felt a bit queasy.

"Yinan," he said. My name in Shanghainese sounded like a little girl's – "南" (*nan*) has a similar sound to "囡" (*nan*, "daughter"). But when he said it in Mandarin, it felt grown up, formal. Nobody had pronounced my name in this way before.

Mr. Yang led me to sit on the bed, and started to take my summer uniform off. He kissed my shoulders when they were exposed.

"I won't do anything against your will," he assured me. It was either his breath or my loosened hair that made my skin red and tickly. I folded my arms in front of me when I was put down on the pillow. He left my socks on, but took his own off. "Will you let me in?" Mr. Yang asked when his lips lay beside my ears, begging me, his student.

I nodded but didn't really know what I had nodded for. Nothing that happened next registered until a few minutes later.

"When I push in, you can try to meet me upwards," Mr. Yang instructed me in detail. "Put your arms around my back if that's easier." Later, when he was moving more quickly on top, he told me that my "breasts were so soft and cunt so good."

The unthinkable obscene word gave me a sharp pain. And only then my tears ran down my cheeks, as if I had been awakened from a long dream. I felt that if I had ever cared for Mr. Yang, that was the moment when I stopped caring. Perhaps that was the moment I stopped caring about many things.

How absurd, I thought. I had wanted to be closer to Mr. Yang all along. Now that he had entered my body, and told me that he had wanted me for a long time, more intimately than any relationships I knew, all I felt was a deep dismay. I thought of a small cardboard mooncake box I used to have when living on Duolun Road, where I had stored sea shells, travel souvenirs, classmates' birthday cards and cheap jewellery given to me by relatives. How silly of me to have kept all these things in the past! To whom was I going to show them?

Mr. Yang said that it was normal for girls in my generation not to bleed during their first time, because we had played so much sports at school. He mentioned riding a bicycle, long-distance running and doing the splits, all of which could break the hymen. Nothing to worry about, he said, thinking he was consoling me, that he knew "what I had given him." I said that he sounded knowledgeable about sports. And then Mr. Yang told me that he swam thirty minutes every day in our school's indoor pool, and sometimes did a hundred sit-ups in the evening, to retain the physique of a young man. I didn't know why he bothered to tell me these things.

That evening, when I returned home, I spent a lot of time looking into the mirror, worrying that my eyebrows would soon betray my new physical experience. Rumours went around among my classmates that a non-virgin would stop frowning and her eyebrows would grow further apart as time went by. "It has something to do with spreading your legs," said some all-knowing girls. It was how everybody had found out that a pretty, second-year exchange student from Nanjing was sleeping with a boy from our school's volley-ball team. In addition, they said that she now walked with pigeon toes after she had lost her virginity. I didn't want to draw any attention like that in school.

There was one person I wished to talk to, though. Over the weekend, I made plans with Jie so that we could meet for a couple of hours in a public park. And I told her about my visit to Mr. Yang and what had happened in his apartment.

"That turd, how could he?" she said, as if talking to herself, not really looking at me. Suddenly I worried in case I had made her never want to see me in our old way again.

I knew for a fact that Jie had never liked Mr. Yang, even before this.

When she finally faced me, I thought that Jie's eyes were the saddest I had ever seen, dark stars that dimmed very quickly. I started to comfort her that it wasn't terrible physical pain, as they had often said. I didn't catch a cold. And I didn't feel anything else change in me. I thought of the letters we wrote to each other about our next life and our "sacred land." It felt like centuries ago when we talked about "The Red Chamber." And as I started to talk faster, the feeling of an inevitable, irreversible change caught up with the words I had built up as a dam, and my eyes welled up.

"I'm sorry," I said.

"You don't have to apologize," she said. "Come on, you have a problem of apologizing too much!"

She raised her voice. And I thought I had failed Jie even more than I had failed myself. I was something in her world that was not supposed to change, a constant, so that she could be entirely pragmatic and fearless with everything else. But how long could I play that role? And what was Jie's role in my life? Would just knowing she cared give me a little hope to carry on?

Elderly strollers and opera singers in the park looked in our direction when they passed by. Young teenagers usually didn't come to their terrain. We had too much homework to do. And now one of the teenagers kept kicking the little pebbles on the sidewalk, hands in her pockets. The other had swollen, woeful eyes. I turned my back on them and quietly wiped away my tears.

12
In Seventh Heaven
欲仙欲死 (*yu xian yu si*)

A few days later, Mr. Yang came back to class. At first, students exchanged looks when he walked in. But Mr. Yang acted as if nothing had happened. He didn't behave any differently towards me in front of the other students, either. Once, he even called my name for a question, a thing that an adult was capable of doing that comforted me and frightened me at the same time. Sometimes, I thought I caught a look from him while he was talking, and there was something desperate in it. I would turn my head away, pretending to look out the window. But no matter where my eyes landed, the voice of the teacher still echoed between the classroom walls.

I tried to forgive Mr. Yang for using the foul word only the most vulgar people I imagined would say, but found it hard to do so. I didn't know how to express the way it made me feel at the time. Words didn't come easily into the most intimate realm. And people sometimes experienced sufferings for a long time because they couldn't put a name to them. There were few references to sex in the literature I read, and the few scenes that I remembered were vaguely reportorial, filled with shame. I realized that I didn't want to acknowledge the experience and treatment as something original from Mr. Yang alone. I wasn't educated to think in this way. But no matter how much I blamed the language itself, his words, new words tied to new desires, were the ones that had taken over my mind. I couldn't erase them, nor could I find any peace.

One afternoon after my last class, I ran into Mr. Yang in the corridor, and he invited me to "walk a few minutes" with him. Without much conversation on the way, we returned to his place together. As the door closed behind us, Mr. Yang embraced me tightly in his arms and kissed me. I thought he was going to loosen my hair soon like the last time. Instead, he led me to sit at the round kitchen table and started to cook us a simple meal of fried rice with eggs and green scallion, perhaps what he had often fixed for himself in the evenings. And I found myself smiling at the few scallion pieces he had clumsily dropped on the floor, unnoticed, as if I had finally found the evidence that we were on a real date together.

Later, on his chest, I untied my hair myself – female students were required either to wear a ponytail or cut their hair short for school, and I chose the former. This time, Mr. Yang told me that my body should be able to climax soon.

"A lot of women don't really know that pleasure. But I'm sure it will come for you soon," he said.

He tested me with his hands and said that it would make me like him better. And then he stood behind me, because he liked it better. I felt that I was falling into a time loop with Mr. Yang, later seeing him kissing up from my knees, as if none of it had anything to do with my high school or my life. Perhaps after the new millennium, I thought, the old log of time would be dropped into a deep well, never to be seen or heard from again. Even if we had to describe it later, it could be described as a past very far away. In the new time-line, memory might work differently.

I imagined the speculations to be true that our planet would be hit by a shooting star, and explode in a few months. Our lives on earth would be wiped clean. Then I had no regrets about being here right now. It wouldn't matter anymore that I was now making this kind of damp, lingering love with my thirty-eight-year-old teacher.

Afterwards, Mr. Yang asked me if I knew how many of my classmates had had sexual experience.

I didn't like the question. I felt sixteen once again, and felt put into a box, one of the many. "How would I know?" I said.

"Your generation is different from mine," he had an ambivalent smile. "We were very idealistic back then, maybe too innocent. People don't care about certain things any more today, as long as business goes well. One day your parents will spend some money to send you abroad, so you don't have to worry."

"Worry about what? Our 'decadent generation' in your eyes?"

"I didn't say that," he said. "Although you learn the decadent things fairly fast..."

I felt annoyed at Mr. Yang. I thought, just because people in his time had fought against something collectively, it didn't give him the right to diminish the individual battles of every generation. But he didn't let me leave his arms yet.

"You know our Party secretary, Old Lin? Is there anything between him and your class president?"

"Jie? What are you talking about?"

"Well, she's no ordinary girl, for sure," said Mr. Yang. He added that he had heard Jie was nominated to be a probationary Party member of my cohort, even though usually only third-year students would be eligible.

"I don't think what you thought is true," I said.

"Perhaps not," said Mr. Yang. "It is none of my business even if it is."

Why did he have to slight Jie, while we were still lying together? Why make things up to push weight off his own conscience? I remembered that when I wanted to close my eyes in the act, Mr. Yang had asked me to look up at him during his deepened movements and my change of breath. His palms pressed on my shoulders with an unbearable urgency and assurance. His request moved me deeply somehow. And I took everything in, everything between us, from second to second. Then, with our eyes locked on each other's, I felt the most humiliation and the most heightened longing all at once. I had wondered if I was falling back in love.

But now, his bringing up Jie in this manner made me extremely sad. Perhaps I wasn't experienced enough to consider his own insecurity at the time, his worries that a young girl was agreeing to be in his apartment not for who he was, but for what he could do for her. It felt as if he was setting me up to defend myself against a crime that I was already condemned for. And a teacher-student relationship was a potential crime towards the teacher, not the student, in his mind.

Back then, I found the accusation familiar, a tradition in the male narrative of my culture. Only much later, did I realize that he needed love, but didn't love me.

That evening, I stayed late and Mr. Yang called a taxi to take me home. And like last time, we kept our distance while walking out of his neighborhood, not conversing. When I looked around from the taxi's back seat, I saw that Mr. Yang stood quietly to see me off, but he didn't wave his hands.

***

During the summer break, Jie finally admitted to me that she was in fact, dating Mr. Lin.

"It only started recently," she said. "At his home," when his wife was at work and son still boarding at university. Jie didn't give much more detail. I tried to imagine the kind of family bed Mr. Lin would have – perhaps purple sheets with mandarin-duck embroidery, and a rosewood bedstead. He had pulled the floor fan close to the bed so that they could cool off afterwards. I felt a throbbing pain in my temples. What kind of key school did we get ourselves into?

I was also convinced that what I had told Jie about Mr. Yang and myself had made it happen. I felt responsible. It almost seemed like revenge on her part. But Jie said that she knew what she was doing.

"He is always talkative when it comes to his son," she said. And all I could think of was that even Mr. Lin's son was older than us.

I asked which university Mr. Lin's son was in, and Jie told me. It was a well-known normal university in Shanghai, although it wouldn't be either Jie's or my first choice in our applications. Jie said that she had seen framed pictures of his son on the dresser, and that she had been introduced to his wife a few months ago, before she and Mr. Lin had started to meet in this way.

"Does that bother you?" I asked.

Jie shook her head quickly, as if a small insect had landed on her hair. "But he talked about making changes so that he could be with me. I don't really want to think about such things."

"You don't. Why?"

"I mean, how could that be possible?" She was deep in thought for a minute. "How could I?"

I wanted to confirm Mr. Yang's speculation that Jie went into this to get her probationary Party membership, but didn't say anything in the end. Things were not either one way or the other, like the painted faces in Peking Opera. Even if it was true, I was resolved not to follow the direction that Mr. Yang had led my mind to. I hadn't forgotten about my ten extra points in the university entrance examination, either. And Jie was protective of Mr. Lin. She didn't tell me much of their intimacy apart from the fact that they were now "together."

"What was his wife like?

"I think she was very nice. Tall and slim, curly hair. She's a businesswoman who has founded an advertising company. I hope I can be like her when I grow up."

"You will. You like the same type of men." I made a bad joke, but Jie laughed. She was wearing a collarless shirt instead of our usual uniform that day. And to my surprise, I discovered that her scent had changed, not in any bad way, but it felt different to be near her. I felt that she had taken a solo trip to a faraway beach, that there was sea salt in her hair, somewhere I hadn't been yet.

"Do you speak Shanghainese with each other?"

"What else?" she teased me back, poking my shoulder twice with her index finger.

"So no love said."

"No love. Who says such things?! Well, we *huoexi* each other." *Huoexi* is "happily fond of" in Shanghainese – there is no commonly used equivalent for the word "love" in the dialect, and people find it embarrassing to speak it in Mandarin anyway. For the first time, I was a little jealous of Jie for their natural kinship.

"He told me that the legal age for sex is fourteen in our country," Jie said. "Are you surprised? I was."

"Fourteen... Some of our classmates hadn't had their first period at fourteen..." I said. Back at that moment, I couldn't figure out why we were suddenly passing around that information; and why, the two of us, talking like adult women about their boyfriends, suddenly fell silent together for a minute.

***

Mr. Yang and I met several more times in his apartment that summer. Now that Jie and I shared a secret, we could cover for each other. And I found ways to push his remarks out of my mind.

In the afternoon heat, Mr. Yang left the windows open for air circulation, and sometimes we heard bird-song. Once the open windows brought in a thunderstorm, when we were too slow to close them. Some of the textbooks on the desk became cockled. In my mind, the papers were now forever wavy with the marks of rain.

He grew familiar with my body, and my limbs often felt sore. I felt our emotions were spent instead of understood. Was it the same with Old Lin as well? Mr. Yang had kissed the faint scar on my knee from when I fell on the school playground four years ago, on the day when I first talked to

Jie. I wondered if Jie had a scar or birth mark that nobody had seen before.

He told me that he had lost his job in Beijing after 1989. Two of his students had been killed. "Two girls, only a few years older than you." Mr. Yang said. "One was stabbed right through the lung." I asked for more of that memory, but he didn't want to talk about it any further.

We watched the documentary "River Elegy", which he had bought from a vendor who sold pirated VCDs, a ground-breaking film from the 1980s that was later banned. Mr. Yang told me that the film marked the spirit of their times – the discussion of a backward-looking "yellow river" civilization, versus an adventure-seeking "blue ocean" civilization, had captured many hearts among the intellectuals of the 1980s. And that afternoon when we made love, the climax came.

It happened unexpectedly that I fell asleep for a while afterwards. I didn't know that I had lost consciousness until I woke up on Mr. Yang's shoulder, feeling embarrassed. I realized that I had imagined only devotion of the mind before. But how to describe a surge of devotion in the body? I didn't know whether it was entirely separate, or even different, from that of the mind. I wished to spend a long time to recall and to understand. Yet, as soon as I woke up, Mr. Yang said that he was looking at me the whole time I slept. He told me that what I had just felt could be described as "欲仙欲死" (yu xian yu si), wishing to be immortal and dead all at once, and it was what he had felt with me – now I had felt the same. He said that I looked like a nude painting coming alive.

The new four-character chengyu Mr. Yang had taught me this time was unfamiliar, beautiful. And my mind had churned with it all day. However, like when remembering the foul language he had used before, I felt once again that my heart was handed a map drawn by somebody else, waiting for me to fall into the experience. Could beautiful words be reductive and misleading, too? I was frustrated by not being able to articulate what I thought in my own words at the time, or not soon enough. I thought I was restless and ungrateful, to be two-minded about my physical pleasure. I knew it was true that I could have abandoned my life for Mr. Yang during that moment. However, when he described that abandonment for me, I wished only to do him bodily harm, to make him feel as confused and ashamed as I did.

The more he told me how I had felt, the more I rebelled against it in my mind. The details I would then recall from our very first time became more and more the opposite of enjoyment. Didn't I force myself to think of something else during the act, and try to see it with more poetry only later? Didn't I do it every time, wearing his words afterwards like a pair of tinted glasses? I no longer trusted even my own experience.

I felt cooped up and sometimes lost my temper in the small and bare room. One day in August, Mr. Yang asked me to pee on a stick to make sure that I was not pregnant. I found it humiliating as I had not seen a pregnancy test kit before, nor had I even considered the possibility.

Schools and parents of my generation believed that sex education was only for married couples who needed it. As teenagers, we were taught nothing more than we learned from watching a fifteen-minute introductory video of the reproductive system, as part of the Biology class; male and female students watching in separate classrooms. It was Mr. Yang who had been calculating the timing of my period.

I found waiting for the result unbearable.

"How many students did you sleep with in Beijing? Maybe it was why you were divorced by that senior official's daughter – or was she your student as well?"

The test showed negative, and Mr. Yang was calm. He collected the kit and dropped it in the rubbish bin with the same swift manner he used to throw away a snack package.

"Don't make me feel that I have over-estimated you," he said. He had the talent of not answering the questions I wanted most to know the answer to. And he knew how to make it about my character instead of his own when questioned.

"I see. In your over-estimation, I should never ask questions or be angry."

"Look, I know why you are so nasty today," said Mr. Yang. "Believe me, I know it. Don't be so *renxing*, okay?" He wanted to pull me to sit on his lap.

The way he hugged me and the familiar words brought tears to my eyes. Don't give rein to your temperament but be amenable. I was not acting my usual self, I knew. But I didn't believe in him. If he had the ability to truly care, he would stop giving me words for my experience. It was not fair from the beginning, I thought, not fair at all. And he was not really that original, either. The map wanted to foresee every step I took. And I had carried that map all my life, for too long. I wanted to throw it away. I would rather be lost.

13
Paper Crane
紙鶴 (*zhihe*)

When the fall semester of the second year started, I noticed that Lily and Xiaofen had formed a quiet alliance. They had been going to the toilet together during class breaks, and sat in the same place in the canteen.

I wasn't surprised to see them become friends. Lily's father was an executive in a state-owned Chinese bank, and Xiaofen's parents had two children without penalty despite the strict One-child Policy that prevailed in big cities like Shanghai. They carried the best-looking backpacks among the girls in class, and knew the latest mainstream American music instead of following Hong Kong or Taiwanese pop singers like everyone else. Some of my classmates admired them, even though, in the past, the more popular students tended to be the ones with the best scores or leading roles assigned by the teachers in our school setting.

When we were all being tutored at Mr. Yang's place, Xiaofen told us stories about her brother and his classmates in a Canadian university. The father of one of his classmates had been a provincial governor in China for a long time. And the classmate was invited to school galas every year, until his father fell under *shuanggui*, was detained and interrogated by the Party. Nobody bothered to socialize with him after that. The story stayed in my mind because at the time, in my own naivety, I was surprised to hear that the foreigners in question were just as snobbish, after they had figured out who had the privilege and means, even though they didn't necessarily agree with the system of selection here.

Mr. Yang was a little more patient towards Xiaofen because she was the landlord's daughter. But I could tell that Lily was the one who adored him.

One day towards the end of the new semester, I saw that Lily was crying in the classroom during break, and that a circle of people had gathered around her. She had her head in her arms and refused to raise her face. Xiaofen stood next to her and petted her back, while looking in my direction from time to time. I felt nailed to my seat, but watched Lily all morning. I thought that something had finally been brought to the foreground that would unravel our lives. The new millennium had just arrived, yet the earth was not hit as I sometimes hoped it would be. We still had to study for university and deal with the problems we ourselves had created.

It was Jie who told me later that Lily and Xiaofen knew about Mr. Yang. Perhaps it was a nosy neighbour who had reported us to the landlord. Or maybe they had followed one of us after school.

"She called you names," said Jie, "but she didn't tell who her crush was that you ended up with. Gosh, I didn't know he was that popular."

It was indeed absurd, I thought. And frankly, who was Jie to judge? But now I recalled a story I had glanced through in my mother's "Readers" magazine recently, that somewhere in Russia, a group of young women had lived underground with a priest for over ten years, doing his laundry and fighting for his favours. When they were finally rescued by the police, these women didn't even know that the USSR no longer existed. Why on earth did these women want to live in a cold, dark room below ground for so long like hibernating bears? Didn't they have other places to visit in this big wide world, or other people to talk to?

When Mr. Yang heard about Lily, he seemed frightened.

"Does anyone else know about us?"

"Lily didn't say your name," I said. "I thought you would be pleased to know this, about her feelings for you."

I realized that Mr. Yang was much more afraid of being discovered than I was. It was true then, I thought. He would never have bothered to defend himself otherwise. Maybe he didn't think he needed to.

"If the school finds out, I might go to jail for this," he said.

"Maybe you should marry me if everyone finds out!" I meant this as revenge, but regretted it the moment the words escaped my mouth.

"Nonsense," he said quickly. And then, after a few seconds, "It's not possible."

Mr. Yang moved close to take my hand. But I felt that the blood ran out from wherever he had touched me. He took my clothes off, but I was not alive. We made love and I cried when it finished. Mr. Yang seemed bewildered by my tears, but didn't say anything. He waited quietly next to me until my eyes had dried. From that day on, I couldn't remember a time that I didn't cry when in bed with him.

***

I couldn't face Mr. Yang in class anymore, seeing him behind the podium and interacting with others, cracking jokes that made my peers laugh. Their laughter tore me apart. I no longer wished to discuss anything with Jie. I thought that because I was so hurt by the lack of any future, I was not as strong as she was.

Before the Lunar New Year break started, I mentioned in a phone call with my father that I wanted to switch to arts instead of sciences when applying for university. And because of this, I wanted to leave the Advanced Science Class and take History as my elective in the university entrance examination. I wasn't particularly interested in the history that was taught at school, but since I was not bad at memorizing textbook facts, my marks on the subject had always been above average and consistent.

"Think about how hard she has worked to get in, in the first place!" my mother complained to my father while I was still on the phone. "Many people in her cohort would be happy to switch places with her."

"They are welcome," I said.

My father was more accommodating than I had expected, however. "You can't do anything well in the long run if you don't really enjoy it," he said. "If you are sure about arts, allow yourself to change your mind." And that was just what I wanted to hear.

He agreed that I should talk to my class teacher soon. I submitted an official letter to Mrs. Xue and was informed before the break that I would become the first in my school's history to quit the reputable Advanced Science Class and become an arts major. I didn't feel as much of an outlier as I thought I would – maybe I was simply so pleased with the change that I didn't care what everyone thought. I told Mr. Yang later that the decision was partly made to avoid Lily and Xiaofen, so that with my exit, they might stop passing gossip around. And he wouldn't get distracted in class, either, I said.

***

But I went to Mr. Yang's place less and less. After school, I avoided the corridor where I might see him. My new classroom was on a different floor, so that made things easier.

In the new class, my overall marks started to improve after dropping Physics and adding History, which gave me some confidence to think about the first-tier universities in Shanghai. In addition, the new class teacher had seated me next to a group of student athletes so that I could help them. As it turned out I became good friends with them and needed much help from them myself, in every aspect other than academic matters. They invited me to play volleyball with them, and held after-school gatherings to strengthen our bond, which my Advanced Science Class peers would never do. Among these athletes, a few of them were dating each other. And I also grew close to one of them.

Jeremy was not particularly good at English, but like some of my high school classmates, he preferred to use the new arbitrary name assigned by the English teacher. "My parents gave me a first name too much like a girl's," he admitted to me once, "and now I finally feel free from it." I found his reasoning amusing, but at the same time, it was almost inspiring that such a simple change could be liberating. I told him that, if he liked, he could call me "Nancy," too, my own temporary name from the English class. Apart from our names, however, we talked to each other mostly in Shanghainese.

He wore glasses and wore a button-down shirt even outside school, which made him look less like a stereotypical athlete. Once the group played a prank on us while we were watching a film together in someone's home, locking Jeremy and me in the bathroom. The group must have detected something between us, and were hoping to "do us a favour." As I knocked on the door with mild frustration, and negotiated terms with them to let us out, Jeremy seemed to be less bothered. He looked around the bathroom and found a stack of decorative paper made in the popular fluorescent style.

"I bet they use these to make stars," he said. It was a pastime in school at the time to make a glass jar of paper stars for your best friends.

Jeremy took one piece and folded it into a paper crane in no time, and then another in a different colour. He put both into my palms and I found the gesture touching. My favourite paper art in my childhood was boats. So I folded a couple after him, surprised that my fingers still knew how to do it in. Later, we put all our artwork down on the counter. The boats and cranes lined up illuminating the dark. We were not having a bad time. In the end, I forgot how long we were in the bathroom. Jeremy had a quality of calming the atmosphere around him.

The first time he asked me out on a Saturday, it was in the midst of spring. We decided to walk around the Chenghuang Temple area and browse the stalls that sold snacks, fans and beaded accessories. Jeremy bought me a Buddhist-style praying bracelet made of small green stones. On the way back to our district, we stopped by a few record shops and then had bubble tea. Later, as we waited for the traffic lights, he took my hand quite naturally. His palm became wet, and he kept quiet the whole time. I found the streets with tall sycamore trees beautiful, as we stepped on the fallen brown leaves still lying on the ground from the year before, making soft, crackling sounds.

At one crossroad, we ran into Lily. She was chatting with a group of university-age boys and girls in front of a convenience store, a cigarette in one hand. I had never seen her smoking before. Feeling startled, I let go of Jeremy's hand when Lily walked across the street towards us.

"Are you two friends now?" She stared at me for a while, and it made me uncomfortable. This was the first time Lily had talked to me since the day she had cried in the classroom. She sized Jeremy up. "What about Mr. Yang, then?"

"This has nothing to do with Mr. Yang."

Lily turned to him. "Do you know that your girlfriend is sleeping with our Physics teacher?"

Jeremy didn't question me afterwards. I wondered if Mr. Yang had ever taught him. It didn't really matter. He let his hand drop when I pulled mine away in front of Lily. But that was probably what any boy that age would do. Had he confronted me back then, however, I might have tried to open up to him, even though I didn't know where I could even start at the time.

We stayed friends within the group and Jeremy didn't mention what he had heard to anyone. Only each of us knew, in our polite avoidances, that we wouldn't go out over weekends again. And that avoidance stung my heart in a controlled, grown-up manner, like Jeremy's, or the person he would naturally become.

I had thrown the stone bracelet into my desk drawer. I managed to convince myself that it was rather old-fashioned to wear a Buddhist ornament like this for a person my age. Nonetheless, I folded many paper cranes that spring, enjoying an old form of art almost lost in time. I couldn't, and wouldn't forget those slower childhood days in the 1980s when there was not much to read, not much to watch on television, and a lot of time was spent waiting for my loved ones to come home. I missed their simplicity.

**

A few days after meeting Lily on the street, I went to Mr. Yang's place. We had been seeing each other secretly for nearly ten months now.

"I can't come here anymore," I said, and walked straight into the room before he had a chance to close the front door. I had always waited for us to be safe in our intimacy, and for the door to be completely locked before I made the faintest sound. Sometimes I walked so carefully up the stairs that I might as well be tiptoeing like a cat. How much effort I used to make in eliminating the space I took up in the world! Mr. Yang leaned against the desk in front of me.

"Soon it will be my final year of high school and I need to concentrate on my studies." I hadn't expected myself to put it in such a disingenuous way, but continued, "You said before that we didn't have a future. We are not going to marry or anything."

"I always knew that this day would come," he said.

If so, then why the hell, I thought. It just came to me that unlike me, he knew this from day one. He already knew this when he showed me his story. He just needed someone like me to read it.

"You have all of your twenties in front of you, and I'm almost forty. There's no reason for me to keep you here, really."

I waited but he didn't say anything else. He accepted the breakup calmly, making a hardened part in my chest ache again.

"You are used to this, aren't you?" I found myself saying. "You are used to being close to your students in the way that we were and then separating. At least I'm not lying cold on a Beijing street. Who could ever compare with them? I don't belong to the generation of people you miss every day. I'm not that brave, nor that foolish!"

"I don't think you want to talk like this. It doesn't do anything, does it?"

"Yes. Nothing."

I suddenly realized that in Chinese, when we say "yes" or "no," we always agree or disagree with the person, and never with the statement. "Yes" and "no" are used to express our feelings towards the person we talk to, and not our stand in regard to any issue. I felt my throat dry.

"Yinan, I don't expect you to understand. You are so young. But I don't want to lose my job again here, in Shanghai."

"Oh, that I understand," I said.

I didn't stay long, before storming out of Mr. Yang's flat. In the end, it was I who lost my temper and couldn't speak in the right manner. The one who had to leave the other felt no acceptance nor peace. That was why it was so unfair.

In the next few days, I replayed our conversation over and over again in my mind. I thought of his former university students, and remembered that he once said he was the one who had influenced them politically, and who, "had encouraged them to think one way more than the other." Was it guilt he had felt, that he was the one spared in the end? Was he capable of feeling guilty? He didn't allow himself to forget them, however, even though it would be much the easier thing to do. Or was it only a version of himself that he couldn't forget and wanted to relive?

I thought of the day, a decade after June 1989, when he was dressed head-to-toe in white linen, refused to teach and walked out of the classroom, leaving me enchanted with a bitter-sweet feeling. At that very moment, I knew now, I felt he was protesting against my whole childhood education, on my behalf, and on behalf of us all. How far away that early June day only months ago already felt.

On campus the spring leaves had deepened in colour. Soon the first spring of the new millennium had gone. I called Mr. Yang only once during the next few months. Being in a different class had helped. Still, once I saw him from a distance in assembly, talking to the foreign music teacher, Mr. Eriksson, and couldn't tell whether he was sad or not. That day, I wandered the streets for half an hour after school, afraid that I would end up at Mr. Yang's door again.

In the end, I dialed his number from a public phone booth.

When Mr. Yang picked up the phone, his voice sounded different. I had always considered him as having a young voice for his age. But now, that voice had also aged. I listened to the cars passing by for a few seconds before speaking. "Can I come over?"

"I don't think that's a good idea," he said. For a moment I thought he was angry and was trying to hurt me, to get revenge. But his voice was flat. "You were right. We shouldn't see each other again. It was not good for us."

"I've missed you," I said. The truth was, most days I couldn't bear this separation. But sometimes, words already knew their answer before they were tossed into the air. I had a feeling that Mr. Yang wouldn't reply in the same way this time. I only realized then that I had made my parting from him official.

"I remember how you looked when you slept," he said. And the following silence made my tears fall in the phone booth. I didn't know how to respond to the idea of not being able to see him ever again. And this time, I felt that

Mr. Yang was not quoting anything vulgar or beautiful, from any books or anyone else. They were his own words and for this reason I couldn't pull myself together.

Some people walked by in the evening mist. The small, rusty phone booth stood in the middle of nowhere. "You shouldn't say that now."

Years later, I realized that I had wished he would tell me that I was his only one at that moment, that he had preferred being vague as to our exclusiveness to create a façade of popularity – a product of his own insecurity – and that I had misunderstood him. Instead, for the first time, he said that he loved me, in Mandarin. "*Wo shi ai ni de.*" I am in love with you. To my ears, however, it was something more believable before he had said it. "I've spent three months to recover from it."

Big deal, I thought.

In the end, Mr. Yang still wanted to confuse me. He didn't own the words he had just uttered. He didn't know me at all, or care about my pain. Let alone, that, given our circumstances, a real love wouldn't have announced itself so prematurely, least of all in the physical way as had happened. What was the use of telling me now? Why name it now? How could he think that by putting a name on it, he had summarized and justified everything that had happened over the past year? But before my tenderness for Mr. Yang again turned into anger, he had already hung up. He said what he wanted to say, but he didn't wish to hear my response.

That was the last time I spoke to Mr. Yang.

14
Love
愛 (*ai*)

In Mandarin, the word love sounds like a sigh: *ai*, in the fourth tone, short and assured.

The written character of love, "愛," consists of four parts – paws (爫), roof (冖), heart (心) and crossed legs/arrival (夂). The simplified version used since the 1950s and 60s in mainland China, is "爱," without the "heart" radical.

The simplification might be the reason why, more than once in my life, the announcement of love always felt like the opposite. It felt like finality, a swan song.

When I was a child, and when beginning to learn the written language, I used to fill three sheets of new characters each week for homework. And now in my thirties, it had been a long time since I had routinely practised calligraphy. Back on Duolun Road, my grandfather used to sit in front of the desk, lay out his rice paper and lose himself for hours in writing. He wrote in traditional characters. And he had a beautiful ink stick and stone set made in Lanting, Zhejiang Province, the place most famous for its gathering of calligraphers. My grandmother was often the one who helped to grind the ink.

The amount of ink on the brush, the thickness of the strokes, the flow of the running lines, and the knit between characters, I was taught, had all played a crucial part in written expression. My grandfather knew how to write a poem in both Yan Zhenqing and Liu Gongquan ways – significantly different styles referred to as "the muscle of Yan and the bone of Liu." But why, like my grandfather, was I also naturally drawn to calligraphy? Was it because the inherited words in printed form were not enough, form devoid of vital emotion?

During those early years, I didn't consider the time spent as worthwhile, not writing down any new ideas, but running the brush over and over again to take each character apart, and examine our tools from the beginning of time.

***

In my final year of high school, I seemed to have lost both interest and ability to read in Chinese. Memorizing textbooks was one thing. But whenever I opened up a "leisure book," the once beloved square-shaped characters started to dance around without forming any meaning. I only saw bits and parts, dots and strokes, stems, branches and radicals.

My father used to say that, to his German colleagues, Chinese characters looked like tens of thousands of variations of little houses, or innovative drawings of spiders. And we had a good laugh about it.

Now I wondered if what I had been seeing all along had also been lines of houses, molding and containing my every thought within their four walls. Or were they armies of spiders, weaving the same symmetrical web with alluring silk, waiting quietly for the human prey of every generation. Did I mistake these webs for my own heartstrings? But without any instrument, how do I hear my own heart?

15
University Entrance Examination
高考 (*gaokao*)

After I left the Advanced Science Class, Jie and I were not in touch. It must have been on purpose. Because during the final year of high school, every ounce of our energy seemed to be spent in front of our desks, in preparation for the *gaokao* − the "high exam"− the most important and final sprint in our academic marathon. Even in my History class, there were no more after-school parties. The present moment had completely surrendered to working towards the future, the ideal goal of our school training. Seasons went by without notice.

Nobody had bothered with the camera at the back of our classrooms for a long time. Sometimes in the school news programme, I saw that our lunch break activities were recorded – students taking a short nap at their desks, quarrelling with neighbours, or throwing a badminton racket down in the classroom – and thought that everyone now viewed these replays of recordings as simply routine. It was easy to get used to a new status quo, I thought, if one followed it long enough. And there were always ways to drain the energy of even the most vocal protestors.

I let my mother cut my hair above the shoulders for the first time in my adolescence, ridding me of any distraction possible in her view. A few other female classmates did the same before the *gaokao*. It reminded me of the induction ritual in which Buddhist nuns have their heads shaved, to farewell the "three thousand strands of worries," and I found the ritual somehow necessary, comforting.

When the three-day nation-wide examination eventually ended, it was already the height of summer, July. I enjoyed the blazing sun over my bare neck during the days that followed, and walked around in different parts of the city by myself, to stretch out my body which had been indoors for so long.

One day, Jie called and we agreed to meet in the park that we used to go to all the time, the same park, now renamed after author Lu Xun, where I had told her about the first night with Mr. Yang. When she saw me, she said that my bobbed haircut made me almost unrecognizable from afar.

"Good or bad?"

"Now it's easier to see your expression," she said.

Jie was only a little tanned. But since she had told me over the phone that she had just returned from a vacation in Hainan Island after the *gaokao*, a tropical tan was what I was expecting. I noticed that the thin hair on her upper arms was gone, too. We were applying to the same university, where my father worked. Her first choice was the World Economics department, which demanded the highest scores among all the admissions, given the expectation that China would soon join the World Trade Organization.

"Ready to be a future businesswoman?"

Jie only smiled at my question. But when she told me that she had a new boyfriend, in fact the person she had gone to Hainan Island with, I was surprised. They had met not long ago, when the Party study group in our high school had invited a university political and ideological advisor – these were usually PhD students working as part-time administrators – to deliver a talk. And he was a PhD student in the department Jie had applied to. She had recently ended things with Mr. Lin.

"How did he take it, Mr. Lin?"

"He said he could get a divorce," said Jie. "I don't think he meant it. He hadn't said it before. And he said it now simply because it had become safe to say it – the fault was mine afterwards, as he would lead himself to believe. So I just did him a favour by telling him that my boyfriend had all that he had, but could give me what he couldn't give. He cried."

I tried to imagine Mr. Lin crying in front of Jie, sitting on the bed with mandarin-duck embroidered sheets, and unable to make her stay. I thought that perhaps neither of them had known when the other had made the final decision. Being with somebody else does not necessarily mean that the heart has made a clear choice, sometimes quite the opposite. I had had that experience. But I was pained by Jie's last statement as well. Because she sounded so free, so reasonable, and so matter-of-fact. And also because of just how plainly rehearsed it sounded.

"So it's settled," I said at last.

"Funny thing – you know that, while we were all busy with the *gaokao*, our school built an online forum? The Internet seems to be an amazing thing. You can talk with virtually anybody in the world. Anyway, in one of the discussion threads, someone posted a 'warning message' to future applicants that 'our school's Party secretary Mr. Lin liked to put his hand on girls' thighs.' Ha! Of course, I didn't mention it to him."

I wondered whether it was before or after Jie had broken up with him. I felt a little nauseous.

Jie was fumbling with the content of her bag to find a few prints of vacation photos to show me. But as she raised her head, I saw that her eyes were suddenly moist. And I understood at once why she had called me. Without thinking, I reached out my hands across the table to cover hers. Jie's fingers were thin and cold. She lifted her chin a little.

"You know," I said, "because of the way you talk and shrug things off, people don't take your tears seriously. People don't take *us* seriously." What I didn't say was that the "people" would eventually include ourselves.

"Well, who wants to live in victimhood? We live in a world where victims are not seen as complex beings."

"I think," I searched for words, but they came very slowly, very inaccurately at the time, "sometimes circumstances put one in a place where one feels that there is no other choice...other than to lay out the most precious and vulnerable things in our lives to gamble for a future. I think the question is, how do people end up in this place? If people in this place are not victims, I don't know who is. If these people are not complex beings, I don't know who else can be."

"Only you see it this way, Yinan."

I thought that what she didn't say was that, in our mundane world, those who matter will not see it in this way, and those who see things in the way I do don't have a chance to matter. I didn't have a response to that, either.

Jie pulled her hands back from mine, and blew her nose into a tissue. I worried that I might have offended her. She had big dreams for life and was ready to move on. All I wanted to tell her was that I had figured out lately that borrowing words from the powerful doesn't make one powerful. If anything, it can make things worse. It left part of us behind, strangled, unheard.

"Remember how our parents liked to tell us that our childhood was 'the happiest time in our life'? Strangely, every time I heard that, I was willing to forget the cramped attic apartment and my annual chilblains for a moment, and thought 'that's right, it was indeed an innocent, blissful time.'"

"Compared to a very tiresome adolescence," Jie said. "I don't know if you've ever noticed, but there isn't a single photograph of me smiling ever since I became a teenager, or since going to school. Almost nobody smiled in the class group photos, either. But now we are older and exhausted, we can still repeat the mantra to each other that 'high school was the most carefree time of all.'"

"Exactly. I guess sometimes we all need that to stay strong, to gloss over things and even to transcend them. But our adolescence is different. I just...don't want you to forget about this. No matter how others describe theirs. No matter how few others remember theirs. You have to promise me that."

"I see that you are very introspective today." Jie's smile seemed to return, but like a faint moon hiding in the late afternoon daylight. "Who would have guessed, the classical lady Lin Daiyu from 'The Red Chamber' now wants to be a Foreign Language major! Sounds like the end of an era – maybe one day you will even become an interpreter at the 2008 Beijing Olympics."

"In my opinion, learning a foreign language is exactly the kind of thing Lin Daiyu would be doing if she had had the opportunity to do so in her day. By the way, you talk like all my relatives did when they heard which department I applied to. The Olympics are the last thing in my mind. I hate the rhetoric that relates choice of major with national service. There are only selfish reasons for my decision."

"But it has to do with him, hasn't it?"

I didn't reply.

Jie stared at me for a while, and let out a long sigh. "You know, I worried about you."

"I felt the same."

"Well, maybe I said cynical things last time we talked, but you never left my mind."

I teased Jie for sounding so soppy all of a sudden, and turned my head to look at the families who were rowing boats in the man-made lake nearby. The slow rhythm of their arms was calming on a summer day.

We walked alongside the lake for a while, and later saw that the renovation of the Lu Xun Memorial Hall – a black and white Jiangnan-style building in the park– was finally complete. Close by was the familiar brass statue in front of Lu Xun's tomb, and the vines of wisteria which both Jie and I knew well, blooming with purple flowers this time of the year. I felt time passing. So much work was being done towards the future, and towards separation. But I just wanted to stay with Jie in the present moment for a while longer.

"I don't remember any of our Chinese teachers mentioning that Lu Xun's wife was his student," I said.

"Only that he wanted to 'wake the dwellers who were suffocating in the dark, windowless room', but worried that he shouldn't wake them. Since there was no way out."

"He was an unhappy author, for sure."

"Always a cigarette in his hand and a long, dreary face."

"We read and analyzed so many of his stories. But now I only wish to hear from his wife's perspective." I remembered an old photograph I had seen of Lu Xun's funeral, his body covered in a banner that read, "Soul of the Nation."

"I bet we would be surprised," said Jie.

In front of us, it was hard to miss the golden inscription "Lu Xun's Tomb" in Mao Zedong's hand-writing. Who would have guessed the irony, I thought. The writer was still held in high esteem here only because he had died early enough, and was naturally silent for what was to come in the second half of the century. Had he lived longer, he too, would be put on the wrong side of history.

"I'm going to set his books aside for a while," I said. "I wish to read from someone who can make his own life happier for a change, and doesn't believe in the 'no exit' bullshit. Even if that means I will read in a different language."

"That sounds like a very good idea to me," said Jie. "Do whatever makes you happy."

***

Before the day ended, Jie suggested that we go together to get our ears pierced in the mall. I was hesitant at first, thinking of my parents' disapproval should they find out – my mother would likely frown at me for being vain, and my father would quote Confucius that "every hair and bit of skin are received from our parents, and therefore we must not wound them.' But soon, I realized that my thoughts – of filial piety governing these minor decisions – were rather laughable. Didn't they come too little, too late?

The piercing on my left earlobe turned out to be more difficult, and I had a mild infection afterwards. As a result, I would need to be careful in choosing the material and size of my earrings in future. I didn't regret our whim of that day, however. In the following years, the occasional inconvenience of an uncomfortable earring would always remind me of Jie, and that we had done this together.

We each bought a pair of thin, silver earrings from the shop that gave us the piercing, and later found an instant photo booth in the mall to mark the occasion. It was the first and only photo which Jie and I took together since we had met as twelve-year-olds. We were both wearing light, earth-tone colours, and our new earrings showed their sparkle. I was looking straight at the camera, while Jie tilted her head to rest her chin on my shoulder. We had decided to smile for this photo. So Jie was smiling with her teeth and I was smiling without.

The then-novelty machine soon printed out our photo, and sealed it in protective plastic, like a bookmark. We inscribed the photo with the date, and "Jie & Yinan, after *gaokao*" in cursive. There was only one copy and I let Jie have it.

I felt that, in a way, we were celebrating becoming adults together at eighteen, and aligning our timelines again, so that, with university days ahead, our paths wouldn't diverge too quickly from each other. It was the reason behind all the other reasons why we had reconnected that day. The notion of the futility of certain relationships hadn't yet come to mind for Jie and me.

Two weeks later, we would both receive the good news that our scores had passed the respective admission lines. I didn't mention to Jie that, in the end, I had no need for my father's extra ten points. Meanwhile, there were a couple of people in my History class who had higher scores than me, but didn't put down a good university as their first choice – it hit me then that the *gaokao* was a confidence game all along. And a confidence game was not really a fair one, although "fairness" was advertised here. I realized that it would be one of the cruelest things to bring up with Jie, so I didn't.

When I was younger, like most people, I had credited the changes I made in life to my own resolve and discipline, and took the advantages I had for granted. Even though I knew well enough that privileges in my country were often fleeting, little privileges were nonetheless something. It was not an easy thing to realize, especially when all you wanted was to get to another place, to break away from your own restrictions, and had worked so hard for it. It was not easy, to truly see someone else in the process.

It was Jie, however, who had kept me visible to her like a kite to a string in the years when I seemed to have lost a name for everything. If only I could have made sense of her tears sooner, and understood her better, instead of being comforted with the mere, faraway presence of her at the other end of the thin thread, I thought over and over many years later, maybe a tragedy could have been avoided.

16
Military Training
軍訓 (*junxun*)

In the summer of 2001, I enrolled in university in my
hometown, the one my father was teaching at. I became a
boarding student for the first time.

In my dorm, there were three bunk beds made of iron, a
long, skinny table in the middle of the room as a shared
desk, and a couple of uncomfortable-looking old benches.
It was surprising to me at the time that the facilities in this
prestigious university were a step down from my high
school dorms, where everyone had her own wooden bed,
desk, chair and bookshelf. Here, male and female students
lived in different buildings. And inside the buildings, each
floor shared a big bathroom of ten sinks for washing hands
and brushing teeth, and open toilet stalls with no doors.
When I lived with my grandparents, I had prided myself on
being able to go to the toilet in a skilled squatting position
to avoid touching the filthy shared toilet seat. But I still
found the open plan unbearable: I would go in and nod to
everyone I knew and when somebody flushed, all of their
business would travel in front of my eyes before it went
down the drain.

However, I found the shared sinks quite entertaining in
the mornings for us foreign language students. Apart from
the half of us who were English majors, the rest of the
students in my department studied "minority languages." I
enjoyed seeing the French majors in the mornings, when
they would drink a mouthful of water from their brushing
cup and practice the "R" sound diligently with water. The
Russian majors would join them sometimes and produce an

even louder and more dramatic "R." The Japanese and Korean majors, on the other hand, often came in with headphones and hummed their own J-pop and K-pop songs, as if these songs were the reason for their chosen major. We even had a few international students coming from Taiwan and Brazil. They soon joined us, perhaps reluctantly like me, to wash their hair at the sink with a basin and a big thermos of hot water, and to bathe in the public shower room where there were no doors, curtains or privacy.

My parents thought that living in an "egalitarian" dorm and meeting peers from outside Shanghai was a good lesson to teach me to be grateful for having competed only within Shanghai and for being one of the luckier ones in the game. At that age, I was more than fed up with the "grateful education" we had already repeatedly learned at home and in school, a language forced down my throat.

I began to realize later, however, as I started to get acquainted with my roommates, that most of them, coming from the neighbouring Provinces of Zhejiang, Jiangsu and Anhui, took a different, more competitive *gaokao* exam than their Shanghainese peers. From my high school, almost all students got into universities, and one-third went to first-tier schools. In contrast, some of my roommates were the number one or number two students in their whole province.

For instance, Lynn from Jiangsu Province, told me that her high school had a "hell-style" training for senior students, where they woke up at 5:30am every morning and returned home from school at 10:30pm. They had only a ten-minute lunch break every day, when some of their parents delivered their lunch boxes to school. During the three days of *gaokao*, many of her classmates had checked into a local hotel, presumably so that they could have the quietest environment possible in which to perform. Lynn told us that the hotels would often end up being overbooked and filled with verbal fights among anxious parents, which in fact defeated the purpose.

"We tore our textbooks to pieces the day after the *gaokao*, and threw them out of the school windows. It was like a ritual after being released from prison," said Lynn. "Later the janitor complained that it took her a whole day to clean up the mess. And she had to do that every year."

We felt sorry for Lynn, and she felt sorry for the janitor. Without feeling sorry for others' misfortune, how could one come to peace with her own lot? The art of acceptance was taught many times throughout our school years, but there was not a single lesson in the art of questioning.

After orientation week, in late summer, before the first semester officially started, our military training began. And it was the physical ritual of disciplining us again into grateful eighteen-year-old young adults. We soon learned that unlike the freshmen who entered university during the years from 1989 to 1992, who had a whole year of military training in the aftermath of the Tiananmen Square protests, ours would only last for a month.

It was, however, still one of the hottest months in the city. We wore a baggy camouflage uniform in school every day. Each class was assigned an officer from the People's Liberation Army who gathered us in the basketball court every morning. We stood or sat on the cement ground to learn army songs, military theories, and spent the rest of the day practicing standing with good posture, marching in unison with goose steps, and shouting out loud when we had to reply to our officer.

Once in a while, when the rules were relaxed a little and we were allowed to take short water- or ice-cream-breaks, I would hear some students talking about our young officer as being quite nice and charming. Such conversation made me roll my eyes in aversion.

I was not enjoying any of it, I knew, as I discovered that goose-stepping was not an easy feat. It sure looked easy. But who would have known that there was a certain angle that everyone was supposed to comply to, and a certain sound the shoe should make when it touched the ground? For hours, the officer made us stand with one leg up to practice that angle and our balance. Some classmates who hadn't put on sunscreen turned red very quickly. And the unbreathable camouflage uniform trapped all the sweat, making me wonder why I hadn't fainted. I thought back to a few years earlier, 1997, when all my family gathered in front of the television to watch the handover of Hong Kong. I thought that the People's Liberation Army walked with such cool, unified steps, while the Hong Kong army marched with their knees up in a strange way and didn't lift them at the same time, or move their arms with the exact same angle. When I saw the two armies exchanging flags, I had even laughed at the chaotic marching style of the Hong Kong troops. I only realized now how much work there had been behind those goose steps, and wished that every soldier in China would simply follow the Hong Kong style in future.

You see, Mr. Yang, I thought, one day during training, who said that our generation could afford to be decadent? In this country, they make sure that every generation pays for the problems caused by the previous one.

I was still conversing with him at times in my mind, and would later regret it deeply, for the impact his words had on me, even after he was no longer in my life. I realized that if anything, it was my mind that needed the military training.

***

In September, we finally took off our camouflage uniform and started classes. All the students were already exhausted. A week later, the news of the attack on New York and the fall of the twin towers reached us, making the atmosphere in the English department rather solemn. In contrast, I heard that some Electronic Engineering department students living in the dormitory behind us had a soccer game that evening to celebrate. Later, in the Marxism

Theory class, which was mandatory for every freshman across all majors, the professor led the discussion by comparing the Taliban's strategies with Sun Tzu's *The Art of War*, in the academic and political, but not humane light. I wondered if the differences in reaction were reflective of which languages people read or conversed in. It had strengthened my resolve to turn more into my new language, and stay away from the old.

Every morning before 6:30am, we had to get up and have our "morning run" record paper stamped near the campus lawn. While some roommates went back to sleep afterwards, I would sit under the ivory-white Mao statue and read a few pages of English books before heading back to my dorm. It was a convenient place to study quietly with my morning energy and fresh air.

Most major universities in China still kept one such Mao statue into the 21st century. If there was any difference between our statue and the ones in other schools, however, it was that our Mao had his hands folded behind his back instead of sporting his usual waving position. It was due, in fact, to cutting corners during its construction, I later learned. Some students commented that this made him look more devious, as if he was hiding something. One of my English professors, who was once publicly denounced during the Cultural Revolution, joked that he would always keep a wary distance when passing the Mao statue, since Mao held a hat behind his back, and "if you are not careful, he will throw the 'hat' onto your head." "I've already had a 'counter-revolutionary' hat once," he said, "and I don't need another!"

In English, some of our professors didn't refrain from their otherwise "counter-revolutionary" opinions. I heard it said once in another class, "As long as Mao's picture remains in Tiananmen Square, we are all a single generation." The simple statement not only made me gasp for a moment, but also made me wish that, with all the diligence of my school years, I should have listened and read more in a different language than I had done in the past.

So, under the Mao statue, I now devoured books from *The Epic of Gilgamesh* and *The Odyssey*, to Chaucer and Shakespeare. I read the Old Testament and the New Testament. And I also enjoyed the short stories of James Joyce and Flannery O'Connor. In class, we debated Dolly the Sheep and mercy killing, analyzed fairy tales and the morals of olden days, and later practiced writing *The Book of Genesis* from a woman's perspective.

I found myself less hemmed in and much more gregarious in English. Even small talk was a way to practice the language with my classmates and professors. And everyone was less afraid of making mistakes, too. Now that I was older when I learned a new language, I could sometimes tell whether I liked a word or not when I first encountered it, and therefore started to build a vocabulary more honest and precise to myself. It is a luxury one could never have with one's native language, I realized, especially when one's native language doesn't encourage an idiosyncratic vocabulary.

The tenses and voices in English had once given me tremendous trouble as a child. But now I saw that they were just artificial prerequisites set by our education system to create unnecessary barriers, instead of encouraging interest in the foreign language and its way of thinking. In university, I finally came to appreciate the clear distinction of the past, present and future tenses in English, as well as of the active and passive voices. For example, "I have suffered" is simply not the same as "I am suffering," and is not an indication that "I will suffer." The tenses in English remind its speakers that one's identity always stays fluid in time, and choice is forever one's own. In terms of the active and passive voices, I also found it useful to see whether my heart was leading or being led in the past, trying now to narrate familiar memories in English.

It was liberating, really, to break the monogamy of language in my mind. Given enough time and effort, I hoped that those heart-breaking first words and first experiences wouldn't have a definitive power. I would understand my past better, and therefore I would have a future less attached to it. I would have power over my own present. I used English as if it was a compass in a dark forest, carefully and full of hope.

17
Coffee Shop
咖啡館 (*ka fei guan*)

During my sophomore year, I worked in the Hard Rock Café off campus.

It is probably not right simply to call it the Hard Rock Café, as the coffee shop had nothing to do with the international franchise that sold burgers, city-name T-shirts and other memorabilia. It only served bland coffee and fruit salad chopped by me, and was not known outside our school. In short, it was essentially a university coffee shop. Yet it was called the Hard Rock Café nonetheless.

I wasn't familiar with "咖啡" (*ka fei*, "coffee") until entering university. My father had always been a tea connoisseur – his brother, Uncle Jingchuan, would send us the first pickings from Zhuji every spring before the Ching Ming Festival. Therefore, I was spoiled, knowing good tea from a very early age. In my childhood, I often opened my father's tea tins when he didn't notice and snacked on the dry tea leaves themselves, as if the fragrant bitter taste would have an underlying sweetness the more I chewed them.

Coffee, on the other hand, was a much simpler drink to me at the time. Even before working at the Hard Rock Café, I had already seen classmates carrying it in a thermos to morning classes. And now I learned to make coffee with a machine myself. It felt industrialized and less atmospheric. The caffeine effect was more straight-forward and noticeable, too. I could always feel the quick surge in my mental energy.

Since the coffee shop was located opposite the Institute of International Students, it was popular among foreigners. On winter mornings, I saw exchange students coming in with an open down coat, shorts and slippers, and was impressed by their health and fashion choices. Soon, I found out that they could wear shorts in winter because the Institute and their dorms had heaters, a luxury during Shanghai winters in those days. I was envious at first but then realized that because of the close proximity, I could now hang out in their lobby on colder days to read a book or go over my study notes – it was a secret few people on campus knew about and I felt lucky. The lobby had sufficient sofas, tables and chairs, and was always quite empty.

Chinese students visited the café as well, usually on film nights, when there were indie films shown from a small screen hanging up near the ceiling. I helped make space for such occasions so that a roomful of people could stand for an hour or two to view the film to the end. It didn't occur to anybody that more comfortable arrangements could be made. I picked up phrases such as "avant-garde" or "new wave" quickly. And sometimes the coffee shop showed controversial, banned films such as the ones with gay sex scenes, pro-Fa Lun Gong content, or simply a fuller version of the films which were censored before they hit the mass market.

Once, after he got to know me a Chinese-American student was curious about my motive for working there. "I know that the cost of tuition is low here, so I haven't met anyone who worries about student loans. I thought you must be very poor to moonlight here," he said, "but you don't look poor. I remember you said that your father teaches in this university. My friends told me that intellectuals are not treated very well in China, though. You see, I'm already a little confused."

I was amused that he took an investigative interest in me and told him that I didn't work for additional income.

"The owners were an English department alumni couple and I was helping out. It was good for me to do something new, to be around people, after so many years of solo studying. Maybe I want to get into the world as soon as possible, when I can still make some big mistakes, before it's too late. There are free films here, too," I said. "But you are right about intellectuals. University professors here don't have as much freedom or earn the same as those in America."

"Ah," he bobbed his head in a good natured way. "I'm hoping to go into academia someday myself."

Simon was one and a half years younger than me, tall and lanky, and had spiky hair which set him apart from most people on campus. He had downturned eyes, straight teeth but a very awkward smile – as if he was a nonchalant tourist often forced to be in the photos of his travel companions. When he walked, I noticed that his arms, like his legs, were disproportionately long. He said that he grew up in Maryland, in the suburbs of Washington D.C. He was a Cognitive Psychology major, a subject unknown to me at the time.

"What do you study in your major?" I asked.

"Well, the mental processes that underlie human thinking basically. Memory, attention, learning, and language, etc. How to help university students remember better, for example, or how to evaluate the reliability of eyewitnesses in a courtroom."

"Mostly in an academic way?"

"I'm going to be a research psychologist, yes, so not really as talented as the clinical folks!"

"Sounds impressive to me."

Before meeting Simon, I didn't know anyone who had studied psychology. There used to be a counseling room in my high school that was available to students. But as far as I knew, nobody really went there or wanted to be known as too weak to endure hardship or simply "having illness of the spirit," which in the Chinese context equals being crazy.

Instead, people unkindly described the Chemistry teacher who volunteered there as an intimidating old maid, which further discouraged anyone who might otherwise seek help.

Memories came back to me, but I didn't mention it to Simon. Meeting new people was always a good way to discover an unknown part of the past, while introducing myself to them. And I found it very easy to talk to Simon. I noticed that, unlike other exchange students, he often came to the coffee shop by himself and was in no hurry to return with a take-away cup to his heated haven. In fact, he was probably running away from other people, for I noticed that if there were more students sitting at the next table, he wouldn't speak as much. He was the only one who tried to practice Chinese with me so much, especially when there was nobody else around in the small space.

"*Tian hen leng* ("weather very cold"), *yao ka fei* ("want coffee")."

"Is it a little late in the day to have coffee?" I replied in Chinese, and we talked in the language for a while.

"Americans drink many coffees. Not afraid." He said.

"Did you practice your writing characters today?" I asked. Simon had told me previously that he had bought a few grid notebooks from a nearby stationery shop.

"Write each character eleven, twelve times."

"Sounds like a punishment we had in primary school, when we had to stay after school and write our name a hundred times. Of course, one was out of luck if his name happened to have more strokes!"

"Wouldn't it lead the students to become narcissistic?"

"I never considered it this way," I said, and found his response funny. "If anything, it made people hate their own names, unfortunately."

"My name is not too hard to write," he said. Simon wrote 袁小雨 on a napkin. In his handwriting, his last name looked like a dancing person. The two characters of his first name mean "little rain."

"I guess you were born on a rainy day."

"My mother use to say this," he said, "when I was young."

Simon told me later that he had lost his mother in an accident when he was sixteen. His parents had moved to the U.S. from Taiwan in the early 1980s, both as graduate students, and settled in the country. Like me, he was also an only child.

I asked him if he spoke Chinese with his father. "Did you have to go to those Sunday schools that I've heard of?"

"Yeah," Simon said. He shrugged his shoulders, something I had often seen in Americans, perhaps an equivalent of knotting the brows for Chinese. He had decided to switch back to English.

"But I don't talk to my family much. And my dad just uses English with Chinese – if there is a word that I don't know, or actually a word I didn't know when I was eight, he will use the English word. By the way, do you want to know why American Born Chinese are bad at learning Chinese? At least for me, it definitely felt like a "parents' language". The only time I used it was talking to my parents or someone else's parents. And as a kid, sometimes we don't feel like talking to our parents. You always want to be young and cool."

"It must feel strange to find out that young people here speak Chinese, too." I said.

"Exactly! Why didn't I meet you when I was eight? Now I am old. It's too late!"

"Silly. I don't think you would have wanted to grow up in China."

Humans are funny creatures, I thought. There was me, who had wished never to have known any of those square-shaped Chinese characters that had walled my thoughts all my life, and an American guy who had regretted not picking them up earlier. Didn't Simon's parents take the hard journey so that their children and their children's children could grow up on the new continent? What was he doing here, erasing the track with his own shoes? However, when Simon and I spoke in Chinese, a very warm feeling rose in me, almost catching me off guard. During those days, he was the reason I still allowed myself not to depart completely from the language.

***

We often talked for a long time and in the end, there would still be coffee left in the cups, turning cold. Simon told me a story, that once when visiting relatives in Taiwan with his father, everyone was speaking in Chinese at the dinner table about the engagement of his cousin, and they didn't bother to translate it for him. So he only figured it out days later.

"It doesn't bother me anymore," he said. "I was annoyed at them before. But there were a lot of years when I was distant from my family."

Just like my earliest memories of becoming literate, most characters I taught Simon to write were nouns, or made up with noun radicals. And he saw them as simple pictures that trace what our eyes see in nature, such as the character in his own name, "雨" (*yu*, "rain"). He also liked it when I practiced the term "訂婚" (*dinghun*, "engagement") with him so that he wouldn't miss the next announcement. "訂" is made up of "言" (*yan*, "language/words") and "丁" (*ding*, "nail"), and "婚" is made up of "女" (*nü*, "woman") and "昏" (*hun*, "dusk"), so engagement in Chinese already implies a custom and a ritual – nail down the commitment with words, and a woman would come to your house at dusk. People who share the same Chinese language, I told Simon, would often not only share the culture as well, but also without realizing it, the same imagination.

I thought back to the time in my childhood when I mimicked my grandfather's calligraphy and ended up wasting his rice paper, yet how excited the family was to witness the occasion. And how pleased my parents were when they saw me practicing new characters as homework in primary school. How would a parent feel, knowing that his child would never really share his imagination?

***

We met outside the coffee shop a few times. Once Simon and I made a day trip to Zhouzhuang, a traditional water town north of Shanghai and walked on bridge after bridge. Simon told me that he believed in "forger le caractère" through walking.

"Well, you live here," he said. "But in most parts of the U.S., people don't walk as much. However, we always hear jokes about parents telling their kids, 'When I was your age, I walked two miles to school every day, uphill both ways!' Something like that."

"Ha! I never thought about the 'character' part," I said. And I considered the landscape where the parents in Simon's community came from for a while.

"Does your father miss Taiwan, or the places before that?"

Simon told me that his paternal grandparents were initially from Shandong and Zhejiang Province. "I don't know. He's kinda quiet. I'm sure he's pretty smart, but he doesn't teach me anything new. You know, our family dynamic changed a lot when my mom died when I was sixteen. I think she did a better job of keeping things under control. I spent a lot of time blaming my dad for that lack of structure."

"What was she like?"

"She liked to read. One book she enjoyed was a Dutch fairy tale called *De kleine Johannes*. I remember reading the beginning about the young boy conversing with animals when I was quite little. But I didn't read the whole book until much later."

"I think I would like that story."

"Yeah. My parents used to be really good. My mom loved taking our family on vacations. She always tried hard to make everything perfect, you know. But I don't remember all these details from my childhood…sometimes it just feels like I'm missing part of myself."

"The feeling you have about these memories now is more important than the details," I said.

Simon didn't reply, but turned his face and smiled. It was a smile that brought me a little mixed joy and sadness. He did, however, become more relaxed while we were on our feet, not having to worry about people listening in at the coffee shop or looking at each other all the time.

So we often took circular walks on campus in the evenings that fall, and went to student plays. We spent New Year's Eve together in front of a mall on Huaihai Road which had a countdown party, and we lit up sparklers sold by a street vender for the occasion while sitting on the sidewalk. The fireworks made buzzing sounds as we waved the sticks in small circles like a dance of bees. And in the remaining light, I saw Simon's profile to the right, eyes closed, as if making a wish. Later, I asked him what he had wished for, and he only smiled, not intending to move an inch of his body. Nearby, some party-goers were already shouting songs and smashing their beer bottles. The sparklers burned out very fast.

I knew that after one semester with the Institute of International Students at my university, Simon would head to Hong Kong in the spring to complete his studies. He said that he had relatives there from his mother's side, whom he could visit. The university in Hong Kong also had a well-established Psychology department.

I thought the way we handled things was for the best. We were friends who cared very much about each other, and promised to visit one another in the future. I repeated these lines in my mind for a while. However, when a few weeks later, I invited Simon to a karaoke party held for Jie's birthday, I came a little closer to my own feelings and therefore my disappointments.

***

The karaoke place was decorated like a night club in a trendy part of the French Concession, and people had to line up to enter. It was the first time I had been to a place that fashionable – it was quite different from the karaoke chains I had been to near our university. I had never experienced any sort of "night life" before and it felt like a novelty.

Jie was wearing a sparkling dress for the evening and strappy sandals that looked a little cold for winter. Her PhD boyfriend, however, drove them there. It felt to me, later, that Jie rather enjoyed having a chauffeur. Soon, six or seven of her other friends arrived, mostly in couples. Apart from myself, wearing jeans and winter boots, all the girls were showing off their painted toenails. The guys, however, were quite casual, and therefore Simon didn't look too out of place.

I didn't expect it to be such a big crowd. But it was Jie's birthday, and she had made new friends. While we were waiting for the karaoke machine to be set up, I heard her mention to one of the girls, how her boyfriend had almost hit a professor on campus with his BMW last week. They both made pretend-horrified faces afterwards. Jie looked in my direction and brought me into the conversation.

"Pei has such a ridiculous high profile with that car on campus, you see, Yinan. And has absolutely no idea. I think you understand why I can't stand it!"

"Tell Yinan and Simon about the piano," one girl with a heart-shaped face nudged Jie.

The PhD boyfriend called Pei jumped in, smiling, and putting his arms around Jie's neck. "Well, I was trying to do a good thing, okay?"

"He is just an embarrassment," Jie said, while she almost glued her eyes on me, as if talking specifically for me to hear.

"I thought you always wanted to learn to play the piano when you were a little girl." Pei was facing Jie, but his comment was for the rest of us as well. Their conversation style reminded me of Uncle Jingzhang and his wife in family gatherings when I grew up, always seeking an audience in their performed exchanges.

"Come on," continued the girl with the heart-shaped face. "So last Christmas, Pei ordered Jie a Yamaha as a surprise present. Wasn't that the sweetest? Only when it was delivered, they realized that the piano was too large to make it through Jie's front door. Poor piano had to be returned."

Memories of the small apartment room Jie had shared with her mother came to me. I doubted if Jie's new friend could imagine the situation. But that might be what Jie had always longed for – people who had no idea where she came from. Back in our middle school and high school, there were a few girls who had learned to play from a very young age. When asked about the experience, they mostly complained that if they had a choice back then, they wouldn't want to spend a childhood cooped up indoors all the time. I didn't realize that Jie was envious of them, and had that dream. There were parts of her that we still didn't get to share, even after all these years.

Simon told me once that he grew up attending piano contests, too, but hadn't played for a long time. In our dark karaoke box, though, I could see that he had no interest in joining the conversation. Apart from initial greetings, he didn't speak a word with the rest of the crowd, either. And I felt guilty for dragging him along.

"Do you have a favourite song?" I turned to him and lowered my voice.

He thought for a minute, "I guess it's 'Brown Eyed Girl'. I like Van Morrison."

"Haven't heard it yet."

"I think you will like it. It's one of my favorites."

Jie and her friends started to browse through and pass around the dog-eared song book, and registered their picks on the karaoke machine in turn. When the book was passed to me, I saw that the English section was thin and that the songs were old: "Sukiyaki," "Y.M.C.A," and "My Girl." I looked at Simon and he shrugged. I passed the book on to the girl next to us.

Later, the group went on stage one after another – in the middle of the room – and sang their hearts out. Jie selected a 90s Cantonese song with a dancing beat. And I could tell that she had had a great deal of practice with it, as if she were a native Cantonese speaker. Her movements were carefree and quite lovely. So, within just more than a year, I thought, Jie had become a natural part of this new social scene, one where it didn't seem that Simon and I would ever be comfortable. I didn't know if I was happy for Jie, or whether I felt both sorry and a little envious at the same time.

Her PhD boyfriend, Pei, had selected "My Girl" and made a half-drunk speech that it was a song dedicated to Jie. How maudlin, I thought. But when the lyrics appeared on the big screen, I found myself quickly immersed in them.

Everyone joined the chorus of the "my girl" verse and I found myself singing along. "Come on, Simon," shouted out Pei, "your chance to sing it to Yinan. I've heard that you're leaving Shanghai soon!" He grinned and tried to stuff his microphone into Simon's hands. The crowd cheered and whistled in encouragement.

I could see Simon's face turning pale even in the grainy light. And before I knew it, he put the microphone down on the table in front of us, making a loud and piercing sound, which suddenly filled the room. Everyone paused what they were doing and looked in our direction. Simon didn't protest or give any words of explanation. It made Pei freeze for a moment in the middle of the room. And I could see that his expression had changed, almost turning a little hostile.

"Wow, wow. We seem to have pissed your ABC off," said Jie to me in Shanghainese, but for the whole room to hear, leaving the abbreviation in English. "Are you sure he is a real American? Never met one like that." She picked up the microphone. And another guy patted Pei's shoulders and navigated the machine to skip to the next song. I felt irritated, but didn't know who had irritated me more.

Later, when we finally left Jie's party, I decided that I would never join any of her gatherings again. She and I had barely exchanged words, even though I could tell that there were things she wanted me to know. However, I felt that I had betrayed my quiet alliance with Simon, in a world where words were uttered quickly and the volume was high. He wasn't in a talking mood as we made our way back to the campus.

Yet still, I felt disappointed. Jie's new relationship had somehow made me face my expectations about Simon head on, even though I really regretted allowing her the chance to pass judgement on Simon and not fighting back for him. I knew that we had only known each other for one semester, and would be apart for much longer. With all my good reasoning, however, I wished that Simon would sing to me once, somewhere, if not in the crowded karaoke room, and using some other words, if not that song.

In a few months, I would finally listen to some Van Morrison and I recalled Simon's favourite song, "Brown Eyed Girl." Was there a reason why he had mentioned that song to me when I asked? I could not know. But I played the CD many times during one of the loneliest semesters in both of our university lives. At the time, Simon had already gone to Hong Kong.

18
Epidemic
溫疫 (*wenyi*)

The Hard Rock Café started to lose its customers in the early spring of 2003, when students first learned about SARS (severe acute respiratory syndrome), a virus much more deadly than the usual flu, which had first broken out in Guangdong Province a year before and quickly spread throughout the country.

Classes and seminars were cancelled. When students heard that we could skip the mandatory Deng Xiaoping Theory class and only hand in an essay for our credits, we were even delighted with our good luck. But soon, as the death toll began to rise in Guangdong, Beijing and Hong Kong, the mood changed. Many discovered that the government's initial reaction to suppress the news had exacerbated the situation.

Shanghai, on the other hand, saw only a single-digit number of cases, much less than other big cities in China, or even Toronto. My parents said that after the 1988 hepatitis-A epidemic spread through raw clams, the Shanghainese had become more aware of food safety and personal hygiene. However, I could see that they were not entirely convinced by the low official numbers given in the evening newspapers, which explained their fear and continuous vigilance. My mother purchased liquid hand-soap for the first time, to replace our usual bar-soap, and managed to get a few thick, medical grade masks, which were in high demand at the time, from her hospital, for us to wear outside.

Many university students, local or otherwise, chose to stay in the dormitory to wait the epidemic out. Living away from their parents gave them more freedom, and they could enjoy easy access to computer rooms on campus. Most peers I knew, who all grew up as the "luckier generation" after 1980 and had found no harm in taking official words as they were, were less anxious than my parents and carried on their routines and social lives as usual. However, many international students decided to suspend their studies and return to their home countries. I still worked at the coffee shop for a couple of weeks after the cancelation of classes, until the owners closed it down. And then, without a useful purpose on campus, I went back home.

My father had purchased a computer about ten years ago, when I was in middle school. Owning personal computers was not common at the time. My father was fortunate to have taken up the trend earlier. Before SARS, however, we didn't use it much other than for typing articles or playing video games. It seemed that now, as instant messaging, online forums and blogs all suddenly gained mass popularity, my family computer became an extremely useful tool for information and connection. It was also the only way I could form a link with Simon during those days.

That spring, Simon was staying in a single-person dorm in Hong Kong, which he said was a small, modest room, but had a balcony facing the green mountains. According to him, Hong Kong had been in a grim situation ever since the semester started. He was communicating with his professors and handing in assignments through the Internet. Apart from grocery trips, his only excursions were in the form of solo exercise, since the university was near several hiking trails.

"It was definitely strange," he typed to me on instant messenger. "I felt that I was closer to the animals on the trails than with anyone else these days. You know, the spiders, birds, cicadas, and quite often a family of wild boar, whose piglets were born earlier in the season. I thought about *De kleine Johannes* a lot…and how he is not above, but part of nature."

I replied that his walks sounded refreshing, and I wished someday I could visit his piglet friends too.

"Just to get away mostly," he said. "There is a vibrant media scene here, unlike in mainland China, so you hear updates all the time – words such as 'we will get through this.' It makes me a little sad thinking of the 'we' actually. Not including those left behind I guess."

"Survivor's language. I don't think we should take these words too seriously."

"Yeah, it's absurd. You are right – I shouldn't take anything too seriously."

Simon told me that he'd placed his laptop on top of a small refrigerator, "small by American standards. It's the right height for my computer when I'm standing." He said that he didn't have any chairs yet. The running water had been off a few afternoons that week as the ventilation pipes were being checked after it was found that a fatal cluster of SARS cases in a housing estate was caused by a failing drainage system. In the evening, Simon was sleeping on an inflatable mattress.

It must be tough to live in prolonged isolation after moving to a new city, I thought, without an end in sight. He didn't sound like he was considering returning to his father's place in the U.S., either.

"I guess you haven't had the opportunity to figure out your furniture yet. After this, you'll get to enjoy decorating your room."

"Do you enjoy decorating?" Simon replied. "I'll ask you to be my interior designer when you are here. Not sure that would make me a good host though. Having you run errands for me on your vacation!"

"As long as we can have a drink on your inflatable mattress to celebrate your move."

For a minute, I regretted what I had just said. I realized that I was bolder than I used to be, now that Simon couldn't see my face. Flirting was never something I was good at since adulthood, always worried that I would send the wrong message. Fortunately, he seemed to have missed that sentence. It felt both disheartening and reassuring for me at the same time.

I knew that some classmates had bought cheap web cameras, but it didn't occur to us to use one. I asked if he had had a chance to visit his mother's relatives in Hong Kong. Simon replied that, when he had first arrived, he had stayed for a night at an aunt's place in Sai Kung, a peninsula in the New Territories.

"They cooked me a nice dinner including homemade tofu. And later there was homemade ice cream! For breakfast, there was homemade banana bread."

"Always so impressed by food, Simon."

"Coming from master chef, Yinan!"

Simon was teasing me about the food blog I had started since living with my parents again, acting as an apprentice to my mother. Her best dishes were river shrimp, *malantou* tofu salad, green tatsoi with bamboo shoots, scallion stewed crucian carp, red braised pork, mini wonton soup and stuffed lotus roots with sweet sticky rice. I had tried to reproduce a couple of them on my blog already.

I thought for a while and typed, "I'm paying more attention to the seasons lately, too. It is probably the old farming culture wisdom, for me a quintessentially Jiangnan wisdom. When I was growing up, my mother and grandmother always put bamboo shoots on our plates in the spring and hairy crabs in the autumn. Ching Ming Festival never passed by without us celebrating with green barley grass rice balls filled with red bean paste, or a Mid-autumn Festival without yam and chestnuts. I admire these things; a way to find joy in the moment for those who face a lot of hardships in life."

"My only concern is whether you will bring me moon-cakes when you visit."

"Well, sounds like you had a good time with your extended family there. Thinking about visiting your aunt again soon?"

"Not for a while, I guess," he said. Simon later told me about an exchange with his aunt while they were having breakfast, when, out of the blue, she had mentioned that Simon was the right age for a girlfriend. "She said that she was not worried about my academic future, but that I was really lonely. I just looked at her blankly because I was completely caught by surprise."

"While you were having homemade banana bread."

"Yeah, I should have changed the subject and asked her about her work or something. But I just stared at her silently. And then she said, 'You have all the right ingredients! Really!' So, that breakfast was very, very awkward."

"She seems to care about you, though."

"That was the first time she started talking to me like that. I actually thought about the Taoist proverb you taught me some time ago, 'two gentlemen's friendship is as bland as water.'"

"Yes, gentlemen's boundaries. Although in *Chuang Tzu*, where the quotation comes from, the story is that, during time of war, refugees would leave behind precious jade and carry their infants with them. Unions bound by interest would break easily when tested, even if it was as 'sweet as wine' at times, but unions bound by natural instinct would always contain each other, despite being 'bland as water.'"

I felt that, given the opportunity to type long paragraphs, I was suddenly talking like my father, so I stopped.

"Well, I'm not sure if my aunt and I will ever understand each other. But in terms of her concern, I just don't want to use relationships as a security rope, to have something to fall back on in case there are difficulties in my new life here."

"Right. You want to figure something out for yourself first." I echoed what he said and decided not to say anything more.

"Yes. By the way, I think you're the only person to hear that story! For some reason, I feel it's really easy and natural to talk to you," he typed.

***

We chatted online almost every day throughout SARS, even after Hong Kong was no longer considered an "epidemic zone" that summer. Meanwhile, travel had resumed. And as Simon and I had already discussed, for the first time since the founding of the People's Republic of China in 1949, residents from large mainland cities such as Shanghai could now enter Hong Kong for personal visits of up to seven days.

Simon, however, was still sleeping on the inflatable mattress. His meals were often the same dish of chicken and spinach. It seemed that the epidemic had had a prolonged effect on him. In contrast, the people around me quickly put those months behind them, and moved on to live life as before. The booming Internet forums were soon surpassed, if not entirely replaced, by internet shopping. The only evidence of the epidemic was that my parents now always had liquid soap in the restroom and masks in the medical cabinet. I hadn't heard anybody in my small circle, apart from Simon, talk about the ones left behind. Many were excited about having the opportunity finally to visit Hong Kong. We decided to wait for a few months to see each other, however, for Simon to become more comfortable in his environment, and for me to finish my internship.

Some nights, after our conversations, I couldn't fall asleep easily. I dreamed about going hiking with Simon in his subtropical city, south of Shanghai, where the air was humid, summer longer, and culture an enticing fusion. I remembered those school days when Jie had introduced me to many Hong Kong television dramas, and I knew that some of my father's favourite books and films were written by Jiangnan intellectuals who had managed to sail south after 1949. My father had made a shrine to the city in his imagination, as if Hong Kong belonged to everyone who wished that the best of their regional culture could survive and be preserved somewhere else. It was a city for immigrants and immigrants-to-be. Looking back to 2003, Hong Kong was certainly scarred deeply by SARS but was about to see an even bigger impact from the shift of political power that came in the following years and which few of us fully anticipated at the time. During that summer, however, it was still a city which held a dream for me.

19
Consumerism
消費主義 (*xiao fei zhu yi*)

I found my first internship through one of my father's former graduate students. Kai and his wife, who were now in their early forties, had founded a popular weekly journal in Shanghai. The journal was a hybrid of newspaper and magazine – articles longer and more thought out, and the layout modern and playful – a new introduction to a market that started to desire weekend reading. A few girls living in my dormitory had already been familiar with the journal over the past couple of years as a touchstone of local fashion and pop culture.

When I met Kai again in his office, I couldn't superimpose the blurry image in my memory of a skinny young man in a white short-sleeved shirt – almost a university students' "uniform" in the early-1990s – on the trendy-looking person now sitting in front of me.

"Remember the day when my students helped us move to our first apartment?" my father had reminded me a few days previously. He said that Kai used to be head of the poetry society in our university, a known idealist, but had now switched gears and in turn enjoyed great commercial success.

My first impression was that the appearance of the former graduate student had been transformed. He wore an expensive pair of black-framed glasses which resembled the style of the last emperor, Pu Yi, and groomed himself well. Above all, he looked healthier both in build and posture than the student I remembered a decade ago. Kai gave me a tour of the office, and later introduced his journal specifically designed as "a leisure read for the emerging middle-class in China."

In recent years, I discovered that the phrase "middle-class" had become primarily aspirational and positive, unlike its former incarnation "middle bourgeoisie," which had been the target of the iron fist in the Mao era and remained a laughing stock for decades afterwards. Thinking back, however, I realized that my uncle Jingzhang and his family had been celebrating wealth for some time, as had many of my high-school classmates who summered overseas. Nevertheless, it was a surprising new trend for me that people would now want to label themselves middle-class, despite having witnessed the painful losses that members of that class had suffered only a generation back. Or had most people, in fact, forgotten about those stormy decades, as they had forgotten about the early summer months of 1989, when encouraged not to remember?

I wondered if it was the general optimism of the time, which allowed people to harbour good will towards each other, become less risk adverse and more willing to forget the violent egalitarian experiments in this country over the past century. Meanwhile, I found it difficult to erase my own memories of my great-grandfather's execution, my grandfather's imprisonment, and my father's former classification as a member of the "Five Black Categories." At that age, it was already a weight I sometimes wanted to set aside, but could not easily do.

Several of my classmates in the university, who had overcome greater odds to study here, were especially hopeful, perhaps because their families were on an upward trajectory and were not yet acquainted with the cycles. And I realized later that even these formative friendships were hardly close friendships for many of us, without a shared history, and without a tradition even to speak about certain things in this country. Loneliness enveloped everyone who didn't have a communicable story of their own.

***

One of my projects as an intern was to interview a woman in her late-twenties who lived a life of leisure. A photographer followed me to the interviewee's renovated apartment on one of the quiet, tree-lined French Concession streets. The beautiful woman who greeted us was meticulously dressed, and had an open closet waiting for us. In detail, she introduced me to her collection of tailored and designer dresses, bags and jewelry, as well as her method of caring for them. She shared with me useful tips such as a specialty detergent and sale seasons in European cities. The woman also claimed that she was a patron of local art galleries, as I noticed a few emerging artists' signatures on the walls. The photographer took pictures of the interviewee's personal possessions as well as of the apartment's interior design.

When asked about her background, however, the woman wearing designer clothes suddenly turned a little shy in front of me. She said that she was from a mountainous village in Sichuan Province and didn't attend university. As a child, she grew up with her grandparents because both her parents went to the city to work and were later divorced. She was the eldest of three siblings – unlike most people in my generation who were only children – and spent a lot of time on household chores at a young age. In high school, her grandparents wanted to marry her off, but she ran away to a classmate's home in town to hide. Later on, by chance, she found a job as a flight attendant for a private jet company. And after that, she visited many countries before settling in Shanghai. She said that she was quite content with her life now, and had a "pure" relationship with her collectables. She regarded them as a sanctuary away from "all the other things in the world."

On the way back, the experienced photographer told me that our interviewee was a mistress of a wealthy businessman, in fact an acquaintance of my boss Kai. "A kept bird in a gilded cage," he said. I asked why he had already reached a conclusion, and the photographer told me that it was simply his intuition.

I found the story of the woman's upbringing more interesting than her closet. Nonetheless, that part of the article that I wrote was swiftly taken out by the editors, since it didn't fit in with the "leisure reading" standard of the journal, as insisted on by one of the editors. I later imagined my revised article being read by young girls in their dormitories on weekends, and how some might admire the interviewee's present way of life, without knowing her hardships, trade-offs and loneliness. It seemed to me then that it was the epitome of how popular media wanted to tell a story. It was a rising trend in the early 2000s, as people of Kai's age commercialized their intellectual expertise. For a moment, I was happy for the former flight attendant that she had at least found a sanctuary among silk and wool in this world.

***

Later, I shared my intern experience with Simon over instant messenger.

"I'm two-minded about consumerism," I typed. "It certainly seems addictive. However, decades ago, people in China didn't have the option, at least in the material sense, to find out who they were, using this comparatively low-stake trial and error. You know, my interviewee seems happy now, even if it is a little delusional."

"Yeah, simple pleasures," Simon responded. "They seem so hard to find these days. I definitely have a complicating mind. Not complicated, just complicating."

And then, I decided to tell him something else from my work experience. I discovered recently when I attended press conferences, that all the journalists would be offered "red envelopes" of a couple hundred *yuan* each time, usually along with a typed-out press release. The journal I worked at was a "lifestyle" one, and didn't cover political or social news. Yet the rules seemed to apply equally to cultural events. And my boss, Kai, told me that it had been a common practice in China over the past decade to compensate the low wages of journalists in this way.

"He said that before starting his own journal, he worked at a traditional local morning paper, and attended up to seven or eight conferences a day. The red envelopes he received constituted a third of his monthly income then. Not taxed."

"Hmm...I don't know about this. I guess I never read Chinese papers while I was in Shanghai. It sounds quite bad, actually, to manipulate the press and public opinion in this way." He paused typing for a while. "In fact, I have something to share with you, too."

Simon told me that earlier in the summer he had been on the street with half a million local protesters, opposing a new "anti-subversion" law drafted for Hong Kong, right after the city emerged from the SARS health crisis. He had read about the protest on a popular online forum. It seemed that many from his university would be going. It was the first time he had walked with such a large crowd, Simon said, feeling less like an outsider in the city all of a sudden, even though he was acquainted with no one around him.

As I listened to his descriptions of the humidity that day, how his shirt was "entirely drenched" after the walk, and the enthusiasm he had described among the city's old and young, I realized that it was not, and never would be an event mentioned by the media on my side of the border. The main news here regarding Hong Kong during the past few weeks was the upcoming possibility of travelling to Hong Kong as an individual and not as a member of a tour group, the hope of a recovery aided by the government in the epidemic-hit economy, and future shopping sprees for visitors. I felt certain that one day Kai's journal would publish feature articles on these cross-border travels, as if every consumer was doing their bit to lift Hong Kong up again. But how many of the mainland visitors would know, or really care about the heavy changes and struggles that had just taken place in the city?

Lately, Simon didn't seem keen to ask me to teach him Chinese anymore. I was aware that the distance had made it harder to practice together. After SARS, however, I found it becoming awkward, to really tease him about this. I wondered if at the moment, the entirety of Chinese culture would be perceived more as coming from top down rather than from bottom up, and language as serving political agendas rather than defying them. Had Simon already suffered a disillusionment?

It shouldn't have been a surprise to me, I thought, as I had more or less been keeping my own distance from the language ever since I was eighteen. Then why was it that suddenly, it pained me to witness an apparent wane of interest in Simon, even though I should be the most understanding of it?

***

Simon and I were still planning to see each other in Hong Kong. And for our reunion, I handed in my application for the special individual travel permit. One day after submitting some forms for the paperwork, I thought of Jie, who was working as an intern nearby in the city centre, and caught up with her for coffee. This time, she took me to another stylish place, the rooftop restaurant of an art museum.

Jie was interning at a multinational consulting firm at the time. She seemed to work much longer hours than I did and also "partied quite a bit in the office." Her team recently went on a training trip to Los Angeles, and visited Las Vegas afterwards. In one of the photos she showed me on her new digital camera, Jie was wearing an eye mask with feathers and a white boa around her neck. All her team-mates were in dazzling formal wear as well. And the current person she was seeing, Jie said, had taken this photo. He was their supervisor and a senior executive of the firm.

We sat across from each other and sipped coffee under the transparent ceiling of the rooftop garden. Jie described the beginning of her new affair. It had started with them alone in the office, working late on a weeknight. "There was always wine kept behind the shelves in his office," she said. The sheer banality of her tone made it sound like she was explaining industry jargon to a layman instead of mocking it as a cliché, which annoyed me. Yet, she knew what details to tell, I thought, as if provoking me to voice my judgment about her, so that she could in turn argue against that judgement. Later, I learned that she and Pei, the Economics PhD from our university, had split up.

"How do you feel?" I decided not to let her get her way this time. I thought of the piano Pei had once delivered to Jie's place. It felt again, as with many shared memories between Jie and myself, like something that had happened in a past lifetime. At a younger age, we used to scribble a few lines on our notebooks and turn the pages rather hastily, impatiently. Sometimes it was the only way to stay sane, I thought. But one day the scribblers might find out that there were not many pages left to write on. Even though Pei had caused a scene with Simon in the karaoke that day, I didn't have a bad impression of him.

"I could consider myself happy," she said. "I think it's just managing expectations in the end. I tend not to get too attached. And he likes me for that. Besides, he's not particular about his diet, so he likes to worry that one day I may find him appalling."

For years, Jie always sounded so certain of what she wanted, a talent I didn't master at a young age like her, especially in my private life. And it seemed that she had made it a habit to leave a crying man behind. However, as time went by, her invincibility worried me deeply, while I started to see the presumed invulnerability of those men she dated, who in fact were not afraid to, and sometimes willfully presented themselves as emotionally vulnerable.

Is it because of reading and writing in English for over a decade, and now constantly thinking in it, that I am finally able to put these thoughts into words? Perhaps any new language would do in this case. When a woman has desires, the world always seems more than ready to lead her astray. Therefore, learning a new language helps her break the custom of an old one. It has allowed me to go back to the path where it deviated and listen to my own heart closely, before it was shaped by formal education.

I still didn't know yet, however, the right things to say to Jie back in that rooftop restaurant. There was always a part of me that wished I could believe in her happiness, even if it was a counterfeit happiness in my own dictionary. In the end, in my memory, we just moved on to discuss the news about the closure of The Great World earlier in May.

The Great World was an amusement centre, built in 1917, a landmark in Shanghai's heyday in the 1920s and 30s. In Jie's and my childhood, we used to share with one another, that both our mothers took us there regularly to see performances. I still recalled the twelve distorting mirrors at the entrance, which in Shanghainese were referred to as "Ha Ha Mirrors" since they gave every visitor a series of laughs upon arrival. During SARS, however, the almost century-old business could no longer sustain itself. The journal I worked at had recently published an editorial about its closure.

"That's too bad. The little that remains of old Shanghai is disappearing in front of our eyes. I loved the 'Ha Ha Mirrors.'"

"Maybe old Shanghai has gone elsewhere," I said. And after initial hesitation, I told Jie that I was planning to visit Simon in Hong Kong.

"Oh, I remember that ABC well. He seemed a little standoffish, though. I'm surprised you are still in touch with him."

"You have only met him once."

"I'm concerned whether he will ever know you, is willing to or has the ability to. And I'm also concerned whether you can live with that unknowing. I remember you said it once yourself that people with our upbringing are not easy books to read. I don't know if the books need to be read, though."

What Jie said was that, unlike her, I couldn't be with a man who didn't know me, which sounded almost like a character flaw, the way she said it. I found it again a typical, irksome comment from her, even though I couldn't completely disagree.

"There is only one way to find out, isn't there?" I said.

My reply seemed to surprise Jie. Maybe it was because I had a firmer tone than usual. She studied my face for a few seconds and then nodded. And I was in turn surprised by her quick retreat and avoidance. We were not people who could stand being with each other all the time and not say what was on our mind. Those unspoken words must be very hurtful now.

I thought of an old proverb that my parents used to repeat when reminiscing over their own past friendships. "The tree grows taller, and the branches grow further." This shouldn't have been a surprise for us though, because, when Jie and I first met, we already anticipated our parting. After that day, however, melancholy overtook me. For a while, I believed that I was not going to see Jie anymore. This impromptu meeting in the city centre of our hometown, casual as it was, could be our last. I didn't imagine then that, not too far into the future, we would meet each other again when our lives had set forth on different paths further apart.

***

That summer and fall, I listened to many old and new songs while commuting from campus to my internship. I had purchased my first cell-phone for work. And because of those interview assignments, I went to neighborhoods in

Shanghai that weren't familiar to me before, feeling that only now had I begun to get to know my home city. Lots of *shikumen* were disappearing and more shopping malls had been built. I could now say with little ambivalence that I disliked these changes more and more each day.

And I often thought of the distorting mirrors at the entrance of the Great World Amusement Arcade as I transited from place to place. In my native cultural context, the idea of truth is often discussed in the *chengyu* as "a blind man feeling the elephant", what one feels can either be described as a radish, a dustpan or a rope, depending on whether one touches the elephant's tusk, ear or tail. I found the metaphor seemingly sagacious, yet on the other hand deeply troublesome, especially when those who are familiar with the *chengyu* at a young age would so readily accept their own "blindness" and their bounded reach. "I think it's just managing expectations in the end" – I couldn't forget these recent words from Jie. We may never see the whole outline of the elephant no matter how hard we try, I thought, but I am not going to close my own eyes voluntarily. I might have enjoyed the "Ha Ha" mirrors in an amusement arcade as a child, but I wouldn't find it so laughable if every mirror I looked at in my mundane life turned into a distorting one.

My parents mentioned that a few of my older cousins, including Small Dragon, had already bought an apartment and a car after working in Shanghai for a few years. Life felt settled for them at a very young age. And there were boxes to check and events to celebrate. Besides, "lifestyle" journals such as the one I worked for made sure that there would be commercial milestones to hit one after another. Small Dragon turned out to be a sales manager who liked to collect expensive whisky from Scotland, despite the prediction of the divination stick from the Taoist temple in Zhuji. However, he had finally returned to the city from where his father was sent down to the countryside. And I thought that his new-born son would one day learn from a textbook similar to the one I used. In fact, since his apartment was bought in the same district that I grew up in, his son might even end up in my primary school or middle school after rounds of intense competition.

My childhood neighbor, Weiwei, was said to have recently married a Japanese man of our age, and had married so early since she went to a short-term vocational school instead of a university. It was the first time, after a long time, that I had heard anything about Weiwei. And it was hard to believe how quickly time had moved through us. Perhaps in a few years, my parents predicted, she would also start to have children. I still remembered her high-pitched voice as a child herself, and her lit-up smile while feeding her pet pigeon.

20
Chinese Diaspora
華僑 (*huaqiao*)

I wondered often during my senior year in university whether I lacked sufficient imagination of the darkness of the human spirit, or whether I was simply too slow to identify its symptoms. I knew that some systems could bring out the worst in people. On the other hand, I spent much time wondering if there was a shortcoming in me during my younger years, whether I had lost opportunities to alter or walk away from situations when they first manifested themselves. Perhaps it was common for people to be like that when young. Anyone lacking understanding of darkness may also lack the courage to face the whole of themself head on.

It was my childhood neighbour Weiwei who had suggested that we raise the chicks in the alley so that they could stay far from the household dining table. Little did we suspect then the other predators lurking outside our homes. Do people possess better imagination as grown-ups, I thought, and therefore wear thicker armour over their hearts to prevent aggression and disappointment? But once the armour is worn all the time, will it grow into the flesh and become inseparable from it? How I wished to reconnect with that innate vulnerability of my childhood.

In fact, I wasn't surprised that Weiwei had become part of the Chinese diaspora. Many people with a family history similar to ours might eventually embark on the journey which their parents hadn't had the opportunity to take. Now I wondered whether, like me, she had thought about how to understand her history when growing up, or whether she had been influenced by any diaspora culture.

On the flight to Hong Kong that November, I recalled my father's all-time favourite film, *The Three Smiles*. It was made in Hong Kong in the late 1960s, a comic take on a Ming Dynasty legend, when a well-known painter Tang Bohu disguised himself as a servant turned family tutor, to win the heart of Qiu Xiang, the beautiful housemaid of the state chancellor. My father told me that all the tunes in the film were Jiangnan folk songs, which he regarded as the most beautiful music in the world. The story was also set in Jiangnan, with the familiar views of lakes and pagodas and scenes of people drinking green tea infused with fragrant yellow osmanthus (it was no accident that the meaning of the girl Qiu Xiang's name was, "Autumn Fragrance"). We could see different aspects of daily life in the area south of the Yangtze River, such as travelling by boat and praying at local temples. I heard later, however, that aside from a few video clips, most scenes were shot in a film studio in Hong Kong.

It was one of the hundreds of productions made by artists, writers and intellectuals who had fled to Hong Kong from Shanghai back then. My father felt that the film had kept the essence of the distinct "Jiangnan Culture," which traced back two thousand years to Wu and Yue times. What kind of emotion did my family feel, having just survived the Cultural Revolution, when he finally watched the film with my grandparents in the 1980s, on our black-and-white television set? And like my father, could I also subscribe to the idea that a significant part of my cultural heritage had already taken root in Hong Kong, with the migration, even before I was born?

I thought of the tunes in *The Three Smiles* film, and found out that I could easily hum them in my mind, one line after another. When I was younger, however, I wouldn't take the time to indulge in an old-fashioned film like this with my father, let alone sing with him.

Those immigrants who had moved to Hong Kong fifty, sixty years ago, did they feel the same as the painter Tang Bohu did when he could only waste his talents teaching the two dim-witted sons of the chancellor, or painting Buddha statues for the chancellor's wife? Was it like the Chinese saying, "a tiger fallen on level land gets insulted by a dog, and a dragon stuck in shallow water gets teased by a prawn"? At least Tang Bohu had played along well enough to impress Qiu Xiang, and walk away with her as a wife. Now sitting in the airplane on my way to Hong Kong for the first time, I thought about my father watching this film over and over again as I grew up in the cramped third-floor apartment on Duolun Road. The ceiling of our third-floor apartment was very low, since it had originally served only as an attic in Weiwei's grandfather's house. It wasn't a big issue for my grandparents, my mother or myself, but it often caused my six-foot-tall father to hit his head. I thought about the burning desire to move away that had been inside me since my childhood, a desire that had not been clear to myself until recently, but was already recognized by my family back then, as they called me a child who "liked to hold the far end of the chopsticks while eating", predicting that a son would travel and a daughter would marry away from her birth family. And now, with the plane making its final turns above the blue ocean and the outline of the silver skyscrapers below, a deep sorrow suddenly descended with the memory of that prediction.

***

I almost didn't recognize Simon when he met me in the lobby of his dormitory building. His hair was unkempt and his face covered with stubble. For some reason, he appeared slightly taller than I remembered, even though his back was hunched. Simon was never a fashionable dresser, but I had always liked his green polos and blue shirts worn with neat khaki pants. Now he was wearing a pair of strange, oversized jeans that reminded me of the "export rejects" stores from my childhood.

"I'm sorry, Yinan. I just saw your message. I had no idea that my phone was off."

The security lady gave us a nod when I folded the chair and thanked her for it. I had been waiting in the narrow lobby for forty minutes with my backpack and suitcase, after I couldn't reach Simon on the cellphone number he had given me a few days earlier.

"Studied too hard last night?"

"No, I just...didn't sleep well. Look, I screwed up. To keep you waiting for me like this, especially when you came all the way."

"It's okay," I said, although taken aback by his quick and harsh indictment of himself. A few residents came out of the elevator on their way out, and glanced casually at my suitcase as they passed. The security lady was friendly, but we had a hard time understanding each other's respective Cantonese and Mandarin.

"I have had trouble falling asleep lately, even when I haven't slept the night before. Strange. I must start keeping a more consistent schedule."

I looked around his studio room and saw the inflatable mattress. It was in fact on top of eight or nine other mattresses of different design and thickness, all stacked together to form a very high bed – I guessed every occupant had left their mattress behind, and no one wanted to sleep on an old one or bothered to pay someone to have them removed. I was reminded again of the fact that Simon was all by himself in a foreign city. I decided to tease him.

"Have you finally discovered the pea at the bottom of all those layers?"

"Ha! Not yet. Try it yourself, miss."

What Simon suggested, later in the evening, was that I take the bed of layered mattresses and he would sleep in a sleeping bag nearby on the floor. It was settled rather easily, but the arrangement left a lingering dullness in my mind, similar to the prolonged exhaustion from the physical journey.

That evening, when I finished showering in the bathroom and before going to sleep, I noticed that Simon was rolling something from a small dish into a cigarette. It was the first time I had found him smoking, and not the usual cigarette that I was familiar with. I was ruffled, but tried not to let my feelings show. He asked me if I minded and I just shook my head, not knowing what to say. The childhood memories of my mother constantly rushing me out of the room to escape my father's cloud of smoke came to my mind. I wondered how long ago Simon had taken up the habit.

The ceiling light made the green herbs appear brighter. And a pungent smell traveled towards the slightly opened window. Simon moved his face away from me every time he exhaled. Seeing that I still sat a little stiffly next to him on the rug, he asked me if I wanted to try it.

I once smoked a cigarette with my university classmate Lynn at the beginning of our freshman year, sitting on the basketball court next to our dorm, after we complained about our daily military training. I coughed the moment I inhaled my first breath of smoke, which made Lynn laugh very hard. I decided not to make a fool of myself another time. Later, when I found out that the green herbs were marijuana, one of the "capitalist vices" branded as an absolutely untouchable substance where I came from, I grew quite worried for Simon.

"It's no big deal," he said, "just to get a better night's sleep."

"What would your father think?"

In retrospect, this was not the best thing to say – even possibly the worst thing – because Simon showed an "I don't care" expression with curled lips. I could tell that he was also concealing disappointment.

I didn't realize at the time that Simon had already stopped talking to most of his older friends. He had told me that he and his father used email for communication, which worked best for them both. Lately, however, there had not been much exchange between them. If I had known then how reliant on me Simon was in those months, as his single outlet, I would have been less straightforward in my opinions.

Simon said that he was worried about the prospect of teaching. He saw himself going to graduate school, but knew that he would have to apply for an assistantship. And he would need to give a guest lecture in one of the instructors' classes next year.

"It really makes sense, but I've been panicking about it a little. It's difficult for me to focus in class and pay attention even as a student. I keep asking myself how I could ever manage to teach a class."

"My father used to tell us that, when he first started teaching, he practiced giving lectures to the walls."

"Well. Just gotta keep trying and survive as long as I can, and see what happens."

"You are going to be an academic too, apart from being a teacher."

"I know, right? In a perfect world, I should be able to do both. In reality, I don't mean to sound pessimistic, but I honestly don't know if I can be successful. There's just too much practical knowledge that I miss out on. I thought I wouldn't need any common sense in academia, but it seems that I should at least have some."

Poor Simon, I thought. He wanted this so much. But I didn't fully understand then that he saw it as his only option to prove his worth in life.

"Sometimes I cannot see a map in my head," Simon said. "But everyone else seems to know naturally where to go, and for some reason I don't. And it's frustrating not understanding why. I actually have to think about it...a lot...to figure out where I am these days."

"You have to give yourself some more credit in a new city..."

Simon paused but didn't let me finish. "Part of my problem is that I can't see the big picture all at once. I can see different parts individually, but I can't see how everything fits together. It's like trying to collect water with a bucket that has a hole in it – it doesn't matter how much you try, the result is always the same."

I didn't know if it was the marijuana, but Simon started to sound far away. It would be the feeling I was to have throughout my entire stay in Hong Kong. I wanted to bring him back to his normal self, but didn't know how to do it. It was already past midnight on my first day in the city, and my washed hair had dried in the air. I had changed into lounging clothes, and Simon seemed comfortable in his oversized jeans. The thought of touching him didn't come to my mind at first. But at one point during our conversation, my fingers seemed to brush against the side of his body and Simon instinctually moved away.

"Sorry, I'm a bit ticklish."

I didn't respond to that verbally, but moved to sit a few more inches away. Minutes later, the conversation dried up and we decided to lie down for the night, him in the sleeping bag, and I on the very high inflatable mattress. Soon afterwards, I descended into a deep, dreamless sleep. One of the studio windows was still left open.

***

The next morning, as planned, we went for a day of hiking in Sai Kung, the scenic peninsula where Simon had once visited his aunt. It was bright and warm outside and we packed hats and sunglasses to go with us. The section of the MacLehose Trail that we headed for promised panoramic coastal views and sandy beaches. This was what the hikers' guidebook I had bought for the trip said. It was the first time to go there for Simon as well.

The beginning of the trail wasn't too strenuous, so we chatted like we used to while walking along the streets of

Shanghai, both of us facing forward. It always made Simon more comfortable this way.

I asked him if he still visited political forums online, or joined protests. Simon didn't seem to want to share too much detail about this with me, but he said, "I think it will be a long game in the future, especially now that the mainlanders have more and more influence in Hong Kong."

I felt my face suddenly burning with the term "mainlanders," while at the same time knowing it was an overreaction that I couldn't help. Growing up in mainland China was one thing, but in the Hong Kong context, the term "mainlanders" was derogatory, reductive, often targeted towards ordinary people from the mainland.

Sensing my silence, a few seconds later Simon added, "I don't mean you, Yinan, of course."

That didn't sit well with me, either. I felt that, however I might respond to what he had said, I had already been put on the defensive, needing to prove that I was different, and that I had a soul. No one should be put in a situation like this. Still, I was cynical – I thought this was how the world was – the oppressed abroad bear the sin of the oppressor from home.

We walked past a narrow path of low, flowering bushes, Simon trailing behind me. I was pleased to see flowers in this season. So I tried to shift my attention to nature itself. Once in a while, blue and brown butterflies flapped their wings and danced up and down along the steps. Some butterflies landed on branches after circling for a while, full of grace. The beaches were never far away. And even before the trail opened up to overlook three sweeping white sand beaches, one after another, we could smell the fresh saltiness of the ocean.

"小雨," I called his name in Chinese, perhaps because there was something brewing in my sub-conscious. I wanted to tell him that Hong Kong was really a one-of-a-kind, beautiful place. And I was grateful that I was able to see it in my life, and to see it with him. But at that moment, a loud noise coming from the nearby bushes interfered with my musings and we both stopped short.

At first, I thought it could be a wild boar, said to be frequently seen in the city's country parks. But it turned out that the noise came from two fairly large macaques, swinging down from a nearby tree. Swiftly, they landed on the trail in front of us. And seeing us freeze, they started hooting for more company, showing their sharp teeth. Shortly afterwards, an army of more than ten macaques joined and cornered us.

It was in the middle of a weekday, and there were not many hikers around. I never thought that macaques would appear in such a large number. Living in Shanghai my whole life, the only sizable wild animals that I had seen were in the zoo. Both Simon and I were caught off guard. Soon, one of the macaques I had made eye contact with stretched out towards me. And in no time, several long, red scratch marks appeared on my calves. Another tried to jump higher to my right arm to bite.

By the time this happened, Simon had already found an opportunity to run ahead on the trail. The macaques who surrounded me didn't take any interest in chasing him.

First, I was too afraid to move, as had always been my habit in the face of danger, and I was very worried that I could soon become a scratching post. But then, I remembered that my hikers' guidebook had mentioned that wild boars would sometimes charge those with bags of food. I didn't have any food with me, apart from two fig bars in my backpack. Trying my luck, I swiftly took off my backpack and threw it a few feet away, hoping to divert the macaques' attention.

And it worked. The group soon disintegrated and ran off to my backpack, searching feverishly for its contents. In the end, a pair of older local hikers appeared on the trail behind me. Watching the scene, they tried to scare the macaques away with their hiking sticks. Eventually, faced with a larger human population, and unsatisfied with the offerings in my backpack, the macaque troop retreated into the woods.

"You should see a doctor," the woman from the pair of older hikers suggested, looking at my wound, "so that you don't get rabies. Better to be safe than sorry."

After making sure that I was okay, they went ahead. Collecting the things in my backpack, I suddenly thought about the tragedy of Aunt Jingyun's son, who had died as a child after a wild dog attack in Zhuji during her "Sent-down Youth" years. My heart rate quickened at the long-buried memory – how easy it is for us to inherit fears from older generations. It seemed that I had traveled miles in my life, and miles to come here. But how far could people travel, really, just in one lifetime and one generation? The conversation with Simon about Hong Kong's political situation rang in my ears again. Here I was, finally, in this in-between city, where many transit passengers had made their home and put down roots. But for just how many generations could people continue to stay here?

After a while Simon turned around, obviously embarrassed at leaving me alone. I didn't know if the two older hikers had passed him by and suspected that he was with me. He looked at the scratch marks on my legs and didn't make a comment. He just walked behind me silently. And for the first time in our reunion, I didn't feel like talking to him, either.

***

Later, Simon and I sat on the beach. We took off our shoes and felt the soft touch of the white sand under our toes. A few boats were scattered on the turquoise water in front of us. Afar, two large green islands appeared like Charlie Brown's famous pet dog lying down on its back, with his round nose and belly facing the sky.

Simon, however, fixed his gaze on the dramatic clouds over the ocean. And for a minute, I thought about the 1980s poet Gu Cheng, the one who met his wife on a train ride, and his poem called "Far and Close": *"You/ Look at me for a while/ And then look at the clouds for a while/ I feel/ You are faraway when you look at me/ And you are close when you look at the clouds."*

"I'm sorry that I've disappointed you," Simon said, still looking ahead into the horizon. "You deserve better."

The formality of the tone surprised me. But Simon continued to mention that he was pretty disappointed with himself as well. He said that it was not worth it for me to waste my time and money to come all the way here to see him.

"That is for me to decide, though."

I was not looking at him either, but at a handful of swimmers in the water, one of them standing on a kickboard and playing with a small dog. Tanned, happy and carefree-looking young people. The "Snoopy Island" in the background. It was too beautiful a place to have this conversation. I had a sinking feeling in my chest.

Simon said that he had had two neuro-psychological examinations in the past, one as a child and another four years ago. The results were generally fine apart from showing he had a learning disability. However, the testing didn't show the severity of the problem, according to Simon, or fit him into a specific category. And because he did quite well on IQ tests, everyone assumed that he was smart and things would be okay.

"But I know that my brain is impaired, and I don't have a name for it. People telling me that there's 'nothing wrong' just increases the disappointment when I can't hide the problem anymore. So eventually, I will just be a failed adult."

"Have you seen a counsellor in Hong Kong?"

Simon told me that as a matter of fact, he had.

"Talk therapy doesn't really help me, though. Anyway, the person I saw was not a psychiatrist. But I was supposed to see her first so that she could refer me to one. There were also some examinations to go through to 'demonstrate' my problem before the next step."

Simon said that he used to bring home a great deal of anger. And he couldn't stand to do that again to someone he cared about. Was that a confession of the heart, finally? I wondered about this. If it was, it was a rather sad one. Simon continued.

"I wish I could just think more naturally instead of having to analyze everything, and run around in circles."

"Maybe it isn't natural. But you have always been original," I said.

"Yeah, special." Simon looked at my wound and then looked away again. "I hate it when I hurt you. I hate it that I just couldn't be there for you when something happens."

He banged one fist on the sand over and over again, leaving a round-shaped dent. The sand had absorbed all the sound. I thought of a saying that my father used to mention that love is like holding sand in your palms, and if you hold it too tightly, the sand will simply slip away.

"You didn't hurt me. Who would imagine macaques behaving like that, in broad daylight?"

But as I said these words aloud, I had to hold back the tears which came to me like an uninvited friend.

***

At the end of that hiking day, Simon and I took the speedboat from the beach to Sai Kung pier. We waded into the water to board the small boat, shoes tied to our backpacks.

Simon got in first and he lent me his hand to help me step in. His palm was parched from the sun. Only many days later did I realize that it was the only physical intimacy we had ever had. For a short moment, it felt like the beginning of life, even though our hearts were heavy. We barely spoke that evening. On the speedboat, with the strong wind on our faces and in our hair, and seeing the beach quickly receding, it registered with me just how precious was every encounter on earth. And how rare it was that Simon's and my paths had converged in the dark obliviousness of time and space. We are living in the same time, I thought, and are even similar in age. With just a twist of hand from fate, our circumstances could be immensely different. We could easily have missed each other, without even knowing it.

It was the first time in my life that I had thought of someone in this way, I realized with a sudden excruciating pain. Because I was afraid that Simon was slipping away.

21
Sailing South in Fine Garments
衣冠南渡 (*yi guan nan du*)

I decided to cook some meals with Simon during the rest of my week-long stay.

If it hadn't been for Simon, I wouldn't have realized how old-fashioned my culinary life had been for someone living in a large city. My family barely ate out. For festive gatherings with relatives, such as at Mid-autumn or Lunar New Year, we mostly just gathered together several dishes of each family's specialty cooking and enjoyed them together in a pot-luck style. My grandmother used to go to the market every day for fresh produce, and my working mother several times a week. When I was apprenticing with my mother during SARS, however, we mostly went to grocery stores to stock up.

It wasn't difficult to find the ingredients I needed in Hong Kong, thanks to the Shanghainese diaspora which had settled here for decades. The dark Jiangnan style vinegar was available in most stores. There was a good selection of white rice cakes in a special shop in Causeway Bay. I bought osmanthus petals in a local teahouse to add flavour to both tea and dessert. We even found the square-shaped, thin wonton skins that I grew up with, a bit different from the usual round, thick ones. Then, one night, Simon helped me to wrap wontons from scratch with minced pork, ginger and cabbage, all bought from the wet market in Central. It was the happiest he had been since I arrived, although we had stopped having the tough conversations about his career and our future.

In the evenings, we used the bathroom in turn to shower and change into sleepwear, then said goodnight in the dark. Simon didn't smoke again in my presence, nor did we sit as closely as we had that first evening.

I didn't realize that it was Thanksgiving until breakfast on the morning of my second-to-last day, when Simon mentioned that he had agreed to see his aunt in a dim sum restaurant. He said that I could tag along if I wanted to.

"The aunt you mentioned earlier, who asked you questions?"

"I agreed to meet her today, the last time we saw one another. She sent me an email reminder a few days ago."

"I see."

I felt unalarmed, yet still curious and nervous. Simon didn't know how to turn invitations down, so he would push himself to go through these things. I was disappointed that he hadn't told me sooner since we only had one full day left. On the other hand, I thought it was generous of his aunt to offer him company on the American holiday. In the end, we went together.

***

My first impression of Simon's aunt, Eunice, seeing her dressed in pearls and elegant tailored clothes of dark green, was that she reminded me of the phrase "衣冠南渡" (*yi guan nan du*). Even in a bustling dim sum place, she didn't slouch or relax her posture.

The phrase *yi guan nan du* was first coined in the Jin Dynasty (266 – 420) when, in order to escape successive wars, noble families migrated in a large-scale southbound exodus from the central plain to the area south of the Yangtze River. People who had the resources to move at the time wore fine clothes, and hence were referred to as "衣冠" (*yi guan*, "garments and headdresses"). Since then, the history of southern China and its variety of dialects is said to be the result of waves of migration, away from famine, wars and tyrants, as well as assimilation and forming new identities. Simon told me that his aunt and his mother's side of the family traced their roots back to Shandong Province, and their journeys were a result of the most recent exodus of the last century. Aunt Eunice, however, as a second-generation immigrant, grew up in Hong Kong and spoke Cantonese and English only.

"You have brought a friend!" She greeted us in a slightly raised voice when Simon and I walked over.

After we introduced each other and sat down, Aunt Eunice washed all our bowls and cups carefully with the tea served, before pouring it out into a larger bowl. She then rinsed all our chopsticks, including the serving pair. Later, she poured the remaining tea into the three cups – it was *pu'er*, a fermented tea from the southern provinces, and especially popular in dim sum restaurants.

"I didn't ask you guys – hope *pu'er* is okay."

"Yinan is a bit of a tea connoisseur." Simon said.

"Well, not really…" I jumped in quickly. My thoughts still lingered on the utensil washing routine and wondered if the SARS epidemic had made it a more rigorous practice here. I also felt embarrassed that someone older had served us tea. "I told Simon that my family had the tea-drinking habit. I don't have *pu'er* very often but I like it, too."

"Oh, do they? Where is your family?" Aunt Eunice asked.

"In Shanghai. I'm only here for a visit."

"So you are a mainlander…it's hard to tell from your clothes though," she said, looking back and forth between Simon and myself. "It must be a cultural shock to see Hong Kong for the first time then, isn't it?"

"Yes and no." I said, trying not to react too hastily. "I certainly notice the difference in manners. However, in the short time I have been here, I have found some familiar culture here. Hong Kong is a mosaic in that sense."

Aunt Eunice smiled and commented that my English was pretty good, and the juxtaposition irked me. She signaled to a nearby waitress and ordered five, six dishes for the table, without needing to look at a menu.

"Forgive me for making the decisions for us, but you have to try their specialties. We can start with these few dishes and add something else later," she said. "As for the mosaic culture you have mentioned in Hong Kong, it is due to different waves of migration. My parents were among the capitalists and military people who came before 1949. Then there were the refugees in the famine years of the 1960s. And intellectuals fled here after 1989. Of course, more and more people from the mainland are thinking about coming today, now that it has been made easier for them to study, live and work here."

"In my view," she paused for a few seconds and continued, "the mosaic lies only on the surface. People will and have to melt into the mainstream here, unless you are a fresh-off-the-boat mainlander…"

I glanced at Simon, who seemed to welcome the fact that Aunt Eunice was talking with me most of the time. He poured himself tea again, and drank silently.

The dim sum arrived at our table, still hot with white steam. This time, I poured tea for the three of us.

"Simon," said Aunt Eunice, "You should add tea for your girlfriend. How could you let the guest serve?"

I could see Simon's profile, his neck and ear turning red all of a sudden. He was looking down at his own bowl and plate.

"Yinan is not my girlfriend. Stop making assumptions."

"Oka-aay," Aunt Eunice was taken back and ended the word with a hesitant, rising tone. Her gaze landed on me for a minute. But soon, she changed the topic and I couldn't keep up with anything she said for the rest of the meal. My stomach felt bloated even though I ate very little. And the cold air-conditioning in the restaurant was giving me a headache.

***

Later that afternoon, instead of returning to Simon's place, I went by myself to a nearby public hospital to get the rabies vaccine that I had been putting off. It was the weekend and the registration area was crowded. I waited a couple of hours for my turn.

After the treatment, the nurse told me to report to the police position inside the hospital and leave a record of the "wild animal assault."

"The virus can live inside the human body for two to three weeks without showing any symptoms," she said in Mandarin after seeing the *pinyin* spelling of my name. "But the animal which potentially carries the rabies will die within a few days. So it would be helpful to trace the animal."

I described to the on-duty policeman the location where we had encountered the macaque troop. After speaking with the nurse, I started the conversation with the policeman in Mandarin as well. But he didn't reciprocate.

"Do you remember which monkey scratched you or bit you?" the policeman asked. His tone was rather impatient.

"Eh...I don't think I remember his specific features." I remembered that the one whom I had mistakenly stared at had an angry, red face. But didn't they all?

"Well, then what are you doing here, missy? How am I supposed to find a monkey if you don't know which one?" The policeman closed his book and waved me away as if waving away a buzzing insect on the trail.

It all felt rather futile and foolish, even though I knew that everything was just customary precaution and paperwork. However, the policeman had reminded me that in the chain of events, I couldn't locate a single macaque to direct my anger at, and therefore he didn't bother to take me seriously. It felt as it I had never really glided through life. Under other circumstances, I knew that my associative thinking simply wouldn't let me find an easy scapegoat in a single sentence, a single action, or a single person in order to move on. And for that, I had always suffered on my own.

Additionally, for the past few years, I had lived in the cocoon of a foreign language, to rid myself of the influence of my original thinking tool and see the shape of my true heart. But what trade-offs were there from all this understanding? Had I made myself lazy, relinquishing responsibility for confrontation and avoiding the search for real justice because there was another rhetoric available to explain things and reshape history? All this knowledge didn't translate into action.

On the way back, I saw, through the taxi window, a faint moon lurking behind the clouds. The moon traveled by itself, leaving only its reflection on the surfaces it touched. And I realized that, even though I was visiting Simon in Hong Kong, I was still very much alone.

22
Joyful Loss
喜喪 (*xisang*)

My grandfather passed away that winter, two months after I returned from Hong Kong.

My parents didn't arrange for my grandparents to stay with us, after all. Nor had Uncle Jingzhang taken them in. Ten years previously, my grandparents had moved to a nursing home in Pudong, some time after my grandmother started to show signs of dementia, and hired a private nurse there. The cost was shared by the two sons in Shanghai.

My grandfather's nurse had recently discovered his difficulty in eating, and it hurt for him to swallow water as well. The doctors advised against esophageal surgery, however, because of my grandfather's advanced age. With intravenous fluid treatment, however, his condition stabilized for a while. My grandfather's mind was very clear, as I heard him still complaining about my grandmother when we visited, commenting on certain "despicable faces" which he didn't wish to see at the home, and asking my father to arrange a trip to Zhuji a few days before he passed.

He was ninety-two years old. In Chinese custom, people consider it a "joyful loss" when someone who has lived beyond ninety passes without too much suffering. All the same, at the funeral, our candles were still white and so were the flowers of the wreaths. My father wore a black arm-band, and my mother wore white cotton in her hair. After we had all seen my grandfather for the last time – lying in the cedar-wood coffin, wearing the new clothes my mother had changed him into, lips tightly closed – my father, as the eldest son, put in the first nail to seal the coffin.

Because it was a "joyful loss," we didn't hire professional mourners, but seven Buddhist monks led close relatives to circle around the sealed coffin, slowly, three times, before the cremation procedure. Two of the monks played percussion instruments, wooden fish and brass cymbals. The sons of the family – my father, Uncle Jingchuan and Uncle Jingzhang – each carried a small red lantern in his hand, lighting the way for the departed soul.

Among the loud chanting of monks, and the rise and fall of the family's wailing, I looked towards my grandmother, small and frail, being held by Aunt Jingyun, as they walked on the other side of the circle. Her eyes were swollen red, and she opened her mouth slightly. She also had been crying. But I wondered if her husband's death had really registered with her as yet.

***

After the funeral, while my family was having the ceremonial vegetarian meal together, I heard Aunt Jingyun asking my father quietly whether she should write a letter to Heng in Taipei. "Not sure if it is still the same address," said my father, "but we can try."

I asked whether my grandfather had a relative in Taiwan. And my father said that she was not a relative, only a friend. I found the name Heng familiar, but didn't know where in my memory it had once lived.

During the fifth "seven-day week" of the 49-day mourning period, my father received a call from Aunt Jingyun, telling him that she had got in touch with Heng. According to Aunt Jingyun, after hearing that my grandfather had passed away, Heng was quiet for a long time on the phone. But she eventually said, "since he has already passed, I won't come to see him off." Some days later, in a letter, Heng told Aunt Jingyun that, after the call, she sat on the couch for a whole afternoon, not knowing that the food she had been cooking on the stove had already turned into hard charcoal.

"A sleepless night. And I couldn't close my eyes," she wrote. "When it was dawn, I wanted to come to Shanghai again, and see him off. But I hesitated – there was Qing and all his children, I thought, and they were the ones at the altar. So I didn't come in the end. And I failed to do what your grandfather and I had promised each other: after we came to the end of this life, we would meet on the journey to the netherworld, sailing along the 'yellow spring' together."

It is said that, after forty-nine days, the deceased will no longer wait, wander, or come back to visit his family. His sons and daughters can now take off their white linen and the black cloth from around their arms. Family members are allowed to eat meat again. As for the files of the deceased, they are closed for this life, before opening as another book. All the life-time love and resentment will be considered resolved, like incense rising to join the wind.

***

Later, my father told me the story.

In the mid-1930s, when my grandfather was studying at the medical university in Shanghai, he had first met Heng, his professor's daughter, six years younger than him. Heng was a native Shanghainese girl who had some "foreign air" features: deep-set brown eyes, and slightly wavy hair, which made her stand out among the young girls he knew. When she smiled, a sweet dimple would appear on the left side of her cheek. And she smiled often. My grandfather had admired her from a distance at first, not knowing that one day they would become close.

In August 1937, just before my grandfather's senior year, their university's red-tiled building with the Red Cross flag on top was lost by bombing, only a few days after Shanghai had been thrown into the Sino-Japanese War. His professor,

Heng's father, decided to move a few students into his home in the French Concession, to continue their studies. And my grandfather was among them. Heng's mother was a kind, educated woman who taught the boys how to cook. And Heng, just attending high school at the time, used to join the students after class to help put away the laboratory equipment. When they had free time, my grandfather and Heng often went to the rooftop of the house, and sat there chatting for a long time.

It was an autumn with much bad news. Every few weeks bombs fell in the middle of the commercial area and killed hundreds of people: in front of the Great World Amusement Arcade, the Sincere Department Store, as well as the Shanghai South Station. In the beginning of November, the Sihang Warehouse Defense Battle was lost, after eight hundred soldiers had fought to the very end. And then, refugees, not only from north of the Suzhou Creek, but from neighbouring provinces as well, rushed into the British and French Concessions. From Heng's rooftop, they could see that people had put together "rolling dragon" homes overnight with uneven brickwork and bamboo scaffolding. Once, my grandfather saw a child drinking from the nearby dirty sewer, since these homes didn't have running water. The number of infectious diseases rose sharply over the months. And soon, even in the Concessions, people would see bodies that hadn't been buried in time, decomposing in public.

Maybe it was the war, knowing so much suffering and not knowing when the next bomb would fall. Maybe it was simply after spending a lot of time together, but my grandfather and Heng were in love. The next year, when my grandfather decided to follow one of the Nationalist generals from his hometown to work in an army hospital behind the frontline in Wuhan, Hubei Province, he made a promise to Heng that they would write to each other every week.

After high school, Heng found a job in Shanghai as a kindergarten teacher. And after she had received her first salary, she bought a kilogram of woollen yarn and knitted a light blue waist-coat for my grandfather. My grandfather wore the waist-coat for many years, until his old age, even though we often mocked him for wearing a colour so bright. Perhaps, I thought, that woollen waist-coat reminded him of the story of Lady Mengjiang and her husband who built the Great Wall. After all, many patriotic songs written in the 1930s mentioned Lady Mengjiang and a soldier's winter clothes.

Wuhan, Changsha, Yichang. My grandfather moved through the inland provinces with the army, closer and closer to the springhead of the Yangtze River. What did he feel seeing the source of the water, after living all his life in Jiangnan, the fertile coastal plains created by the river? Did that give him a different view of history, or about the borders of one's identity? Then, after writing to Heng for a few years, during which my grandfather had been back to Shanghai to see her only twice, an unexpected person appeared in his life.

My great-grandparents back in Zhuji considered my grandfather to be at the right age to marry, and found him a suitable wife in the same county, my grandmother Qing. Although my grandmother was from a poor farmer's family, she had the egg-shaped face of a classic beauty, and a diligent yet tender personality which soon won over my great-grandparents. They invited her to stay with them as if she was already their daughter-in-law, and occasionally let her help in the restaurant they owned.

In early 1943, my grandfather received a letter from his parents, with a photograph of Qing, demanding he come back and get married. According to them, his elder brother who went to join the Communists in Yan'an in 1938 had never been heard from since. The parents already considered him dead. Therefore, my grandfather shouldn't take his "eldest son's duty lightly," wrote his father.

My grandfather was at loss. On the one hand, after being in the war for years, he longed for a simple, family life. On the other hand, Heng was the only woman he had ever wanted. He decided to go to Shanghai first, before heading back to Zhuji.

However, when he arrived in Shanghai this time, he realized that life in the Concessions was now completely different, cut off from what was going on in the rest of China. People had got used to the comfort of the Concessions, and would no longer frown at a refugee's body on a side street. Movie theatres were again filled with young couples, waiting to see the latest Hollywood film. After not seeing Heng for an entire year, he found that she had now grown into a bona fide woman – her green *qipao* and nylon stockings on her hourglass figure looked like a different world from where he had just come, where people died from plague and starvation every day in front of his eyes, and soldiers were left with only straw shoes and bamboo helmets to wear.

He had brought her a box of red-bean-flavoured rice cakes. And as they hung out in a park near the Bund, she teased him, "Why didn't you get a few savory ones – you know that I don't like sweet snacks." After hearing her comments, my grandfather threw the whole box into the Huangpu River, causing some pedestrians to stare at them.

And another day, when they were walking together on the street, Heng bumped into a colleague whom she greeted with the nickname "fountain pen." Her colleague was a tall, young man called Xinming, whose name shared the same characters as a popular fountain pen brand at the time. But my grandfather became angry in front of the colleague, and lectured Heng that she shouldn't give nicknames to male colleagues, as it made a girl look frivolous and cheap.

When Heng made *longjing* tea for him in her parents' house later, my grandfather once again criticised her in her mother's presence, for using a mug with the name of his former medical university on it. "How could you serve me tea in a cheap mug?" he said, "I want to use your mug instead." Within just a few days, my grandfather embarrassed Heng on many similar occasions. And she didn't know what was going on in his mind. She didn't have any idea about my great-grandparents' letter regarding Qing, or understand that my grandfather had wished to use her mug only to kiss her indirectly.

That meeting in Shanghai left both of them dismayed, more so in a way for my grandfather. He didn't speak to Heng from his heart. Soon, he was back in the family house in Zhuji. Nobody knew what his feelings were when he first met Qing or whether they got along at the beginning. But to my great-grandparents' delight, my grandfather finally agreed to marry her a year before the end of the Sino-Japanese War. At the wedding, my grandmother was already pregnant with my father.

***

So it was my grandfather who had given her up, I thought.

"How did Heng find out?" I asked my father.

"Well, you know, the Civil War happened right after. And we didn't move to Shanghai until 1946. I guess that was when your grandfather met her again."

According to my father, even though my grandfather and Heng still wrote letters to each other, he couldn't work up the courage to tell her that he was already married. In 1946, however, after my grandfather had decided to retire from military work, and took a job in the Shanghai Department of Public Health as an ophthalmologist, he knew that the time had come for him to tell Heng the truth.

Being happy at first about their eventual reunion in the same city after nine long years, Heng couldn't believe it when she heard that my grandfather had already married someone else and had children. Deep down, she had long considered them to be destined. And what was worse, over the past two years, even though they didn't write as frequently as before, my grandfather had never mentioned a word about Qing.

That evening, Heng's parents discovered that their daughter had collected a large number of match-heads, in preparation for suicide. Filled with anger, her father, once my grandfather's professor, dashed into the Department of Public Health the next day, pounded his fists on the desk, and castigated my grandfather for being a deceiving, irresponsible man. He told my grandfather to stay away from his daughter, better still move to another city, because his whole family wouldn't want to see him on the street in Shanghai any longer. Otherwise, he said that he would not hesitate to take the matter further to my grandfather's superiors and cause him to be "a homeless dog" in the medical circle in Shanghai. After this, with her parents' measures and consolation, Heng didn't try to commit suicide anymore.

But, in the end, it wasn't my grandfather who moved away. Two years later, he heard from a former classmate that Heng's family had gone to Taipei. Her father would continue as a teacher in a university there. And since they had moved before 1949, they were able to ship all their furniture and antiques across the Taiwan Strait. It was a year before my grandfather was offered a position and plane tickets, as the People's Liberation Army was preparing to cross the Yangtze River.

I asked my father if he thought it was possible, that my grandfather had turned the position down because of Heng. It was a factor I had not considered before. By not being in the same city with her, he had fulfilled her father's wish and avoided unnecessary suffering for both parties.

"It is one explanation," my father said, "a romantic one. But I think that your grandfather, like most middle-class people in Shanghai at the time, had also lost his trust in the Nationalist government. During the Civil War, and especially in 1948 and 1949, in order to pay for military debt, the government printed fiat currency in excess, and later the 'gold voucher,' to force or at least encourage its citizens to give up their gold and foreign currencies. And when the economy collapsed, these fiat currencies and gold vouchers depreciated very quickly. The money became waste paper and all commodities became scarce. My parents always talked about how, during those two years, there was barely anything on the shelves of grocery stores. In order to pay for a bar of soap, two people needed to carry a large bag of money to the store between them. In the department stores, your grandmother used to tell me, even the counter that sold buttons had a notice-board that said, 'Limited to one button for each person.' Some people lost all their savings by exchanging into these government-issued fiat currencies. Fortunately, despite the regulations, my parents still kept some gold bullion. But you know this didn't last very long after '49…"

"Because people in Shanghai didn't know much about Mao back then," I said. I thought, perhaps, that my grandfather, being quite irresolute when it came to important decisions, found himself unable to leave everything behind at short notice. Also, people who moved late had to bear the risk of being separated from their family members, let alone their furniture. My grandfather was not just "patriotic" as my grandmother had often claimed. He was also practical. And as someone with a specialized skill, he had always believed that he could be useful to people under new circumstances.

"For a young, unknown government, one was often hopeful," my father said.

***

Now the memory of seeing Heng when I was a child came back to me. It was in the late 1980s – 1988 or 1989, I didn't remember which year exactly. But the three generations of our family were still living on Duolun Road. Back then, it was a real novelty to see taxis. So the adults, in white vests and shorts, and the children who had been playing featherball all stood still to watch the red Volkswagen Santana driving slowly into our narrow *longtang*. I remembered vividly a Taiwanese girl of my age who also had a boyish, short haircut like mine. In fact, we posed for a photo together after their visit in the *longtang*, both of us smiling with our teeth showing. She was wearing a neat white dress with ruffles at the collar, white socks and black leather shoes, and I was in a white pajama set, with bare feet with slippers. We both looked very innocent and happy. As for the adults, I couldn't recall their appearance very well. But now I realized that the "older grandma", similar to my grandmother's age must have been Heng, and the sturdy, middle-aged man must have been her son.

It was her first time coming back to Shanghai after forty years. I did the math in my mind. Forty years – easy to summarize in a history book, but how long was that in a person's life? A young girl with red cheeks and tight *qipao* now had grandchildren. And my grandfather was no longer the handsome, but ill-tempered army doctor who had broken her heart. In my memory, the meeting was mundane though, despite the entrance of a taxi, and rather peaceful. I was surprised at the time that these guests didn't eat much and were full so quickly, even though my grandmother had prepared a feast that filled the whole table. The middle-aged man was surprised, in his turn, that we didn't even have fruit in the house, and he went out to get some oranges for us as a dessert. I remembered the gray-haired "older grandma" Heng apologizing to my grandparents for her son's impulsive behaviour. And I didn't understand at the time why, before meeting them, my grandfather had warned all of us over and over again not to ask anything from them.

What were we supposed to ask for from these Taiwanese guests? I thought, confused. Perhaps what he had meant was not to accept any expensive gifts from them. My grandfather still had his pride. And what had my grandfather and Heng talked about, after so many years, sitting at the same table with my grandmother, their children and grandchildren?

It seemed that in the late 1980s, according to my father, my grandfather and Heng started to write to each other again. Like old friends, he said. They would talk about the past, their health, and their children. Once, Aunt Jingyun went to a jewelry industry trade conference in Taipei, and they arranged for her to stay with Heng for a couple of days. Since 1998, when my grandmother's dementia started to become worse, and all of his children lived far away and were busy with their lives, writing to Heng had become a way for my grandfather to release his stress. My grandfather had never learned how to do housework all his life. Later on, even with the help of nurses, it was still a big challenge for him to manage the daily chores of simply keeping everything in order.

How much did my grandmother know? The thought often came to my mind. "An example of the older generation of women whom we won't see in China anymore" – those were my father's familiar words. Could one practice denial until it became real? In the end, it was my grandfather's twelve years of labour camp and the devastating famine that she would rather remember. Could they be in fact, the most worthwhile years in my grandmother's life?

I realized now, as my grandmother slipped into a world where she couldn't tell who I was, that all I had were questions. Growing questions which would be met only with an experienced silence. My grandmother didn't like to talk about the past until she stopped remembering it. Only then, was she willing to release the burden. She had already lost her maiden name Qin – a seven-stringed zither – ever since we had known her. I thought of my grandmother tearing off the stamps from Heng's letters, and putting them carefully into her albums. She had never learned to read or write, so stamp albums were what she had, an archive of another woman's thoughts and feelings. It felt cruel to me.

But don't we all map the content of our hearts every day through different sets of borrowed and insufficient pictures and symbols?

The lighthouse at Kenting, plum blossom in shades of pink, National Palace Museum ink paintings, and children trundling along with an iron hoop – a window into the lost forty years, and into the hearts of my grandfather, Heng, and of herself. A very small window, but a window, nonetheless.

23
Five-finger Mountain
五指山 (*wu zhi shan*)

After my grandfather's funeral, I didn't talk to Simon for a while. History had pulled me in and made me feel far away from him. I wished that he hadn't left me on the trail where the macaques had gathered. I wished that Simon had a different relationship with his father. But right now, how was he capable of reading beyond the imperfect vehicle of my words and understanding the family stories of a time before I was born? And where was I even going to start?

I thought of my grandfather in his late years, who, after a lifetime of hardship, had put his most tender feelings onto someone impossible, someone on the other side of the Taiwan Strait. It was not the love I had envisioned; not really "愛," either. It lacked day-to-day texture, missed real effort and therefore real disappointment. It had, nonetheless, waited so lonely and so patiently for years, waiting to be loved. But what other choices did he have, when it was already too late, after the cross-strait traffic was closed off?

If Simon and I were ever to have a future, I thought, living side by side, I would first need to feel my own temperature and figure out where I wanted to be. It was still too soon for me to be truly close to someone. Deep down, I knew it very well.

***

In my senior year, I started another internship in a small, newly-established publishing house. It had approximately twenty employees, but was affiliated to the largest publishing group in Shanghai. I was employed in the marketing department, and worked for a year mostly as an interpreter. At the time, the company was introducing an important biography of a former Chinese politician to the market. The book was written by an American author.

The author, Dr. Glen, in his early sixties, was a former investment banker, and a long-term friend of the Chinese politician. His project was to record China's rapid modernization over recent decades through the life of a leader. He had spent several years interviewing senior officials who were close to the politician, as well as people from all walks of life in China. The book was translated into Chinese in the same year that the original English version was written. Before its official publication, I heard that it had already pre-sold a million copies. Many corporations, either state-owned or private, and government bureaus, had made the red-covered biography mandatory for all their employees.

I was assigned to be Dr. Glen's interpreter during press conferences, book signings and dinners in around thirty cities in China, approximately two cities in each province. Thinking back, it was a physically exhausting tour, since we sat in planes and cars for long hours, and moved from one event to another without much pause. It was the intensity I wanted at the time, however, an all-consuming distraction. And back at university, I had no more academic credits left to achieve, other than my thesis, which I still had a semester to work on.

Dr. Glen had some investment interests at the provincial level. However, it baffled me at first what reason the government had, apart from his "trustworthiness" in the eyes of the book's small English-reading audience, to choose to showcase its "success story" through a foreigner's lens. Only later, at dinner tables, did I discover that Dr. Glen had the ability to make even the stiffest government officials laugh. And I understood then what difference a little humour can make in story-telling. His ability to poke fun, of course, came from a more secure, unscarred place. For the first time in my life, I felt sorry for the officials we were meeting. Few of the people in positions of authority whom I had met, no matter their level, had that personal touch and charisma. All officials were well aware of the arbitrary possibility of an earthquake in their lives and were always on guard among people. As a result, they couldn't manage to tell a genuine story with natural human vulnerability.

For example, since Dr. Glen's restrictive dietary list that the publisher had received before the trip permitted only cherry tomatoes, broccoli, tofu and fish, each province had gone out of its way to select local delicacies from the water. Once, when the Party official of a coastal province was briefing Dr. Glen on the five different names of fish on the table, I found it hard to translate them correctly into English.

"These are various kinds of local fish," I began, and then tried to add that the dishes were seasonal, expensive, and rare, as implied by my monotonous introduction of the fish names. Dr. Glen soon understood that having them was a special treat. The official, however, cared neither to explain his staff's efforts nor make a self-deprecating joke about his wish to please new friends.

That evening, on our way back to the hotel, Dr. Glen's assistant told me that the very official we had met that day was the heir apparent of the Party, and would move to Beijing in five years' time. It surprised me that these Americans already knew my country's next top leaders before most ordinary Chinese citizens did. I thought that perhaps I should have learned more English names for fish after all. Otherwise, because of translation problems like this, Westerners would never be able truly to understand the intentions behind the dour introduction of fish names, nor what the head of the Chinese government was trying to imply.

My unusual sympathy for the ultra-powerful in the country, however, didn't last long. There was often liquor at the dinner table. And some officials enjoyed seeing a young female interpreter drunk, since they were too polite or self-conscious to make the male foreign guests drink too much. I often became the substitute target of their power-play business ritual.

One time in Qingdao, Shandong Province, an official in a military uniform insisted on my drinking with him some green liquor containing bitter snake-gall, after I had shaken my head to the scarlet-red snake blood in a full wine glass. I threw up in my hotel bathroom afterwards and decided not to let myself be pushed around any longer. When we traveled to Xiamen, Fujian Province, I finally succeeded in sticking to my principles when it came to exotic alcohol, no matter how often the local official's subordinates echoed disapprovingly that I "didn't know how to appreciate favours." Strangely enough, the next day when the official was showing us around in a golf cart on Kulangsu Island, he put his hand on my waist.

"You must come from some family," he said.

Because I didn't drink last night? Perhaps he was being sarcastic. I moved away from him. But the golf cart was small. Dr. Glen and his assistant were sitting in front of us, enjoying the sight of the red-roofed Amoy Deco Style architecture.

And then as if engaging in casual small talk, the official asked if I would consider bearing a son for him, because he only had a teenage daughter, who had just enrolled at a woman's college in the U.S. His wife, according to him, hadn't been interested in sharing a room for years. "You wouldn't have to translate any more, you see," he said.

I couldn't tell if this was merely an inappropriate joke, which would still be unusual. How long had we been in the province, I thought, two days? His hand rested firmly on my lower back, holding my body, but it didn't move. I felt dizzy as if I was caught by the familiar motion sickness from my childhood bus rides.

The piano museum we would visit was getting close. So in the end, I leaned forward and pretended that I didn't hear clearly what he had said, and started a conversation about the museum with Dr. Glen. And once the foreign guests started talking, I knew that I could avoid speaking to the official directly. After a few minutes, the hand finally retreated.

Later that evening, I took a long shower and when I came out of the hotel bathroom, I heard someone knocking at my door. From the peep hole, I saw the official we had met earlier with his two subordinates, one of them carrying a gift box.

I didn't want to answer the door. Cold sweat started to dampen the back of my shirt. Then, to my surprise, after a round of knocking, one subordinate tried to open the door from the outside. They had the keys for this state-owned hotel, I realized with more distress. Fortunately, I had locked the door from the inside with the latch.

Through the door, I heard that the two subordinates were talking about me being *bu dong shi*, not knowing any better, by not accepting the stone carving gift that was considered premium local artwork. The remark was coercing and intended for me to hear. I bit my lip, and thought that I would just have to let them talk.

Perhaps they didn't want to linger too long and wake up other guests because the three men eventually left. It was almost midnight, but I couldn't sleep in the hours that followed. I felt that my movements could be recorded by everything in the room even with all the blinds closed.

What had I just done? I was "allowing temperament" for sure this time even though I was too scared to fire back. At the time, I didn't think about the repercussions, whether it would jeopardize the book-tour or my internship. I had merely followed my instinct. Nevertheless, I thought about it late into the night and was still unsettled. What would be the price to pay for this in the future? Something dear in my life to exchange for that freedom? "A mound sticking out from the bank will certainly be eroded by the current," said the conventional Chinese wisdom. No matter how much I tried to stay away from the language, the familiar quotation still came to mind.

The next day, however, the official didn't appear to remember the previous night, at least not during the exchange of pleasantries with the book-tour delegation. He even brought his daughter to the meeting, asking if Dr. Glen could find a position for her in his company. The daughter was a few years younger than me, rather friendly, and fetched me to chat with her afterwards. She mentioned that she had grown up in upstate New York, and spent most of the time talking about a recent comedy film starring Asian actors whom I had never heard of.

"We need more of these in America," she said in her native English. "Different kinds, even not-so-good ones!"

I found it interesting, the way this second- or third-generation "red princeling" used the word "we." She seemed to be sincerely happy for what those Asian-American actors represented and embraced the values of her own identity. There was even a dash of an underprivileged experience in her tone. However, I couldn't shake the memory of the day before. I realized that the person who had asked me to consider bearing him a son and almost forced himself into my hotel room late at night, didn't want his own daughter to live in this country. I had used up all my sympathy.

The two subordinates watched my conversation with the daughter closely, but didn't interrupt us. Our delegation moved on to another province later that day and I was finally relieved.

**

When the book-tours ended, I was transferred from the small publisher to the headquarters of the publishing group.

The internship continued, yet I didn't have to work every day, which suited the schedule of the final semester at the university. If everything went well, I was told, I could have full-time employment after graduation. The place where I worked was one of the "core" departments in the group, the Copyright and Legal Affairs Department.

For the next six months, I finally came to understand what it meant to work in a state-owned enterprise, and why so many people wanted to have these secure, "iron rice-bowl" jobs. The two bosses of my department each had a bamboo bench in their office so that they could lie down after lunch to take a nap. The three other young girls who had worked longer than me spent most of their time making phone-calls to the affiliated publishers, and apart from collecting sales numbers, they chatted the hours away. When they were not on the phone, they would browse the online shopping-sites. Every day, we had at least one box delivered to the office for them, containing cosmetics or accessories.

It was a way of life in the workplace, almost in a laid-back feudal fashion, and a way many people would prefer. It didn't seem to suit me at that age, however. I felt out of place.

Once, the girl who was in charge of compiling the numbers for the publishing group's year-end meetings, told me that "out of fifteen, only two educational publishers were making money with their textbooks." Carefully painting her nails pink, blowing air on them from time to time, she nonchalantly continued to provide information from her office desk, telling me that other academic books and books of literature simply had no market. She didn't care about reading herself, she claimed. When the numbers didn't add up, she told me, she would simply make them up. And later in the annual meeting, I saw our two bosses using the excel sheet which the nail-painting girl had compiled, analyzing the report in all seriousness for the benefit of the head of the publishing group.

In one of the copyrights business meetings where I had interpreted, a senior executive in charge of foreign affairs chatted with me during breaks and said, "if I were as young as you, I wouldn't work in a state-owned company for long, being surrounded by people who have already retired at heart." I was grateful for the advice. And, soon after, another incident strengthened my resolution to leave.

It was the year when the Shanghai Party secretary fell from grace. As usual, he was accused of bribery and corruption, and was sentenced to eighteen years in prison. Even though we had not met him on the book-tour earlier, and I had no personal feelings for the former chief of the city, I was fairly shocked by his sudden loss of favour. My parents, and most of my relatives, in fact, held a good impression of the man, who had initiated a few trade and infrastructure projects over recent years, including pushing Shanghai to become a "free trade zone," clearing up the pollution of Suzhou Creek and building several subway lines. In addition, they said that, as a native of Shanghai, he had made some effort to protect the local dialect and culture by introducing Shanghainese children's songs and cultural tours to kindergarten students.

Some of my relatives said that, of course, he was just another victim of the political struggle among senior leaders in Beijing. And perhaps, after all, what he had been accused of was true, others claimed as if they had all the inside information, since none of these officials were corruption-free – evidence of corruption had always been the easiest thing to grab in this game.

We had a really hectic couple of months in the publishing group, however, especially in my department. The two bosses had no time to nap on their benches anymore since we had to work with the Administration of News and Culture in Shanghai to recall all the million copies of the politician's biography written by the American author. In the book, there had been a positive mention of the Shanghai Party secretary, as well as a few photos of him and the retired politician. They had all to be deleted before the book could be reprinted.

The last time we had done such a recall, it was of a few French and Japanese novels that had contained "erotic content not suitable for the Chinese market." As a customary practice, the Department of Administration of News and Culture required our department to send them a copy of every book before we published it. But sometimes, for efficiency, we had only done so when the book was already on its way for distribution, or even after. Years later, I still found it incredible to imagine that in the Administration of News and Culture, there had been an office of employees whose only job was to read every book in the market and spot those with "erotic" or "unsuitable content." In fact, if I had the opportunity, I wouldn't mind doing that job for a day or two.

However, it was not that fun being on the receiving end of it. I made so many calls during the day that my right arm became sore. Couldn't we just let the Shanghai Party secretary live in history, no matter what kind of crimes he had committed? Even the murderers from the evening news had their fair share of personal stories. How about adding a negative biography of him to the market? After all, the English version of the book remained unchanged. So what was the rush to erase him from the minds of all Chinese readers? Well, I thought, I was finally doing a job like dear old Winston Smith in *1984*, erasing a person from history as if he had never existed. And how many Winston Smiths had there been before me, so that "history" became the way it was told? The thought gave me a deep chill.

I lost sleep some nights. And as I closed my eyes, I imagined myself being erased by a solid, white, eraser, like a casual mistake to be corrected. First the toes, and then up to my legs, and waist. The eraser worked at a steady but unarguable pace, moving in a graceful diagonal angle. It hardly made any noise. And there went the chest and arms, my neck, and with some last effort, all of it was gone.

Where my former self used to stand, there remained only some faint marks that hardly resembled a figure, and the annoying black rubber residue.

***

I could find a job elsewhere, I considered, say, in a foreign company in Shanghai. But in the 2000s, that meant most likely I wouldn't be able to find something in publishing or the arts, if freedom of expression was what I wanted. Besides, I wasn't convinced that I could go beyond the "Five-finger Mountain" as long as I remained in the same locale. The reference reminded me of Jie, who always enjoyed *Journey to the West*, where the metaphor of the "Five-finger Mountain" came from.

In the story, The Monkey King had a bet with the Buddha that he could go to the end of the universe, completely out of the Buddha's sight. In order to prove it, he dashed for a thousand miles, passing oceans and continents, until he reached a mountain with five peaks, signifying the edge of anywhere mortal beings can possibly reach. Happy with his accomplishment, the Monkey marked his territory by peeing at the foot of the mountain so that he could leave some evidence, only to smell later his own urine on the Buddha's palm, which he, in fact, had never travelled beyond. Having won the bet, the Buddha locked the Monkey under the mountain for five hundred years, to repent, before releasing him again as the Tang monk's disciple.

Having known this story all my childhood, I had never felt more like the Monkey than now. Could I ever jump off the Buddha's palm? Or was the pursuit of a worthwhile humanity during our short life, instead of becoming a functional chess piece in the set, a mere joke in the eyes of the Buddha?

Chinese politicians have always been very good at blurring the lines between the Taoist and Buddhist practices of breaking the boundary of a self, and their own political interest in requiring other people to subscribe to a complete, selfless subjection. I often wondered which came first, like a chicken and egg question. During the long history of religion intertwined with politics in our particular cultural landscape, however, it has become hard for people to separate the two.

I remembered the childhood days when I was far-sighted, haunted by my own mortality, and learned to expel the "consideration of the self," or at least learned to regard it as the moral and spiritual ideal. Far-sightedness was not the most serviceable eyesight, and it was as inconvenient as near-sightedness, I knew. But to cure it, we had a culture of practicing the abolition of the "self" early in life, as children. At such a young age, could the joy of abandonment really come from within? I didn't feel joy when I practiced it. I felt an amplified fear and a suppressed, nameless discontent for most of my younger years.

I would rather be the arrogant Monkey and test the palm out, no matter what. If I jumped just far enough, at least I would be able to get a glimpse of the Buddha's shape, even if the mission would eventually fail. One couldn't know, really. In Hong Kong, people old and young still braved the streets to protest.

24
Plum Rain Season
梅雨季 (*mei yu ji*)

If I were to leave Jiangnan one day, I would miss the rainy season in June. It was the time when plums were ripe, ready to be made into dry snacks or wine. Each year the humid and warm days felt endless, and it was impossible to keep food for long. I had sensitive skin and reacted badly to mosquito bites, which occurred often during the rainy season. It was a time of year everyone complained about while living through it. But I knew, that if I were to leave one day, I, like many people, would forget about the mosquitoes and the other terrifying insects which awoke after the warm rain. Instead, I would miss the sight of thick green moss on the old sidewalks, the triangular-shaped rice dumplings sold in stores around the time of the Dragon Boat Festival, and my family tradition of making green-bean dessert and winter melon soup to help us cool down in the heat.

I knew that my heart was filled with sentiment and nostalgia, because my mind was made up.

***

It was mid 2005 when I graduated from university and over a year since I had last talked with Simon. So when he asked about my mailing address on instant messenger, I realized that I had missed him. After all, it was I who had dropped our connection. Yet, like a growing plant beneath the earth, he had never really left my mind. The hours we had spent together, and the conversations we shared, had taken up space in my memory.

Sometimes I felt that Simon's and my stories were two sides of the same coin: an immigrant story and an emigrant story. Sometimes I felt that he was my future. I imagined his parents' journeys, too, and finally recognized that it can take more than one generation for each of the body and the heart to both uproot themselves and travel.

My father, in his sixties when I graduated, told me, "Even after so many years, I still feel myself at odds with the entire system here…" For some, perhaps, the heart has traveled but the body still remains, stuck. For others, the body has long settled in a new place, but the heart's journey is only just beginning. And there is an in-between place, like Hong Kong, where the body and heart can be together for a short while. But how ephemeral that peace is.

I messaged Simon to ask if he wanted to chat again. And the next morning, he came online.

"Are you mailing me a graduation present?" I told him briefly of my completed internship and the exams I was taking to prepare for graduate school applications in the U.S.

"I'm really glad to hear it, Yinan. You're a special person and you've touched my life. No matter what happens, I really care about you. And you have a lot to live for. You will do well in graduate school."

"I miss talking to you."

"I miss you, too."

"Hope someday we won't be too far from each other. Someday in the U.S., perhaps." I was imagining Simon's return after his graduation in Hong Kong. However, he still had a couple years to go.

"I'd like to stand by your side if I could," Simon wrote. "I don't really know how to explain myself. I guess you'll just have to trust me."

"I always do," I replied. I felt that neither of us was holding back today, after losing touch for so long.

"I know that I've disappointed you. I just can't think clearly sometimes. My whole life, I have been waiting for something to click, so that everything would just turn around. But I really don't know how to fight it. I see a lot of beauty in the world, but I don't know how to grasp it. My brain is stuck in the internal world and it can't let itself be shaped by anything else."

"But you said we have influenced each other, haven't we?"

"I really want that deep connection," he said.

"We should give it more time."

"I know myself though. It's really difficult for me to have a connection with anyone, even my own family. I just have to choose the right road, and face reality with honesty, no matter how much I might despise it. It's not like with a normal person, where there are thoughts and emotions, and you put them into words. With me, it just feels like constant emptiness, and I have to try to dig meaning out of it. It's like not really being alive."

"But I didn't feel empty with you," I said. "Shall we switch to Chinese?"

I told Simon my thoughts about the language lately, that despite its flaws, Chinese can be a better means of communicating our situation. The pictographic characters trace the shape we see in nature. And since there are no complicated tenses or explicit prepositions, we don't need constantly to make a choice, or make a choice right away. The language that frustrates in certain aspects also frees in others. I said that perhaps, in future, we could use Chinese to build a shared imagination and a better understanding, and I would try to avoid the idioms used in propaganda. But Simon ignored my request.

"Sometimes I can see things from your perspective, and I do understand how silly everything might seem. But you never know. You'll become a different person after you're in the U.S., too. Your priorities may shift, or not. Anything could happen…"

I felt strongly that I wanted to hear from him more, about his daily life. But in a way, I had changed the topic. "How were your recent school projects?"

"Recent projects? We studied capuchin monkeys and chimpanzees in the lab, and their ability to use tools."

"That sounds interesting. What tools did you give them?"

"Well, we tested their ability to align objects to a surface, such as a circular rod or a cross. It was to see if they could manipulate the objects and correctly put them inside the groove. In fact, the chimpanzees were pretty bad at the cross and anything else more complicated; even the straight rod was more difficult than expected."

I paused for a few seconds, thinking about the fumbling chimpanzees.

"Anyway, there is nothing new. I just have to face the future without fear." Simon typed a smiley face after his sentence. He then asked for my address and I typed it on instant messenger. We talked so much about our feelings this time that I almost forgot it was the reason Simon contacted me again.

For a moment, I was happy that I might see his handwriting soon.

"It was nice talking to you, Yinan, as always."

"Next time, you'll have to let me give you a call. I have been using a cell phone for some time, finally not a technology dinosaur."

"Heh. Goodbye for now. I will miss you."

***

The rain came almost every day that summer. The beautiful, puffy clouds of a season ago were now only misty rain, collecting on the city pavements. I spent most of the time in my room over the following week, studying vocabulary or doing exercises for my exams.

From time to time, I thought about the recent online chat with Simon. How I wished I could have heard his voice!

Instead, only a few former university classmates had called. Most of them already had a job offer and were officially working in Shanghai after graduation. Some were baffled at my decision to forego the opportunity of working in the large state-owned publishing group in order to pursue graduate school overseas. I hadn't heard from Jie for a long time, and wondered if she also had joined the workforce.

And then one evening, Simon's letter arrived in my mailbox.

On the envelope, the return address was his father's home in Maryland. Among the five stamps, one showed a scene from a Hans Christian Andersen fairy tale, three were scenes of Ham Tin Wan beach, and the last one, a goldfish. The post date was just a day after our last conversation. It was a short note no longer than one-third of a page, not hand-written but printed out. Simon had signed his name in a blue pen next to the black ink of the printer. It was the most formal letter I had received.

"Dear Yinan,

"Thank you for being such a faithful friend to me. I was really hoping to give this to you in person, but I just want you to know that you've always been in my mind. I like it because it reminds me of your quiet strength. Perhaps you can use it for inspiration if you ever find yourself losing courage. You'll always be special to me, and I'll always believe in you. Please believe in yourself too, no matter what happens. I love you.

"All my best,
"Simon"

Inside the envelope, there was a small white paper bag carrying a sun-shaped brooch. The writing on it was, "Ojo de tigre." I looked it up and found out that it was the

Spanish name of the stone set in the brooch, meaning "tiger's eye."

That evening, I found it impossible to fall asleep. So I sat in front of my desk for a long time. Simon didn't log in online, but I waited. And then, I couldn't stop my tears. It was not only because of sorrow. What I touched on my face, were also tears of a terrible, transcending joy. I recognised the sensation clearly, even then. Yet somehow, I couldn't forgive myself for that feeling.

The next morning, I decided to give Aunt Eunice a long-distance call, since she had given me a name card the last time we had lunch in Hong Kong.

"The memorial will be this Thursday in Rockville," Aunt Eunice said over the phone, her voice soft and drained. "I don't know what else to say. I'm sorry to be the one you hear this from."

I thanked her before wanting to hang up. I didn't want the conversation to sink in.

"Simon will be buried with his mother," she added, as if I might have misunderstood what she said previously. She kept talking for a few minutes longer. I was standing in my own room, watching the rain landing on the street puddles, making echoes of circles.

***

Later, I looked up the word "helium" on the Internet. It was an unusual word that I had not heard of before. In Chinese, it had an "air" radical, similar in shape to the character for oxygen. Two tanks of helium, Aunt Eunice had said. In his single dormitory in Hong Kong. All alone. It was the day after our last chat, and the same day as the post-mark on the mail I had received.

I had waited a few more days for Simon to appear online, but he hadn't shown up. We had only just started talking again after a very long time. But for him, it wasn't the same. It wasn't a new beginning. He was only twenty years old, and I was already a few months past twenty-one. I would simply become older and older than him, as years went by. Simon really knew how to annoy me, I said to myself. How stupid could he possibly be? And how juvenile.

I read Simon's letter over and over again, where only his name was signed in cursive, dark blue ink. The rest was printed in black. He had put down simple words that I could read for a lifetime. But without gazes or gestures, prosody or tones, or touches of calligraphy, the words were empty. He had turned himself into a favourite book such as I had curled up with in my childhood loneliness. Yet I had learned long ago that books were not enough. I wanted to see the movement of his lips again when he spoke, to taste the warmth of his breath, and put my hand on his chest this time so that I could feel his heartbeat. How I had wished to see the stars shining in their time, instead of the ghostly illusion they brought to earth after light years of traveling.

25
Hometown
故鄉 (*guxiang*)

That summer, I pushed myself through the exams and did some research on potential graduate schools. Most of the time, I stayed in my room. When the nights fell, however, I thought of Simon. The night brought me closer to him. I thought of the shadow world he once described to me.

"It's a place where you can't find anything. Even things that you believe in don't make sense. All those proverbs from childhood seem to lose their meaning. It's hard even to feel like a human there. There's no right or wrong, and sometimes you do horrible things because you don't know what else to do. Nothing has any detail, just dancing shadows. Really, it's a miserable, miserable place."

"Shall I come with you?" I had said, "Maybe I'll punch you right in the face and wake you up."

"You are the only one who talked about punching." He laughed. "You are so sweet, and stubborn. The real world is full of simple pleasures... I'll be angry if you don't enjoy them! And some day I hope we can experience them together. I'm used to the shadow world anyway – I've been fighting the shadows for years, it doesn't matter if I fight them a little longer."

* * *

One evening at the dinner table, I found my tears dropping in front of my parents and they were concerned about my stress with all the applications. I knew that they were holding back their emotion about my leaving next year, too. But I couldn't bring up Simon's name. For a long time, it felt like a slight to talk about him with anyone. I didn't want to compromise my feelings by openly putting them into words.

***

At the end of the summer, I made a few trips to my university to get transcripts and references for my applications. Once I ran into Jie's former boyfriend, Pei, on campus. He had graduated a few years previously from his Economics PhD programme and was now employed in an administrative role at the university. It seemed that Pei still remembered me from Jie's birthday party, even though that was the only time we had met.

"I'm concerned about Jie," he said after our initial greetings. "She didn't come to the commencement. And nobody seemed to be able to contact her, either. Her mother wouldn't pick up the phone. But I've heard that Jie moved out some time ago."

I wasn't surprised at her independence. But not receiving her degree in person was not Jie's style. I could tell that Pei continued to care for her, even after their breakup. Maybe I had judged this flamboyant fellow too quickly, I thought. Behind his conspicuous gestures, he must have some understanding of Jie's vulnerability.

I told him that I would let him know if I had some news.

After bidding Pei goodbye, I called Jie's mother's place a few times but as Pei mentioned, the calls didn't go through. Jie's cell phone was turned off. Later, I phoned the consulting firm she had told me about over a year ago, when we had last met. After several confusing transfers of line, one secretary confirmed that Jie had completed her internship two months ago. I also sent her an email, but received no reply. Despite all the new communication technologies, it felt as though Jie had simply vanished from the world, just like Simon. I couldn't stand the thought of it.

I found myself going to our middle school and high school on weekdays, just to see the old and new campuses from the outside. There were often schoolgirls coming out in their uniform, and it was difficult for me to imagine that we were once so slim and willowy. However, I did not wish to go inside again. Knowing that Mr. Yang and Mr. Lin might still be teaching there made my stomach turn. The KFC and McDonald's where Jie and I used to hang out with our sodas had mostly been replaced now by new coffee and bubble-tea shops. Our favourite park remained the same and the leaves were lightly tinted by the new season. I had just started to send out graduate school applications. But without Simon and Jie in my life, I felt as downcast about the future as about the past. I lost some weight due to insomnia. And for two weeks at mid-autumn, I suffered from shingles. The sharp physical pain on my skin and nerves finally eased the numbness of my mind for a while. Afterwards, exhausted from illness, my sleep finally returned, long and uninterrupted.

***

Jie's voice came from the other end of the line as if from another world. I was still drowsy from my afternoon nap and in recovery, so it took me a few seconds to recognize her. But then, my heart beat fast.

"Where have you been?"

"Were you sleeping in the middle of the day? I just woke up myself – we seem to have the same internal rhythm." It felt as if she was relaxed and in a healthy spirit. Was I still dreaming?

She asked me if I could meet her in her new place tomorrow. She had moved to the city centre a few months ago. And her cell phone number had changed.

"Is everything alright? Your former classmates were asking about you." I didn't mention Pei, however.

"Well, I won't ask about them. I'm sure they just want to know which offer I got. People compare these things with each other in my department," she said. I felt that Jie was laughing a little on the other side, and her sarcasm surprised me this time. "Didn't you use to say that it's better to have no peers than to have the ones that will give you all the wrong ideas?"

"You never agreed with it in the past, though."

"True. I don't read as much as you, or seek confidants mostly from a different time. Once in a while though, I think I would like to have that security also, if you ask me."

"It's not all that secure," I said. "It's a shadow world." I felt emotion rising up from my chest. How nice it was to hear Jie's voice again.

"Hmm...you always have an interesting way of putting things. Tomorrow morning," she said. "Please come."

***

I thought about the word "故鄉" (guxiang) during my taxi ride to Jie's place the next day. Outside the car windows, the morning light landed on the distant, changing skylines of Pudong. I had never felt so far away from the last century, and from my childhood. In English, one has a hometown, but the Chinese guxiang is the old countryside which has already ceased to exist the moment you leave it. Jiangnan lived only in my dreams. And Shanghai would soon no longer resemble the world I grew up in. Where would I return to in the years to come, but my memories?

A yellow gingko leaf had got stuck behind the windshield wiper of the taxi, and the driver just let it be. I imagined myself to be a leaf, tied to a branch, waiting. Would the leaf envy my mobility to move in dimensions where it couldn't? Or did I envy its eventual freedom? In fact, I was still tied to the ground, pulled by gravity from my very first day on earth, and waiting to go home.

***

We sat on the small balcony of Jie's new apartment, overlooking the sycamore-tree-lined street. There was an old-fashioned mom-and-pop shop that sold steamed food across from us, and we could smell the white buns. A few men had gathered under a tree, chatting, while listening to something on a radio. The familiar colours, scent, and street noise once again evoked memories of our earlier years, youthful, and therefore filled with desires. The alienated feeling while I was in the taxi had now slowly vanished. I realized that I always felt more rooted with Jie. I noticed that her figure had changed since we last saw each other. She wore a loose-fitting tunic but I could tell that she had put on weight. Unlike before, Jie had no makeup on but her cheeks were flushed.

"I'm eighteen weeks pregnant," she said not long after we sat down.

My mouth opened but no words came out at first. I refrained from showing too much surprise in my expression, but suddenly, I didn't feel like myself. I remembered the day when I told Jie about Mr. Yang in the park. She was the only person I wanted to speak to back then. But now I started to realize that by sharing that piece of knowledge, I had thrust her into the realm of knowing, of new possibilities and experiences, which could not be undone. I wondered how long Jie had kept the secret, and how long it took her to make up her mind. Finally, I asked, "Was he the one in your previous firm?"

Jie nodded and we fell quiet for a while. I had many questions and Jie seemed to know that I struggled to voice them all at once. She took my right hand to place on her belly, so that I could feel the rising shape and her warmth. Her pregnancy had made her more comfortable with physical intimacy, I thought. We had never shared such close proximity. With the touch on skin, it felt real that she was going to be a young mother in just a few months, and to have a family member of her own. Jie smiled when I moved my hand slightly left and right, in hope to detect a movement. She said that it was too early to feel anything from the outside.

"I never expected it to happen at this time of my life. But when I saw the test result, all I felt was an assured determination to figure out what would be next, a strong curiosity. I couldn't possibly pass up the opportunity, even though it was not in any plan I had made before. I knew that it would be the most important relationship of my life, for someone like me." Later, as if as an afterthought, she added, "We are not together anymore, but it doesn't matter."

It sounded like the pregnancy was the right timing for her after all. Still, I worried about the hardships of being a single mother. Jie had guessed my thoughts.

"My mother raised me all by herself and things were difficult, of course. She wasn't very strong. And sometimes I think our roles were reversed at home, that I had to be someone she could rely on throughout the years. It was a different generation and different time, however. She didn't have the opportunity to go to university or receive any kind of training to be a parent."

"What's your plan about school, or work?"

"I'm going to defer for one year. Don't worry. I have some freelance work lined up for the time being."

Jie smiled again and put some stray strands of hair behind her ears. Her round, tanned face still resembled the girl who accompanied me to the school clinic during our Monday assembly. "The most important relationship in my life." I ruminated on her words, how these months far from everyone else had strengthened her.

"Will you leave Shanghai soon?" she asked. "I have that feeling. For a while I didn't want to talk to anybody. But there was a voice nagging me inside that if I didn't see Yinan, it would be too late."

I told her about my plan to go to graduate school in the U.S. And Jie listened to the details carefully.

"It is brave of you," she said.

"I feel the same about you."

"Well, it always takes the first step to realize our real options, doesn't it? And funny that we just couldn't find this out sooner in life."

"I'm glad you didn't, otherwise you could have been an even younger mother," I teased her and Jie laughed.

I thought more about what she had said. Hearing Jie's words this time made me really happy. I felt that the heavy something that had stayed on my mind for years was finally lifted. Growing up in a place like ours, we didn't in the end mold ourselves after the adults we didn't like, even though there was a fair amount of meandering. I realized that, over the years, it was never the situations that Jie was in which concerned me, but her attitude towards them, her preference and talent for shortcuts, her premature cynicism, caused by her acceptance of the restrictions of her situation, and a helplessness masquerading as worldly. But I could see, that even when she had made choices different from mine in the past, it was never done without conflicting thoughts, just as in my case. Now that she had chosen a difficult, unconventional path, I started to feel her girlish courage return, as warm and pure as the autumn sun which left its shadow on the balcony.

***

I accompanied Jie to her ultrasound a few weeks later. And as the doctor measured the height and width of the baby with a transducer, we saw little arms and legs moving rapidly in the womb and a steady heartbeat on the screen. I couldn't see much of the baby's facial expressions. But for the first time after I heard Jie's news, I felt an unforeseen surge of sadness rising from deep. I had not really considered having a child myself at that age. Nonetheless, it reminded me that, no matter what my life would be in the future, home or abroad, married or not, Simon wouldn't be a part of it.

All our possibilities had ceased to live. The future we were not yet prepared for continued to live only in the shadows of our past. Simon and I on the trail in Hong Kong. The crystal blue ocean nearby. The salty wind that messed up our hair in the speedboat. Our long walks in Shanghai. The fireworks on New Year's Eve. In front of the changing, fuzzy captions of the ultrasound screen, I felt now that if only I had understood Jie a bit earlier, the story with Simon wouldn't have turned out the same way. If only I could have listened to him more over recent years, stretched out my arms more, and hadn't let him retreat from the trust we had for each other, and from the world. If only I had been a more patient, better friend.

26
First Snow
初雪 (*chuxue*)

A year later, in late November, I watched the gingko trees change colour outside my rented basement in Washington D.C. and for a moment, forgot where I was. The first few months in the U.S. had fled by quickly among new registrations and new routines. When I took a break from my full graduate-student schedule, however, I walked around the city as much as I could. This was the city Simon grew up closest to – the squirrels that slid down from the tree-trunks and jumped away, the couples who went by with a baby-stroller and two dogs, and young people jogging in Rock Creek Park. Everyday sights that he once took for granted were at first novelties to me.

Simon and I had spent much of our time in my part of the world. And now I was finally in his.

Aunt Eunice put me in touch with Simon's father soon after I settled in. His father was snowy haired, wearing a pair of metal-framed glasses, tall, and a man of few words. He was recently remarried to a woman from the church. And when we first met, they took me to a country club restaurant overlooking the golf course.

I found his father's mannerisms similar to Simon's. We spoke mostly in Mandarin. And I found him not too difficult to talk to, contrary to the impression I had from Simon. He told me that Simon liked cats, and showed me a photo of him playing with a silver Persian, holding a long fishing-rod toy up high for the cat to reach. "He'd always say that 'they don't become your best friends as soon as they meet you, like dogs.'"

There was another photo of Simon winning a piano competition at seven, standing in the crowd in formal clothes and holding a big award with his name on it; and one in a winter jacket in front of the White House, right hand over chest. My favourite was the four-year-old Simon leaning on a large snowman he had just built, eyes closed. He had a serene smile on his face in that photo, and so did his buddy with the coal mouth and a yellow bucket hat.

When I gave them a copy of Simon's letter, his father didn't say a word after reading it. He folded the thin piece of paper into a square and then put it into his shirt pocket. After a while, as we served food to each other again, I saw tears in his wife's eyes, she who had never met Simon.

***

The day after I saw Simon's father, I went to the cemetery alone. From a nearby large grocery store, I bought two bouquets of white roses. An old caretaker drove me to the spot from the entrance. It was a big garden, and where I wanted to visit was not easy to find. Simon's name marker was beside his mother's, half-buried in the tall grass and dry, golden leaves. Simple, unlike the tombstones I had seen in the Shanghai suburbs. Nearby, there was an area with still barren soil and a thin, wooden stick on top with its tip painted orange – a new burial. Compared to its neighbour, Simon's name lay quietly, as if it had already been a long time. I put the flowers down as I sat next to him.

The caretaker offered to wait for me for ten minutes and then drive me back to the entrance. I said thanks, but told him that I would like to walk back later.

It was the end of a season. And the passing wind had just started to bite. While sitting and talking to Simon, I discovered a small, black spider on the flower pot next to his marker, starting to build a rudimentary web. I was very late finally to come here, I said. I told Simon about my considerable loneliness over the past year, and eventually, the strength I had gained from that loneliness. I mentioned his father's new marriage and our meeting. In this novel way of communicating, we also kept each other company in silence for a long time. Then I told him that I had received his letter, the way he had intended me to receive it. I said that I wouldn't let go of his trust. And like my native language and my hometown, I wouldn't leave him behind in my future journeys; I would carry him with me, as a part of me, even now that the same aching feelings of parting no longer contain me.

The sound of the wind sometimes rustled through the trees. By the time I left the garden and walked back, the sun was already setting low. Evening fell much faster here in Rockville at this time of the year.

***

Simon's father invited me to join them for Thanksgiving dinner a few days later. It was hosted in his wife, Aunt Joyce's, house, where he now lived after getting married, in Cleveland Park.

Thanksgiving in a Chinese American family seemed to me to embody a mix of traditions. There was a turkey with stuffing. But instead of cranberry and brussels sprouts, Simon's father and Aunt Joyce had made fried noodles and dumplings. The sweet potatoes were steamed, like my mother would have prepared them, rather than baked in an oven. Aunt Joyce was originally from Shandong Province, so she had prepared seafood as well, such as prawns and squid, more richly seasoned than their Shanghainese or Cantonese equivalents.

Many of Aunt Joyce's church friends had come for dinner, too, mostly Mandarin speakers. They spent the meal debating international politics, which reminded me of my extended family's gatherings during the Lunar New Year. And besides myself, there was only one other young person in his twenties, a family friend, whom most of us didn't have a chance to talk to because he left the house early to line up overnight and snag a pair of sneakers in the Black Friday sale.

"Oh, let him go," I heard Aunt Joyce saying to his parents. "The younger generation have their own world. What can you do about it?"

"The problem is that I have no idea of the stuff in his mind these days," the mother of the young man complained in Chinese. "Sometimes I'm just afraid of him. He will come home and give me an angry look without saying anything, as if I made him sick."

"Well, at least he showed up tonight." Aunt Joyce let out a sigh, mentioning that her two older children from a previous marriage had other plans.

The young man didn't seem to hear what was said about him. He tied his shoes quickly and stepped out, closing the door behind him.

I felt that I was sitting in Simon's place, a place that I wanted so much to treasure on his behalf. Seeing another young ABC leave the Thanksgiving table to be on his own almost brought tears to my eyes. It was a year since Simon was gone, but I realized that I had only just crossed a threshold which I should have crossed a long time ago. I now had a better understanding of the things Simon had left out in our conversations; for instance, the different expectations of a relationship between Chinese immigrant parents and their American children, and both Simon's hesitancy and his desire to bridge those gaps.

After dinner, I baked chocolate chip cookies with Simon's father and Aunt Joyce. While we mixed the dough, Aunt Joyce told me that she had come to the U.S. in the 1980s and decided not to return after what happened in Tiananmen Square in 1989. She didn't speak much English in the beginning and worked for many years as a waitress in a casino, before opening her own travel agency in the late 1990s.

"Young people from China speak better English these days," said Aunt Joyce. "And your journey might be easier.

In those days, it took Simon's father quite some time to complete his doctorate degree and find a suitable engineering job. He even worked as a handyman for a couple of years. Just imagine, someone with a PhD!"

"My father was a handyman in Taiwan, so I know how to do most jobs," said Simon's father. Compared to Aunt Joyce, he sounded very even-tempered. After the cookie dough was well mixed, he started to lay the cookies on the baking sheet in similar sizes. "Back in Taiwan, handymen were sort of Jacks-of-all-trades, unlike here in the U.S., where you have different numbers to call for plumbing, electricity, windows, etc. So I was well sought-after in those days."

"I think it was the same in China," I said. "Jacks-of-all-trades."

"Still," Aunt Joyce spoke as she put on the oven-glove and shoved the baking sheet inside the oven, "he made it sound like it didn't take difficult adjustments. 'A tiger fallen on level land gets insulted by a dog' was what I often reminded myself, back in the casino days."

"My father likes this idiom, too."

"Your parents probably have a lot in common with us, even though they stayed and we came here. We have something to fight against either way, right?" said Aunt Joyce.

And I thought, I had a lot in common with them, too.

After we finished the cookies, I didn't stay long. I knew that my presence was still a source of sadness over Thanksgiving, even after a year. When I bid them goodbye at the door, however, Simon's father and Aunt Joyce both hugged me, not something a Chinese parent would usually do. "Come back soon," they said, "this is your home too."

***

I still remember when the first snow came that November, lightly coating the autumn colours. I hadn't seen snow in Shanghai for years, and I'd forgotten how quietly snowflakes fall, and how they could melt over the course of a morning.

It was on one of those days that I walked around the National Zoo to see the giant pandas. By then, I was already familiar with Tian Tian, Mei Xiang, and their year-old cub Tai Shan. Visiting them and seeing them napping or chewing away at bamboo had become a routine which put my mind at ease.

Simon once told me that when he was in high school, he used to intern at the zoo.

"At the veterinary hospital for three months. There was a baby elephant and it was so playful – always kicking a bucket or just rolling over. Doing all sorts of tricks. Just like a human baby, with an instinct to play."

"What were you doing for all those three months?"

"I don't remember exactly...it was a long time ago," he said, *"In the pathology lab, collecting blood samples or something like that. And I watched operations, and I saw a necropsy – just a term for animal autopsy, you know? We cut them open to see their insides after they had died. To understand the cause of death, I suppose."*

At the time, Tian Tian and Mei Xiang hadn't arrived from China; therefore Simon didn't mention the pandas. How he would have enjoyed watching the panda cub Tai Shan rolling down the snowy slope, I thought.

But today, Tai Shan seemed rather lethargic, staying close to Mei Xiang the whole time. I saw a few workers putting iron wraps on the tree trunks in the yard so that the cub wouldn't climb up too high and "get stuck" like he did a few days ago. It was in the local paper that the staff had to rescue Tai Shan in the middle of the night. I wondered if he was in fact plotting an adventure or an escape.

I recalled that I had read on the gallery wall that Tai Shan would return to China in a few years. The giant pandas were all "rented" guests, the newspaper said, and would be returned home at the end of their lease, except for the cubs, for whom this had already become home.

Was Tai Shan climbing on top of the tree so that he could get a faraway view beyond the zoo? Would he someday put up resistance against the set track of his life? Through the glass, I watched Mei Xiang and her cub's slow movements for a while and felt strangely sentimental. I decided to take a longer walk.

The zoo was filled with families and tourists. Girl scouts lined up all over the Asian Trails, wearing small panda hats. Professional photographers, camped out since dawn, carried their heavy equipment. I strolled around, avoiding the crowd.

On the elephant path, there were giant footprints painted in red. I followed them to a quiet area near the elephants' residence. Yellow crocuses were blooming on either side of the path and the fresh fragrance in the air almost smelled like early spring. It was an unusual sight in late November. A lanky Asian boy was sitting on one of the benches, bending down and burying his face in both hands.

Something about him and the way he sat on the bench made me stop. He was about sixteen, or seventeen, years old, and when he lifted his face up a bit, I could see his downturned eyes and two thick eye-brows. He was in a blue T-shirt and black shorts. It looked as if the boy had waited too long to get his next haircut, making his head puffier.

I was not sure whether he had been crying.

The long-legged boy looked over towards me and his face blushed, like he had been caught doing something that he didn't want people to see. He didn't move, but looked at me in bewilderment.

"Have you lost something?" I asked, surprised that I was talking to a stranger. The impact of a new location, I suppose. A wave of tenderness came to me like drizzling rain. A nostalgic feeling.

The boy shook his head, suddenly wary. It seemed funny that with so many tourists in the zoo today, there was no one else passing by on the elephant path. It was quiet here, as if it was a world of its own. The boy's expression softened after a short while. Maybe he too, found something familiar in me similar to what I saw in him. I was glad he didn't run away. He told me he had started working in the zoo as an intern this year. He was in a public school near Rockville.

"Well, I'm here to see the panda cub, Tai Shan."

"Tai Shan?" The long-legged boy looked like he didn't know what I was talking about.

"Never mind," I said, "What's it like working in the zoo? I had a friend who used to work here as well."

"Oh really? I guess I'm doing okay," the boy looked at his hands. "I get to watch cool operations in the lab. But Kumari is getting worse today. She has had a fever for days and her tongue has turned all purple. I don't think I can work in the lab any longer."

"Who is Kumari?" It occurred to me that maybe he was indeed crying before I walked over.

"I guess that you don't know much about the zoo," he said. "Kumari is an elephant calf only sixteen months old. She's the best. Everybody loves her. But it seems like she's going to die soon, and the veterinarians can't do anything about it."

I said I was sorry to hear that, but sometimes things like that happen. No matter how much you love them.

"It's just really mysterious. The vets can't find any cause of the disease. But I know that Kumari is tired, and she wants to lie down. Her mother Shanthi won't let her because Kumari is new to the herd and she's afraid that the other elephants won't accept her."

"But she should lie down and take a rest if she's really tired," I said.

"I'm afraid we are going to lose her." His voice stayed calm, but there was a heavy weight in the air when he spoke. And then, without warning, I saw tears running down his cheeks, despite great effort on his part.

I didn't know how to say something nice to make him feel better. But I knew that he would like me to listen and just stay around. I also felt glad for him that he was able to cry, and to cry in front of me. I had a feeling that this didn't happen to him very often. Finally I put a hand on his arm, when he was wiping his eyes with the back of his hands. I asked, "Do you want me to give you a hug?"

The boy looked embarrassed at first, but he slowly got up and I hugged him. We stood in the middle of the elephant path, still with no tourists walking by. How long had it been? I lost count of time. I knew it was him. And he was simply waiting for me, not just any stranger who chanced on the trail. For a short moment, the boy broke into an aching sob again. His nails pressed on my shoulders tightly. I felt tears coming to my eyes as well, but I had turned my chin up to let them not fall.

Even though he was a few years younger than me, the boy was still taller. His neck carried a faint scent of soap. I patted his back and felt that his body started to turn a little stiff. With his face blushing again, the boy suddenly stepped back and told me he had to return to work soon. His misty eyes reminded me of the ocean in Hong Kong, the shimmering, endless water that Simon and I had loved when we stood on the lookout of the Maclehose Trail.

"Good luck with your work," I said. "I hope Kumari will get well soon."

He waved goodbye and disappeared at the end of the elephant path, almost running. It took me a while to find the way back to the main road and my bearing.

LIST OF CHARACTERS

Qian Yinan (錢憶南) – Protagonist

Yinan's Husband

Yinan's Father, Qian Jingcheng, eldest of the four siblings

Yinan's Mother, Yueling

Yinan's grandfather, middle son of a landlord, former Lieutenant Colonel during the Second World War

Yinan's grandmother, Qing

Weiwei – Yinan's childhood friend in the *longtang*

Aunt Jingyun

Uncle Jingchuan

Xiaolong ("Small Dragon"), Uncle Jingchuan's son, Yinan's cousin

Uncle Jingzhang

Jie – Yinan's best friend in middle school and high school

Mr. Yang – Physics teacher in Yinan's high school

Mrs. Xue – Class teacher of the Advanced Science Class in Yinan's high school

Lily – Yinan's classmate in the Advanced Science Class, Mr. Yang's student

Xiaofen – Yinan's classmate in the Advanced Science Class, Mr. Yang's student

Mr. Lin – Party secretary of Yinan's high school

Jeremy – Yinan's friend in high school

Simon (袁小雨) – Yinan's university friend from Maryland, United States, Psychology major

Pei – Jie's university boyfriend

Kai – Former student of Yinan's father, owner of a Shanghai journal

Eunice – Simon's aunt in Hong Kong

Heng – Former sweetheart of Yinan's grandfather, living in Taipei after 1949

Dr. Glen – American author Yinan worked with during a book tour

Simon's father in the United States

Joyce – Simon's father's wife

ADVANCE COMMENTS

From Geoffrey Becker

The theme of language and how it shapes consciousness underlies much of this affecting, thoughtful novel. Flora Qian vividly depicts the Shanghai childhood of her main character, Yinan, and her subsequent struggles with the culture she belongs to but must inevitably distance herself from. Qian's sharply observed prose is full of wonderful details and compelling characters, incorporating Chinese history, folk tales, and even a pet pigeon—I loved spending time in her world. As Yinan herself tells us, "I felt that I had to lose my native words so that I could speak my true mind".

—Geoffrey Becker,
    Towson University, Maryland, USA,
    author of *Hot Springs* and *Black Elvis*.

From Emily Mitchell

Told with wonderful precision, insight and vivid detail, *South of the Yangtze* brings to life a transformative time period through the eyes of a young woman doing her best to navigate the seismic changes in her society and her own coming of age.

—Emily Mitchell, Washington, DC;
    University of Maryland,
    author of *The Last Summer of the World*
    and *Viral: Stories*.

From Dami Jung

Flora Qian's *South of the Yangtze* is a beautifully crafted coming of age story of Yinan, a girl with a mature insight and bright mind. Growing up in China in the 1980s and later building a new life in Hong Kong, Yinan's journey to establish her identity is heart-wrenching. The turbulent time of her motherland is challenging for Yinan to define herself. *South of the Yangtze* shows how our personal life is entwined with a political environment and never free from it. I admired how Qian engraved Yinan's life with a brilliant tool of languages and cultures. The comparison and metaphors in the multiple layers of the Chinese language are impressive. But what I loved most about *South of the Yangtze* was what Qian described as the feeling of being a diaspora in her own country. Growing up in South Korea during a similar period, I instantly understood what she meant. Qian's writing also reminds me of my struggle and freedom to write in a second language and the nostalgia it brings simultaneously. Every sentence in her book is dignified and thoroughly thought out. It was a joy to discover the intriguing characters that will stay long after you finish the book.

—Dami Jung,
   winner of the Proverse Prize 2021,
   author of *Jane, Frank and Mia,*.

FICTION PUBLISHED BY PROVERSE HONG KONG

NOVELS

A Misted Mirror. Gillian Jones.
A Painted Moment. Jennifer Ching.
Adam's Franchise. Lawrence Gray.
An Imitation of Life. Laura Solomon.
Article 109. Peter Gregoire.
As Leaves Blow. Philip Chatting.
*Bao Bao's Odyssey: From Mao's Shanghai
    to Capitalist Hong Kong*. Paul Ting.
Black Tortoise Winter. Jan Pearson.
Blue Dragon Spring. Jan Pearson.
Bright Lights and White Lights. Andrew Carter.
Cemetery miss you. Jason S Polley.
Cop Show Heaven. Lawrence Gray.
Cry of the Flying Rhino. Ivy Ngeow.
Curveball: Life Never Comes At You Straight. Gustav Preller.
Death Has A Thousand Doors. Patricia W. Grey
Enoch's Muse. Sergio Monteiro.
Finley's Confession. George Watt.
Hilary and David. Laura Solomon.
HK Hollow. Dragoş Ilca.
Hong Kong Rocks. Peter Humphreys.
Instant Messages. Laura Solomon.
Jane, Frank and Mia. Dami Jung.
Man's Last Song. James Tam.
Mishpacha – Family. Rebecca Tomasis.
Paranoia. Caleb Kavon.
Professor Everywhere. Nicholas Binge.
Red Bird Summer. Jan Pearson.
Revenge from Beyond. Dennis Wong.
The Day They Came. Gerard Breissan.
The Devil You Know. Peter Gregoire.
The Handover Murders. Damon Rose.
The Monkey in Me. Caleb Kavon.
The Perilous Passage of Princess Petunia Peasant.
        Victor Edward Apps.
The Reluctant Terrorist. Caleb Kavon.

The Thing Is. Andrew Carter.
The Village in the Mountains. David Diskin.
Three Wishes in Bardo. Feng Chi-shun.
Tiger Autumn. Jan Pearson.
Tightrope! A Bohemian Tale. Olga Walló
    (translated from Czech).
University Days. Laura Solomon.
Vera Magpie. Laura Solomon. (Novella.)

SHORT STORY COLLECTIONS

Beyond Brightness. Sanja Särman.
Odds and Sods. Lawrence Gray.
The Shingle Bar Sea Monster and Other Stories.
    Laura Solomon.
The Snow Bridge And Other Stories. Philip Chatting.
Under the shade of the Feijoa trees and other stories.
    Hayley Ann Solomon.

FIND OUT MORE ABOUT PROVERSE AUTHORS, BOOKS, EVENTS AND LITERARY PRIZES

Website: <https://www.proversepublishing.com>
Proverse page on our Hong Kong distributor's website:
<https://cup.cuhk.edu.hk/Proversehk>
Twitter / X: twitter.com/Proversebooks
"Like" us on www.facebook.com/ProversePress

Request our free E-Newsletter
Send your request to <info@proversepublishing.com>.

Availability
Most of our titles
are available in Hong Kong and world-wide
from our Hong Kong based distributor,
the Chinese University of Hong Kong Press,
The Chinese University of Hong Kong, Shatin, NT,
Hong Kong SAR, China.

Most titles can be ordered online from amazon
(various countries) and other online retailers.

Stock-holding retailers
Hong Kong (CUHKP, Bookazine)
Canada (Elizabeth Campbell Books)
Andorra (Llibreria La Puça, La Llibreria)
UK (Ivybridge Bookshop, Devon).

Orders may be made from bookshops
in the UK and elsewhere.

Ebooks and audiobooks
Most of our titles are available also as Ebooks and increasingly
as audiobooks.